To Hull & Back

Short Story Anthology 2015

Copyright © 2015 Christopher Fielden. All rights reserved.

The copyright of each story published in this anthology remains with the author.

Cover copyright © 2015 Lukas Miguel. All rights reserved.

The cover features the delectable visage of Radovana Jágriková.

First published on Hulloween, October 31st 2015.

The rights of the writers of the short stories published in this anthology to be identified as the authors of their work has been asserted in accordance with the Copyright, Designs and Patents Act 1988.

All rights reserved. No part of this publication may be reproduced, stored in a retrieval system, or transmitted in any form by any means, electronic, mechanical, photocopying, recording or otherwise, without the prior permission of the publishers.

You can learn more about the To Hull & Back short story competition at:

www.christopherfielden.com

All characters in this publication are fictitious and any resemblance to real persons, living or dead, is purely coincidental.

ISBN: 1517661072
ISBN-13: 978-1517661076

INTRODUCTION

Welcome to the second To Hull & Back short story anthology. I hope you enjoy all the highly imaginative tales that appear within this fun-filled tome. May your senses be tantalised and fun bags filled with merriment.

Some memory in the dark recesses of my brain made me do a quick Google search for the term 'fun bags' after I typed the words. The results brought a childish grin to my chops, but it transpires that it's a poor choice of terminology to use in the anthology's introduction. Please accept my sincere apologies. 'Let your temporal lobe be tickled with delight' might be more appropriate. Let's go with that...

The anthology opens with the three winning stories of the 2015 competition. These are followed by the three highly commended tales from the runners-up, in alphabetical order (based on story title). After that, the other 14 shortlisted stories appear, again, in alphabetical order.

A story written by each of the judges closes the anthology. This is so future entrants to the competition can see the types of stories the judges write. This should give them a better chance of penning a successful entry for next year's competition.

I'd like to express my utmost thanks to all the authors of the stories that appear in the anthology. It's an honour to be able to present them in this collection.

Chris Fielden

CONTENTS

	Acknowledgements	i

WINNING STORIES

1	'Too' by Radovana Jágriková	1
2	'On a Cross of Iron' by Jonathan Macho	13
3	'Parrotlytic' by Adena Graham	28

HIGHLY COMMENDED STORIES

4	'Biking to Find the Boy' by Ian Tucker	39
5	'Joe Lean' by Bernie Deehan	54
6	'Soup' by Dirk Puis	64

SHORTLISTED STORIES

7	'An Eztraordinary Ezperience' by Stuart Aken	76
8	'Barry's Home' by Jade Williams	84
9	'Beneath the Waves' by Olivia Arroy	90
10	'Beståˇ' by Adena Graham	105
11	'Cheer' by Patrick Tuck	118
12	'Fancy That' by John Emms	131
13	'My Week With Kim Jong Un' by Will Haynes	136

14	'Out of the Mouths of Babes' by Sheila Corbishley	151
15	'Shirt Tales' by Adele Smith	155
16	'Tell Us About Your Stay' by Dan Brotzel	171
17	'The Deaths of Arthur' by Georgina Sanjana	183
18	'The Wedding of Ugly Bob' by Scott Johnston	201
19	'To Wyke-on-Hull and Back' by Danny Shilling	216
20	'Ups and Downs' by Mark Rutterford	232

JUDGE'S STORIES

21	'Away Day' by Mike Scott Thomson	241
22	'Bag Packers' by Christie Cluett	254
23	'Central Line Betty' by Steph Minns	263
24	'Devil's Crush' by Christopher Fielden	271
25	'Night Reception' by Andy Melhuish	285
26	'Wonder Woman's Birthday Party' by Mel Ciavucco	293
27	A Final Note	303

ACKNOWLEDGEMENTS

Thank you to Andy Melhuish, Christie Cluett, Mel Ciavucco, Mike Scott Thomson and Steph Minns for helping me judge the competition. Myself, Andy, Christie, Mel and Steph belong (or have belonged – sadly Andy recently moved to Oxford) to a writing group called Stokes Croft Writers:
www.stokescroftwriters.com

Thanks to Lukas Miguel for designing the amazing cover of this book – you can learn more about his artistic awesomeness at: www.lukasmiguel.org

Thanks to David Fielden for building and maintaining my website. Without him, I'd never have created a platform that allowed the greatest writing prize in the known macrocosm to have been conceived, launched and enjoyed by all who happen across it. You can learn more about Dave's website building prowess at:
www.bluetree.co.uk

And finally, a HUMONGOUS thank you to everyone who entered the contest. The volume of entries has enabled me to offer a whopping £1,000 top prize in next year's competition. Without the support of all those who entered, this just wouldn't be possible.

WINNING STORIES

TOO

The winning story, by Radovana Jágriková

The man had been dreaming about a large chunk of cheese chasing him along a cherry-tree lane when he awoke to the darkness of his bedroom. He stared at the ceiling for a while, trying to remember who the woman who set the cheese on him reminded him of, when he noticed an unusual feature of the usually unsurprising room. He turned on the light and blinked. There was a guy sitting peacefully at the edge of his bed.

He looked at the guy. The guy looked at him.

He closed his eyes and opened them carefully again. The guy was still there, watching him with a slightly amused look.

"Er... Hello."

"Hello."

He waited, but nothing happened.

"It's... a lovely night, isn't it?"

The guy nodded. "Oh yes, very nice. A little cold perhaps."

The man smiled politely.

In the silence that followed, the man glanced at the guy. The greasy pony tail and the worn-out 'Keep Calm and Hug a Tree' T-shirt suggested slight disinterest in fashion and good looks, but no obvious mass-murderer inclinations, and try as he may, the man felt no sense of immediate mortal danger. He considered rolling over and getting back to sleep and finding out what would happen if the cheese caught up with him, but some basic natural curiosity took over and he decided to learn more about the visitor.

"Would you care for a cup of tea perhaps...?"

"Oh, that's most kind of you, thank you. Milk, no sugar."

The man sprung out of bed and gestured vaguely towards the kitchen.

"I'll just wait here, if you don't mind," the guy smiled.

"Oh. Right. Sure."

The man prepared two cups of milk-no-sugar tea and, impulsively, decided to include a plate with a selection of digestives too.

"There you go," he said as he put one cup and the plate on the small bedside table for his guest.

"Ta."

The man placed his cup on the other side and, feeling that it might be expected of him – for some surely perfectly logical reason – he got back into bed, though unsure how to pull the duvet from under the visitor without it seeming improper so he ended up just hugging one corner awkwardly. Then, to regain some of his quickly vanishing sense of respectability, he pushed himself into a half-lying, half-sitting position and took his cup firmly in his hands. The guy started with the biscuits, nibbling happily on a small one.

"Forgive me for being a bit blunt perhaps, but – do I know you?"

"No, I don't think so."

"Ah."

"I'm Tooth Fairy."

"Ah."

The man let the information sink in, and when it seemed impossible for it to sink any deeper, he continued, "I – for some reason – always thought that the Tooth Fairy is... well... female."

Tooth Fairy rolled his eyes. "If I had a penny for every time I hear that..."

The man smiled politely. He turned the cup in his hands twice, once clockwise, once anticlockwise. It seemed that it was his turn to start the conversation again.

"So... Is Tooth Fairy both your occupation and name?"

"Yeah. Keeps things simple."

"Oh yes."

Tooth Fairy sipped his tea again with an approving nod. The man, glancing at his alarm clock, decided to speed things up a bit and asked merrily, "Well then...

Mr Fairy... How can I help you?"

"Oh, just call me Too."

"Too. Right. So, Too... Is there anything I can do for you?"

"No, I'm all right, thank you. I'm just waiting."

"Waiting – for what?"

Too frowned slightly and said, with a hint of sarcasm in his voice for the first time, "I'm Tooth Fairy. What am I likely to wait for?"

The man blinked slowly. "You... are waiting for a tooth."

"Yep."

"But I have none loose."

"Well, that's why I'm waiting."

Too stood up with the air of a man having all the time in the world and strolled leisurely around the room.

"This is a great TV, I must say. I've read some reviews recently. External surround-sound speakers would be handy too. I can see that you haven't bought any..."

"Er... no, I'm afraid not."

"Well, the built-in speakers should be decent enough." He reached for the remote control, turned the TV on and skimmed through the pages of the programme listings lying on the bedside table. Suddenly he exclaimed, "Ooh, I haven't seen that in ages. Would you mind moving a bit?"

The man moved, whether he minded or not, and found himself somehow sharing the duvet with the guy. Before he knew it, he offered to prepare some popcorn as well and returned not only with a bowlful of hot popcorn covered in melting butter, but with another round of teas as well. The film was surprisingly good and he found himself cheering for the brave handsome guy escaping from the bad ugly guys.

He was just wondering whether an experienced serial killer would really miss from a distance of just a few steps and whether she could really run comfortably in such high heels when an enormous helpless yawn interrupted his stream of thought. Then he realised it was nearly getting light outside.

"I'm rather tired," the man said through another long yawn.

"Yes, I can understand that. Not used to being awake this time of night," Too replied, not taking his eyes off the screen.

"Er... I'd better get some rest then, I guess."

"I agree. Let me take the popcorn then."

After the popcorn was successfully transferred and Too returned to the on-screen action, the man, not knowing what else to do, wished his visitor good night, made himself as comfortable as possible on his half of the bed and, to the sounds of quiet chuckles, car explosions and popcorn crunches, he fell asleep peacefully.

*

In the morning, the man awoke to the sound of his alarm clock. He looked around. There was no popcorn, no tea cups, no visitor.

No tooth was missing.

What was missing though was his TV, his mobile phone and the contents of his wallet.

~

Radovana Jágriková's Biography

Radovana Jágriková (Radka) has been writing short stories since her early teens, and in her most productive years amassed more than 20 prizes in youth and adult literary competitions. After a few years of focussing on journalism and academic writing, she has recently returned to fiction and hopes to start working on her ideas for a novel and a children's/young adults' literary project in the near future too. She lives in Gateshead/Newcastle upon Tyne, UK, where she works for an international creative learning foundation. She is originally from Slovakia and has also previously studied and worked in the Netherlands.

~

Radovana Jágriková – Winner's Interview

1. What is the most interesting thing that's ever happened to you?

I guess I'll have to say, my birth. I don't remember much of it, but it led to a lot of other interesting things happening later.

2. Who is the most inspirational person you've ever met and why?

Hmm. Tricky. I've probably been influenced by a number of people rather than one big hero and idol of mine. Perhaps I just have an eclectic approach and try to take the best from various people.

3. Which authors do you most admire and why?

There are many authors I could mention, for different reasons.
   One could be Agatha Christie, with her brilliant mind, amazing plots and her dedication to publishing for so long while maintaining the same high standard of writing.
   Another one might be Lucy Maud Montgomery, who created the rich and imaginative worlds of *Anne of Green Gables* and *Emily of New Moon*, and in her books managed to show strong female characters who can inspire and charm you at any age.
   J R R Tolkien, because his immensely well thought-through creation of a new world, his imagination, his ability to involve you in the story and feel strongly about it are all worth admiring too.
   There are also books from E M Remarque or Jules Verne that made me respect the authors greatly, and I need to explore more of their work.
   And from the contemporary writers I could perhaps mention John Grisham for his very readable writing style and the obvious amount of research and hard work he puts into his novels.
   And I'll have to stop there before I get carried away.

4. When and why did you start writing short stories?

I would have been around nine or 10 when I first wrote down something formally and called it a short story I suppose. It just felt natural. I enjoyed it. And I always loved reading, so that must have made me try it myself.
   I was also part of a drama and literature club and we were encouraged to write down interesting things that

had happened to us and share it, to develop our storytelling skills. I came up with this novella – a series of diary-like entries about my adventures with my younger sister and our pet cat – and my teacher found it charming and started asking details about my family, and got very puzzled when I explained that I didn't have a cat or a sister and none of the things had ever happened to me. That amused me and encouraged me to keep puzzling grown-ups.

When I was 15 I submitted two poems and one short story to a competition. I was very proud of the poems and only wrote the story for fun really, just like all the previous ones. I liked the idea of writing moving poetry and was thrilled to get invited to the award ceremony. In the end it was the short story that got a prize though, and I got to talk to a lot of people about it and analyse it and discuss other stories submitted, and it felt great. It was then that I decided to keep writing short stories, for as long as I enjoy it. And I still do.

5. Where do your ideas and inspiration come from?

That varies a lot. It could be an interesting combination of words that suddenly appear in my mind and it becomes the title so I write a story around that. I might be inspired by my own current or past emotions and dilemmas. I could think of a fun sentence to start with and then just keep writing. I could think of an interesting character I would like to portray and explore, or a twist I think others would really like. These things can come out of the blue, be based on something I've just seen or heard, or be arrived at when I'm doing some short-story brainstorming on purpose. I think I'm open to new ideas for stories, almost always scanning for them unconsciously, and if I have too many or don't have enough time to work on them, I just write down some notes and return to them later. I have plenty to choose from at the moment.

6. Where do you write?

Usually at home on my laptop. But I don't need a perfectly quiet place just for myself or a specific desk or to always be in the same place to 'get in the writing zone'. For me, there are different types or stages of writing; writing down random new ideas, getting deep into an emotionally intense scene, polishing a near-final draft, playing with a humorous story, writing without stopping to see where it leads to – these all need different levels of concentration, so I don't need to have the same 'ideal' conditions for all of them.

Sometimes I also write on random small pieces of paper, often grocery shopping receipts or used printed boarding passes, to capture a new idea, a good-sounding sentence or outline a storyline (and you should see my handwriting – it's tiny, and I use any minuscule space there is, so receipts from three average 20-pound grocery shopping trips could give me enough usable space for a whole short story I guess).

But it all usually starts with writing in my own head – thinking about everything, different possibilities, where something might lead or how to achieve a particular mood, and that can be done absolutely everywhere. This has worked for me at different stages of writing actually, and I've recently done a lot of it while walking or taking the metro home from work. If you haven't got much free time, use whatever you have.

7. How do you cope when your writing is rejected?

I realise that judges and writers, no matter how experienced, still have some subjective preferences. If you don't win a competition that doesn't necessarily mean the piece submitted wasn't good; different readers might value it more. Or there were simply other stories that just seemed a tiny bit better. I think it helps to realise that there are many good writers and many good stories out there, and you can't always be better than all of them, just be one of them.

I generally prefer writing competitions with more prizes and types of recognition; if, rather than just picking one winner out of the 500 entries, they recognise more of the talent and encourage more people, such as by having commended stories or publishing shortlists. And if you're not even on the shortlist? Get other people's feedback and look at what could be done better. And if you can't find anything to improve and are sure you have reached the story's full potential and it's too good for other people not to read it, just try submitting it somewhere else.

8. Who has published your work before?

I self-published a book of Christmas stories when I was about 12. By self-published I mean I illustrated them, printed them, stapled as a booklet and gave to my family and friends. Later it was a respected Slovak publishing house who published three of my short stories for children in their three consecutive anthologies, and my other stories were included in a few other competition anthologies. This would all be when I was 16 to 19. As for my more recent English fiction writing, a story that came second in a competition was published in the *British Czech and Slovak Review* in 2014, and there should be the *Sentinel Annual Short Story Competition 2014 anthology* with my winning story published sometime this year too. And now I'm published again!

9. Why did you choose to enter the To Hull & Back competition?

Firstly, because I had a short story that I thought would deserve to be at least highly commended somewhere; secondly, because Chris who organises the competition seemed like he would appreciate the story's sense of humour; and thirdly, because the competition sounded so fun and unique, and the prospect of being portrayed on the cover riding a Harley Davidson was intriguing and scary at the same time...

10. What will you spend your prize money on?

I'm better at saving than spending, crazy as it sounds. But I'll try to treat myself rather than use it all on my mortgage. I might buy some theatre tickets and perhaps one or two rare editions of some good books too.

11. What has been your proudest writing moment so far?

Can't decide really, when it comes to fiction writing. Perhaps when a competition judge invited me to talk about my writing to her class of 11 and 12-year-olds – I was 16 myself I think – and they all genuinely liked my short story and wanted me to sign their printed copy and stay in touch. And when I learnt from a former after-school drama teacher that she'd heard a couple of my short stories performed by children at several recitation competitions (these used to be quite popular in Slovakia). Or when I won first prize in an established international writing competition for the first time, beating many good writers who have English as their first language. And hopefully there'll be a few more.

12. What advice would you give to novice writers?

Every writer is unique and would benefit from different advice I think; it's hard to come up with a set of universal advice, and there is plenty of that about already. I could just say things that sound perhaps obvious, but some people might find them helpful.

Read a lot. Interact with other writers and readers. Talk about writing and reading. But save some time for the actual writing too. Care about your pieces of writing. Enjoy writing, but don't use the fact it's just something you enjoy as an excuse not to try and improve yourself.

And be aware that one day you might be asked to answer all sorts of questions about your writing and give advice to other writers, and you'll be expected to come up with something very sophisticated and inspirational – which might be even harder than writing a good short story...

ON A CROSS OF IRON

The second place story, by Jonathan Macho

Just imagine, for a second, that the impossible was possible. Take a moment to believe the unbelievable, to fathom the unfathomable, and to comprehend the utterly farcical. I would really appreciate it if you did.

Now, consider this, a concept snatched not from the minds of children or philosophers, but instead from somewhere between the two, the best place to hunt for ideas surely. Consider that, if every weapon in the world was a sandwich, both war and global starvation would end, just like that.

No, stick with it, I promise it goes somewhere.

Just imagine. Every gun would suddenly be a BLT which could feed the starving in the bombed out remains of their homes. Every knife would be a ham and cheese bap, another meal for the poor of the inner city. Every bomb, a grilled cheese deluxe on the plate of those who'd usually go without. The fillings don't really matter, I'm just trying to make a point.

It'd never happen of course. It's just an idea after all, and an impossible one at that. Unbelievable. Unfathomable. Some would say utterly farcical.

But just imagine.

Powell Estate, London, England. 00.35 until Event

Little Tony Lewis was afraid. He sat at the filthy table in his filthy kitchen and stared, just gazed out at everything and nothing at the same time. His brain raced along with his pulse, trying to keep pace. Nothing seemed concrete. The fear was there, in his head, his gut, twisting things, so that his thoughts and its own whispered jibes were too intermingled to tell apart. Was he thinking clearly? He wasn't sure, but he knew a few things for certain; he was out of his depth, and he didn't want anyone to die.

He was 11, for God's sake. Why was this pressure being put on him? Why was he in this adult world of blood and feuds and malice? Sometimes, in those brief moments of respite between school and the fear, Tony would sit, and just imagine a world where none of this nonsense mattered. He would see blue sky, no grey, white or black staining his view like it always was here. He would have company. He would have space to just be free.

But that was impossible. The fear reminded him of that whenever it could. He wasn't free. He was stuck in the filthy kitchen, at the filthy table, staring. He had inherited a prison which always needed an occupant. 20 stories up. Long term sentence. No parole.

His brother was out now, but he would come back, and soon, with more cuts no doubt, blood on his knuckles, on his lip, his mind. He'd have been fighting with the gang again, the boys with sharp words and cruel eyes. They'll have mentioned dad, and he will have just lost it, out of some sense of duty.

Tony never understood Mark's 'responsibility' to defend their father. He didn't understand what they owed him. He'd never been around long enough to leave them anything but an empty chair and a hollow feeling. What had he done to deserve their blood? He never brought it up with his brother though, just in case the lad decided to unleash some of that responsibility on him. Tony thought sometimes that was just the fear again, twisting it, that his brother would never hit him really. But then the fear would whisper at him some more and his dismissal would itself be dismissed. In all honesty, when he saw that fire in Mark's eyes, Tony had no idea what he was capable of.

Like that last fight with the gang. His brother had staggered home, cut and bruised, but not cowed. He hadn't smiled, very rarely found cause to, but still had an air of victory, of pride about him. A brick had sailed through their window the next day, a note tied to it: "YOU'LL GET YOURS, BOY. WE'LL GUT YOU FOR THAT."

Tony had asked what was going on, again and again, the fear seeping into his head and driving him on, but he was given no answer bar silence.

It was when the dead bird was pushed through their letterbox that he became sure that they were going to kill him.

Mark was never going to stop. He'd go to get their dole for the week, he'd go to buy food and, of course, drink, and he'd take Tony to school and back. Sometimes, he'd go and see his mates, leave Tony in charge of their prison in the sky for a while. But in between, sooner or later, he would fight the gang or the gang would fight him. And this time they would kill his brother, and Tony would really be alone.

Tony's imagination world was suddenly corrupted by the fear's fake thoughts. They drip-dropped into his blue-skied paradise like the blood that fell from the bird's neck, staining everything with a red hue. His space was cluttered with bats and chains, his imaginary friends grew fangs and claws, and his youth was taken away by figures without faces. His brother was there, and so was his erstwhile dad, and a shadow that might've been his mum. Helpless? Uncaring? He couldn't be sure. They all just watched. His dream was torn apart.

He didn't know what do to. Everything was upside down and back to front. He couldn't let Mark die, Mark was all he had. But he couldn't stop him by himself. He was alone. He was scared to go outside, but he was far too scared to stay in this cell left to him when his father was taken away to another one.

But then, the cell wasn't all Dad had left.

Tony had been staring for so long now that his vision was full of shapes that weren't really there, his eyes compensating for his lack of focus by giving him something interesting to see. He was never going back to his imaginary world. It was time for him to face the real one.

He pushed his chair out and away from the filthy table in his filthy kitchen, and crossed to one of the cupboards. He was going to have to help his brother the only way he could think of. He was so out of his depth and he didn't want anyone to die, but the fear insisted that there was no alternative. He opened one of the drawers, and pulled his dad's old handgun out from under the tablecloth which covered it.

Breathing hard, he found the safety and turned it off, just as he'd seen his father and brother do before him. The sight of him there, so small, staring at something so powerful... He was going to try and make it right.

Little Tony Lewis was afraid.

The Eiffel Tower, Paris, France. 00.09 until Event

Fadi Ismael waved off another street merchant as he made his way towards the tower, not even bothering to apologise or excuse himself this time. The way to the landmark was covered in them, all shouting in broken English and waving their wares in hope of attracting tourists. They were mosquitoes, any buzzing replaced with cries of, "Eiffel tower, 10 Euro," and, "Keychain, four Euro." Few stopped to give them the time of day, tour guides advising against it to the groups they marched across the space. Fadi was no exception. He had far more important work to attend to.

Now he was this close to the tower, he had to admit he was impressed. It was a remarkable structure, a masterpiece of architecture that dwarfed anything he had seen before. His father, an architect working out of Ar Rutba, would have approved immensely. He used to spend hours pawing through his father's plans in his workshop, awed by the detail, the complexity. He always said Fadi would make a great architect when he was older.

Now Fadi had to put all of that out of his mind. He had a new family to think of. After that day in the rain, alone in the middle of the street in his home town, he had fallen so far into despair that he thought he would never be able to climb out. But then friendly arms had reached in and grasped onto him, never to let him go again. Until now, at least.

They assured him, his new family, that Allah had not abandoned him as he had thought. He was told that his wife and his children had been claimed for a reason, to fashion him into a sword for Allah, a weapon against the Westerners who tore down Ar Rutba and had raised Korean Village in its stead. Fadi had been unsure of why Allah would ever do such a thing to him, to craft a weapon or otherwise, but was told it so much and so well that it soon became an undeniable fact. He needed his new family to fill the void that had opened in him; he couldn't risk losing them.

Months had passed, months of rehearing the words his grandfather had read to him, holy words reinterpreted, words which, like him, became weapons. Then he was told his time had come. Time for him to go and do what Allah had chosen him for. Time to be the weapon. Fadi was given the means and sent to the West, to the loud land, the land of the filthy and the corrupt, and given a job to do for his new family. For God.

Though doubt was now creeping in, in with the memories of that young boy with his dad's work, of the old man who had told him of peace and love, of the woman and the two little girls who clung to him so tightly. What could this possibly serve? How could this possibly end well? He watched a woman with two young girls of her own, one in a pram, another gripping her hand and gazing wide eyed at the tower before them. He had felt such rage. Such emptiness. Allah would never wish him to inflict that onto others, would he?

But then, who was he to question the almighty? He was but a man who had been given a job to do. He was told often enough. And he had been so sure...

No turning back now. He resumed his walk to the tower's base, with a racing brain and a heavy heart, imagining all that was to come. A weapon, until someone told him otherwise.

Give me a sign, he begged as the despair rose up around him again. *Please.*

Military Weapon's Museum, Poznan, Poland. 00.00.
The Event

Maja Zurek was going insane. That was the only explanation. It had finally gotten to her; the inherent stresses of the life of a museum curator had gotten to her and driven her completely bonkers. Her mother had always told her to aim lower, but no. She had a passion for history and she was going to follow it through. And now she was crazy. She could hear Mum's, "I told you so," already. God, she hated that old bat...

Maja had been strolling through the museum, making final checks before they closed for the night. She was in the medieval section, eyeing up a particularly rusty pair of swords, when she'd blinked (that was all she did, she swore, nothing else), and suddenly the swords were sandwiches. Four slices of bread with assorted fillings sat where the priceless artefacts of yesteryear were mere moments before. She gaped, then after a moment, blinked again in an attempt to reverse the process. It didn't work.

Letting out a little squealing noise, then composing herself as much as she was able when she determined her sanity was on the fritz, Maja called in Aleksy, one of the staff she knew was still nearby and who she thought to be fairly cogent. "Aleksy," she said as soon as he had rounded the corner. "Tell me what you see there."

Aleksy blinked. "What?"

"Just – please, just tell me what is where my fingers are pointing. Please. And stop blinking, that might just make things worse."

Bemused, Aleksy nonetheless followed her finger with his eyes and said, simply, "There are two sandwiches there, Mrs Zurek."

"Oh thank God..." Maja found herself saying, relieved beyond belief that she wasn't seeing things. As soon as that relief passed however, she cried, "No, wait, not that. This is terrible. This is a nightmare. This is – completely mad. Where have my two swords gone? Those are priceless artefacts. Why are there snacks where my priceless artefacts should be?"

"I don't know why you're so worked up about these two," the ever bemused Aleksy said. "Far as I can tell, it's happened to every weapon in the place."

Blinking again, the curator pushed past Aleksy into the next room and found him to be right. As far as the eye could see, all varieties of weapons were replaced by what might've been the contents of tomorrow's canteen dinner. The whole place smelt of lunch meat. Maja swayed a little on the spot, looked like she was about to say something, then fainted.

Panic Room, the Pentagon, Washington D.C. 12.00 after Event

The General sat at the end of the long table, glaring at all his men over the pyramid he'd made with his fingers, and waited. Ice blue eyes took in the room, pausing occasionally to hover over any particular target he deemed to be too calm. Once sure that they were terrified enough, he snarled, "Tell me what we know."

"Well, uh, sir," the Chief Scientist began, "As far as we can gather, approximately 12 hours ago, every single weapon on the planet was transformed in some way into, uh, well, a, sandwich. Sir."

The General's gaze locked onto the Chief Scientist, cold and unbroken. He flinched involuntarily. "Sandwiches?"

"Yes sir."

"Every weapon on the planet?"

"Yes sir."

"Have turned into two pieces of bread each, with, what, some lettuce inside? Is that what you're telling me?"

"Well, actually sir, the contents of each sandwich vary. It's quite remarkable – our people are working now to try and see if there's a correlation between type of weapon and sandwich fill–"

"I DON'T GIVE A DAMN ABOUT WHAT'S IN THE THINGS," the General suddenly roared, his hand pyramid breaking apart and slamming onto the table top. There was not a dry seat in the house. "ARE YOU TELLING ME THAT OUR ENTIRE ARSENAL NOW EQUATES THE CONTENTS OF MY KITCHEN?"

"Actually, sir," a young scientist to his left piped up feebly, "the number of sandwiches produced far outweighs that—"

"GET OUT OF HERE BEFORE I HAVE YOU COURT MARSHALLED." The scientist squealed and scurried away. After a moment's pause, the General managed to sink the protruding veins on his neck back into cover, and turned to his Head of Intel. "Who's behind it? The Afghans? The Koreans? The British? Who else would want to cripple us like this?"

"Far as we can tell, sir, nobody's behind it," the Intel man said with remarkable calm. "For one, this has happened to everyone. Reliable sources have confirmed that this... Event is a worldwide phenomenon. Why would any of our enemies do this if it would just mean crippling themselves as well?"

The General couldn't really find anything to yell about in that last statement, so instead pressed, "And two?"

"Nobody has the kind of technology for this, sir. And I mean nobody."

"Well, that's mostly because this is a scientific impossibility," the Chief Scientist added, "sir."

The General's frown sagged lower. "So what else could it be?"

"Aliens? God? The heartfelt wishes of a child?" The Chief Scientist looked legitimately heartbroken, like he'd been cheated on by his long term girlfriend. "In all honesty, I'm the wrong person to be asking, sir."

"Then who should I ask?" When nobody answered for a while, the General took a deep breath, and continued. "So what are our options? Are we going to have to rebuild our entire arsenal or—?"

"I'm afraid it's not that simple, sir," a Sergeant to his right said. "We've had word from our weapon's factories since the event, and it would appear that as soon as they finish putting the materials together to make, say, a gun, then it just pops itself into a sandwich just like everything else."

"Seriously?" When the Sergeant didn't leap up and scream 'April fools', the General pressed, "Then how are we meant to finish our on-going campaigns? How are we meant to protect ourselves?"

"Latest word from the front is that it isn't really a consideration anymore, sir," the Intel man said. "After a little while of just hitting each other, infantry on both sides sort of gave up and went back to base." When the General looked outraged, the Intel man added, "To be fair, nothing was really happening, sir. It was all a bit embarrassing really."

"What about their knives? Tanks? Rocks, for God's sake?"

"Well that's the thing, sir, it isn't just guns," the Chief Scientist answered. "It seems that anything, as soon as someone tries to use it as a weapon, turns into a sandwich. A man in a tank at the time of the Event found himself covered in Bacon sandwiches, enough at least to equate the tank's size. And we've had 100s of police reports that assaults, using everything from kitchen knives, to chairs, to sticks, have been brought to abrupt halts as the weapons in question were transformed into, well..."

"Sandwiches," the General finished, massaging his brow.

"Exactly. It would appear as if the moment something innocent is repurposed with malicious intent – becomes 'a weapon' if you like – it too falls under the guidelines of the Event and itself becomes a sandwich. It's all quite fascin–" The Chief Scientist saw the steel in the General's eyes and decided it best to stop there.

"So you're telling me that all of our highly trained men in the field are now just, what, sitting around having tea parties because of this thing?"

"The situation as it is now is simply untenable, sir," the Intel man said. "You have to see that."

Not answering, the General instead said to the Chief Scientist, "Is there any way to reverse the sandwich process?"

"How do you reverse something that's scientifically impossible?" he replied in way of answer. "We just don't understand it enough."

"But could we ever, in the future...?" The General's mind drifted back to the prize antique Colt M1911 which used to hang on his study wall, now replaced with an unfortunately aromatic tuna mayo baguette.

"Sorry." The General slumped in his chair and the room descended into a deathly silence. "Actually, sir," the Chief scientist tried, building in confidence as he spoke, "we were thinking about trying to instead use the sandwiches produced productively. Most have somehow resisted the passage of time and are still good enough to eat. My department have been talking and we believe that we would be able to, with the redistribution of our resources, get these resilient foods to those who need it. The starving world-wide."

"Are we sure the sandwiches are edible?" the Intel man asked, an eyebrow raised.

"All tests are positive," the Chief Scientist replied, "and we have several reports of people eating them without any negative effect."

"Feh," the General practically spat, "leave all that namby-pamby stuff to the bleeding hearts in congress. No, no, we've got men's work to do..." After a little while, he leant across the table and addressed the room at large with as straight a face as any of them had ever seen.

"Tell me," he said. "Can we weaponise the sandwiches?"

The Eifel Tower, Paris, France. 00.15 after Event

Fadi Ismael walked down the crowded Paris street with the broadest of smiles on his face, the very essence of relief. His jacket was open all the way for the first time since this morning, and in his hand he held the most beautiful chicken sandwich he had ever seen.

He knew that Allah would never allow him to do such a terrible thing. He had asked for a sign and he was given one. And more than just a sign, but a stalemate from above. No more weapons, it said. Try something else. And oh, Fadi would; he was looking forward to it immensely.

He couldn't go back now, of course. He was sure those who had made themselves his surrogate family would never understand. Indeed, if this sign had been Allah showing him anything, it had been that those men did not speak for him at all. They were liars; the truth instead could be found in his grandfather's preaching of peace. Allah loved him, and had saved his life and so many others that day. He would never condone what those who claimed to speak in his name said. He could no longer trust those he considered family, and would have to leave them behind.

That of course meant he had nowhere to go. His future, like that of the rest of the world, was suddenly and startlingly unclear. But then, at least he had a future now.

A man grabbed his arm, part of a frenzied group that

hurried past him, up the street and into chaos. "World's gone mad, brother," he said, grinning at Fadi under terrified eyes. "Don't waste the chance. Take it back."

"My dear friend," Fadi said as he eased the man's hand off of his arm, meaning every word, "I already have." The man clearly didn't understand, but nodded nonetheless, then hurried to catch up with the others. Fadi could see one of them stopping outside the window of a Pharmacy, raising an old chair to smash it, and staring in bewilderment as the wood melted into Panini's upon impact. The bread and cheese slid its way down the glass and the defeated looter moved on. Fadi turned away just as the pigeons started to flock.

Man would still be man, that was undeniable. It would take time to find that other way, a better way, and it would not be easy. But what about in 50 years? What about 100 years from now? What about all the children raised in a world without weapons?

Just imagine.

As he made his way down the street, Fadi passed a homeless man, curled up against the hostile world that surrounded him. Glancing at the contents of his hand, Fadi walked over to the man and handed him the chicken sandwich which had saved his life. "Enjoy it my friend," he said, before straightening up and carrying on his way.

Just outside the Powell Estate, London, England. 24.00 after Event

Little Tony Lewis made his way over the little green hill just past his Estate. He looked up into a clear blue sky and took a moment, letting the sun touch his face, gazing wide eyed at everything and nothing at the same time. He took a deep breath, closed his eyes, and revelled in the relative peace and quiet. After a little while, he decided a direction, took a bite out of the sandwich in his hand, and set off over the hill and to the other side.

*

"Every gun that is made, every warship launched, every rocket fired signifies in the final sense, a theft from those who hunger and are not fed, those who are cold and are not clothed. This world in arms is not spending money alone. It is spending the sweat of its labourers, the genius of its scientists, the hopes of its children. This is not a way of life at all in any true sense. Under the clouds of war, it is humanity hanging on a cross of iron."
Dwight D. Eisenhower.

~

Jonathan Macho's Biography

Jonathan Macho lives in Cardiff with his family, and a talking space raccoon that may or may not exist. A recent English Graduate faced with the big wide world, Jon has always wanted to be a writer and loves making his nonsensical ideas into (a sort of) reality. He has co-produced three plays with the Sherman Theatre's Young Writers Group and had work previously published in Candy Jar Books *Beneath the Surface Anthology*, PageTurners India's *Across the Ages Collection*, and in the Modern Alchemist's Abacus Gallery for an installation.

PARROTLYTIC

The third place story, by Adena Graham

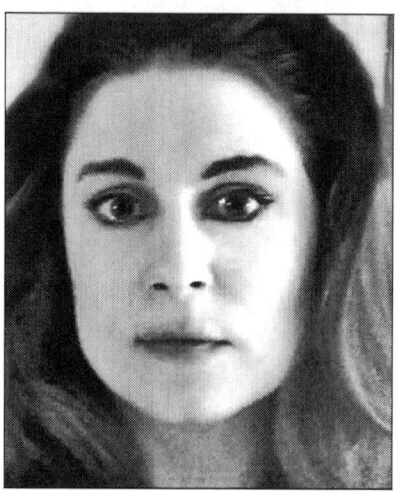

The first time I saw him, he was sitting on a perch, cracking a nut with his beak. I walked over to his cage for a closer look as he manipulated the kernel with a slug-like black tongue, expertly holding onto it with one scaly foot. Eventually he got bored and flung the shell aside. It sailed out of the cage, pinging against the side of my head where it came to rest in a strand of hair. The bird let out a low cackle and began busily grooming its shoulder-feathers. If birds have shoulders. I wasn't exactly sure.

I extracted the peanut shell from my hair and continued to watch.

After the bird had finished rooting about, it glanced up at me, blinked once, then shuffled sideways on its perch before turning around and providing me with a glorious view of it crapping generously onto the sanded bottom of the cage. I was about to give it a standing ovation but its repertoire wasn't over. Swivelling about, the creature proceeded to balance on one leg, making strange clicking noises like a metal detector having a seizure. *He's showing off*, I thought, and pretended to turn away, whereupon he set up a loud, angry squawking until I turned back to him.

"He's quite a character, isn't he?" said an assistant, coming up beside me.

"You could say that. I've had worst first dates. How much is he, just out of interest?"

"This one's a bargain, he's only 250 pounds."

250 didn't sound like much of a bargain to me, not for a bunch of grey and white feathers attached to a less than attractive bird. Turn it into a Stella McCartney handbag and I might be prepared to revise my opinion though.

"He's an African Grey," the assistant explained. "They're not the prettiest parrots around, but they're supposed to be the best talkers. They usually cost anything from four to 500, but we don't know this one's history which is why he's so cheap."

"Cheap, cheap," screamed the parrot.

"Oh hush," the assistant said, tapping her finger against his cage. "The owner found him flying around her garden – it took her two hours to catch him. We put up notices in the area but no one came forward to claim him, so he's been with us for about two weeks now."

"What sort of things can he say?"

"He's not as talkative as he could be, but I think that once he's settled into a new home his owner's going to have trouble keeping him quiet. He's got a wicked sense of humour. He's learned to imitate the phone here and had us running about all day yesterday. The one thing I will say," the assistant whispered confidentially, "is that he's got a bit of a dirty mouth. I'm assuming he picked up his habit for foul language from his last owners."

"Bollocks," the bird suddenly contributed, as though proving the assistant's point, or maybe contradicting it.

The assistant moved off, possibly in disgust, but I stayed in front of the parrot's cage for a while longer to see if he'd come out with anything else. If he said the c-word, it would raise his value in my eyes by about a score. Unfortunately, he didn't seem to have anything further to share, and soon returned to preening himself. Clearly nobody had bothered to tell him that African Greys weren't considered the prettiest of the parrot species.

Eventually I wandered over to the kitten enclosure but the cute balls of fluff weren't doing it for me, and I kept glancing back towards the large grey bird.

I'd originally intended to buy a kitten as a present to myself. It was my one-year anniversary since coming off the booze; 365 days and I hadn't touched a drop. It still wasn't easy but my resolve had hardened and I was proud of myself. I kept a bottle of whisky locked away inside my living room sideboard. It was a mark of willpower. My father, on the other hand, thought it was a mark of insanity – or, to coin his phrase, I was 'a mad bitch with a death wish'. Still, it had remained there for a year, untouched. For some reason, it gave me a sense of power knowing that I was strong enough to fight the urge. I'd tried explaining this to my dad but he'd suggested that if I wanted to experience a sense of power I should just stick my finger into a live socket and be done with it. It would kill me quicker than the booze. He's nothing if not supportive, my old dad.

Anyway, I'd promised myself that if I ever reached this momentous day, I would buy myself a cat. I love animals but when I was drinking I could barely remember to feed myself, let alone a pet. That morning I'd woken up knowing it was my day for kitten-buying. But after just 10 minutes in the pet shop my plan was unravelling. I was already besotted with a ludicrously expensive, rudely verbose bird and now a kitten felt like second best. I wanted that parrot more than anything – if only to teach him how to say 'big hairy monkey bollocks'. But there's a huge difference between a 20 pound kitten and a 250 pound bird, so I left the shop pet-less and depressed.

*

All that evening, I kept thinking about the parrot – he'd seemed so human, as though there was a superior brain ticking away under that feathered head. At some point I must have made the decision to go back for him, because by 10 the next morning I found myself standing in front of his cage again.

"OK arsehole?" said the parrot. I have been greeted in more pleasant ways, but I still felt that he was pleased to see me. The bird eyeballed me curiously and, for a brief second, it seemed like he was sussing me out

– deciding whether I was right for him, rather than the other way round.

The assistant I'd spoken to the previous day recognised me and came over. "So, he's finally got his claws into someone, has he?"

"Yup, I have to admit I'm smitten. He's a bit on the pricey side but I reckon he'll provide me with hours of amusement."

"I'm sure he will. To be honest, I'm glad someone's taking him. I'll miss him, but I was getting a little worried that we'd have trouble finding him a new owner. A lot of people want a bird with hardly any vocabulary so that they can teach them from scratch. And what with his bad language, somebody with kids would never have taken him."

"Well I live alone and I promise not to be too offended by him." Little did she know I'd stopped off at the bookshop first to buy a copy of the *Profanisaurus*.

Half an hour later, I left the shop the proud new owner of a splendid African Grey. They had included the cage and some feed in with the price, so I felt that I hadn't done too badly. Back home, I settled him in the lounge where he promptly fell asleep.

Later that night, while I was hosting the weekly AA meeting, he woke up and shook out his feathers, making a great show of fanning the air. For a while everyone clucked over him but they soon grew bored when it became apparent he wasn't going to speak. A few times, when I looked up, I was pleased to see that he was focusing on me, head on one side, his eyes sharp and black like two tiny raisins. I'd had boyfriends in the past who were less attentive, so I was pretty impressed.

When the last of the group had left, I stood in front of his cage trying to cajole him into speaking, but he remained stoic and eventually tucked his head under his wing in a gesture which could be interpreted as nothing other than dismissive. I decided to name him Torrap – not very imaginative, but it was bound to rhyme with one of his favourite swear words.

For three days the bird kept a very firm lid on things. He contemplated, he groomed, he shat, he ate but not a word burst forth from his well-sealed beak. Then on the fourth day the phone rang at three o'clock in the morning. Or rather it didn't. I was roused from a deep, peaceful slumber by the parrot's first vocal submission, and very impressive it was too. Just as I replaced the telephone back in its cradle, I saw him glance at me with something resembling glee before he started up the ringing again. This went on for quarter of an hour, by which time I felt like throttling him. Just as I was nearing boiling point, he turned his back on me and fell asleep. I thought about rattling his cage, just to pay him back, but reminded myself that he was only an animal and didn't know any better.

A week after the phone incident, he learned to imitate my smoke alarm. This was not so amusing. My smoke alarm is very shrill and whereas a sharp jab with the broom is enough to put an end to its accidental cacophony, I could hardly stick said implement up the bird's arse – although I did come close twice. To make matters worse, whenever I tried to reprimand him, I was greeted by a string of abuse and the furious flinging of birdseed.

His behaviour became both embarrassing and ill-mannered. There was no jolly repetition of lewd catchphrases, as I'd hoped; simply cringe-worthy faux pas. He would make farting noises, the likes of which I had never heard before, whenever my boyfriend came round, and then pretend to be innocently asleep. He would shout abuse when friends came to visit, always somehow managing to home in on some essential truth, so that one of my overweight friends had 'fat cow' repeatedly screamed at her, while another was chastised for being a 'cock-munching slut bucket'. It seemed that the parrot might have actually edited the *Profanisaurus* himself.

The longer I had him, the more I began to suspect that his behaviour was not merely mindless repetition but almost planned malice. The bird had a scheming brain, I was sure of it.

Often I would place food in his bowl, only to be greeted by screams of, "Take it away. Take it away, I don't fucking want this shit. Garcon. Garcon. Bring me some proper food." If his previous owners had taught him all this, they certainly had a lot to answer for. I was not impressed.

In this way, life with the bird became uneasy. It was like a bad marriage. I would dread coming home, never knowing if I would be greeted with vengeful abuse or stony silence. We sulked with each other, we ignored one another and, after a while, for some inexplicable reason, I became slightly afraid of him. I sensed a dark malevolence to his antics and, by week four, decided to get rid of him. My wariness was proved right when, cleaning out his cage, he pecked my hand so viciously that he drew blood. I shouted out in pain but he merely sat in the corner, calmly staring at me while expertly mimicking the sound of an ambulance.

As I left the room to seek out a plaster for my smarting hand, I heard him muttering quietly to himself. Creeping back, I pressed my ear to the door. I couldn't properly hear what he was saying, but I felt a cold shiver of fear pass down my spine as I caught the sound of my own name, followed by a low, spiteful chuckle.

*

The night before I was due to return him to the shop, I was sitting in my lounge reading a book. He was asleep with his back to me, and I hoped he would remain that way until the following morning. Unfortunately it was not to be, he wasn't about to go quietly. He had decided to leave me with a suitable reminder of his stay.

At 10:30 I was getting ready to turn in for the night when I heard a voice. "What's your poison?" it inquired.

I spun around, but the bird had its back to me and appeared to be asleep. Shaking my head to clear it, I made to stand up when I heard a sound I hadn't experienced for over a year. With perfect clarity, came the grating sound of ice being scooped out of a bucket, followed by the crisp chink of it falling into a glass. Saliva flooded my mouth and I panted lightly, fighting down the response.

Looking towards the parrot again, our eyes met. He was surreptitiously peering at me over his shoulder, an evil gleam in his eye, but as soon as I glanced at him he turned away and ruffled his feathers – a performer warming up for Act II.

Again, the sound of tinkling ice – musical and deadly.

Placing my hands firmly over my ears, I started to leave the room but my body jolted involuntarily as I encountered the sweet sound of smooth, golden Jack Daniels being poured into a glass, followed by the sound of someone gulping it down. A contented sigh from the drinker and then, "Same again."

Same again. Same again. The sound of ice, whiskey. Ice and whiskey together. Again and again and again. Saliva dribbled from the corner of my mouth and I began to shake with anticipation.

By the time I'd unlocked my lone bottle of JD I could taste it. I'd already drunk the whole bottle without even touching a drop. I tore off the top and, unable to get to a glass in time, took a long swig from the bottle. I was in heaven. I was in hell. I was back at the beginning, and all the while, the parrot sat in the corner examining its black talons and urging me on. "Same again. Same again. Same again."

I returned the parrot late the next day, once I'd vaguely sobered up, but already it was too late. He knew it and I knew it. The journey was spent in implacable silence, only punctuated now and again by the sound of the bird imitating a cork popping out of a wine bottle and chuckling excitedly under its breath.

*

A few weeks later I returned to the pet shop; although by this time, the assistant didn't even recognise me and I had to remind her who I was. My hair hung in greasy strands around my grey, drawn face, and even in my half-human state, I knew that she was recoiling from my fumy breath as I spoke. But I had to know.

"The parrot?" I asked. "Did you manage to re-sell him?"

"Er, yes," she replied, her voice heavy with a combination of pity and revulsion as she indicated towards the now-empty cage. "A couple of days after you returned him a gentleman came in and bought him. Rather a sad story really, his wife left him a few months back because of a gambling problem. He said he'd managed to crack the habit and thought the bird would be just the incentive he needed to lay off the gambling for good."

As I made my way home, via Threshers, I had the distinct feeling that the pet shop hadn't seen the last of the parrot. In fact, I would have bet my week's giro on it. And I probably wouldn't have been the only one.

~

Adena Graham's Biography

I have had other stories published in various magazines (both online and offline). This includes *Creepy Pasta*, *Unhinged*, *Dead Things*, *QWF*, *Writers' Brew* and, most recently, three editions of *Popshot Magazine*.

I've also had two erotic novels published (under a pseudonym) - I'd like to say it was *Fifty Shades of Grey*, but there are three of those and my bank balance indicates it wasn't them.

I've also recently finished a novel which I'm trying to find an agent for.

HIGHLY COMMENDED STORIES

BIKING TO FIND THE BOY

Highly commended story, by Ian Tucker

The last few inches of soil were basically slurry, which was totally yukky and kept getting under my fingernails and running down the inside of my arm. At least it was easy to shove my hand through and soon I could feel rain dropping on my fingers and warm air blowing against my palm.

Unfortunately, it took another age to get any further. The oozy, sloppy, deluging muck gave me nothing to hold on to and I must have spent 10 minutes just waving my hand around blindly and grabbing at weirdly-shaped things which slipped through my fingers.

In the end, I had to rotate my arm in a circle to make the hole bigger and then push my shoulders sideways so I could get into a crouching position under the ground. There was a fearful, bone-grinding noise as I finally forced my head into the looser earth but, as far as I could tell, everything was still functioning. I would have to investigate the causes later.

The last bit was dragging my lower half from the sucking grasp of the slimy bombsite I had made of my grave. I have curvy hips, meaning a big bum, so it was a bit of a struggle and somehow I managed to crush one of my fingers between two rocks in the process. However, a lot of straining, a good deal of unladylike grunting, one mighty pop and I was sitting on the graveside – born again from Mother Earth like a whopping, grime-laden zombie-cherub.

Being buried does nothing for your hair. Neither does head-butting your way out of a coffin or clambering through six feet of soil. Worst of all, however, is being dead. Being dead gives your hair a lifelessness which would daunt any shampoo. Nonetheless, I was not about to go back into the world looking like a total fright. There's a big difference between being haunted by a buxom, undead demon-queen and being chased around by a drooling, gawky undead-beat with matted hair and a lop-sided running style. I was definitely planning to be the former and, as I'd only been dead a few days, I still had something to salvage.

It was the kind of cemetery with a toilet block so mourners and flower-bringers wouldn't have to worry about being caught short. Very middle class and exactly the sort of place my parents would have decided to put me. I shouldn't complain of course. They must have spent a fortune on the plot when it would have been much cheaper – and in retrospect much less convenient – to have given the job to the crematorium.

Anyway, the loo-block was locked – presumably they don't expect much demand after midnight and are worried about the local goths breaking in and holding some kind of messy orgy involving lager, frowning and candles. It is a moot point whether anyone ever considered the toiletry needs of the more permanent residents.

But a locked door should be no trouble. It was time to try the preternatural strength which comes with being undead. There is no point in holding back on these things. If you have to put up with the drawbacks of having expired, then you may as well enjoy the advantages. I shoulder-charged the door.

And bounced off. It appears that having snuffed it doesn't give you preternatural strength after all.

Interestingly, however, it didn't hurt. I stood staring at the door with my head lolling slightly to one side, contemplating this. I could clearly feel stuff, mud under my fingernails, the torn hem of my grave clothes, the knots of hair which were bouncing on my cheeks and so on. And I could feel temperatures and solidity and liquid-i-ness and the crawling sensation you get when your entire body is clammy and moist and dirty. But there was no pain.

Very interesting. However, after a bit more thought I decided it didn't help much.

I eventually got into and out of the loo block by smashing a window with a rock and climbing through.

On the return I was making efforts to preserve my newly hand-soaped cleanliness and overlooked a few remaining glass-shards, one of which neatly sliced off a finger on my left hand. There wasn't much blood and it didn't bother me much. It was more embarrassing than anything else.

I wasn't sure what you're supposed to do with bits of yourself which come off. Presumably you should take some care to keep as much of you together as possible. However, the torn-nighty thing I was wearing didn't have any pockets so I had to hide the finger behind a tombstone to collect later.

While I'd been powdering my broken nose, it had become obvious to me that the first thing I would need was transport. This I would have to steal and there wasn't going to be anything to steal in the cemetery at night. Hence it was a short walk – well, actually a shuffle, as the undertakers had only made cosmetic efforts to repair my smashed hip and my head did seem to keep tipping to one side – to the gates. Then, after shifting a lawn-mower against the wall to give me a step up, I was out and over onto the road.

No one about. I inspected a couple of family cars parked on the kerb and tried their handles, but, frankly, I have no idea how to break into or steal a car. Being dead doesn't give you any additional insight in that respect. All this stuff about reading minds, x-ray vision and demonic knowledge is just a myth, I'm afraid. Being dead was turning out to be a bit disappointing in terms of special powers.

Maybe I would have to walk? After all, I couldn't feel any pain in my legs so I could presumably go on, basically, for ever. But it would probably take several days to reach Hull and I imagined daylight might cause me some practical problems.

I saw a light approaching down the road. Oddly, only a single light. Perhaps someone with a broken headlamp? I shuffled into the road. The engine was making a deep roar and the light was approaching fast. Motorbike. Best to get out the way.

Or not. I was already dead – how bad could it be? The bike wobbled slightly as the rider saw me, then it tried to veer. I veered with it. The bike swung hard the other way and I leapt towards it yelling comedy ghost-noises and throwing my hands in the air like a vampire. It's fun being dead – all the fear's gone but somehow you still have a sense of humour.

The biker didn't seem to be enjoying the joke. His last movement was to fail to mount the kerb. Then he was sliding into a wall on his bottom and the bike was flipping artistically through the air and landing on top of me. I went down like a blancmange under a paperweight.

My grave-nighty got caught in one of the wheels and jammed it up while I grabbed the other one to stop it spinning into my face. This stopped it blending my nose but unfortunately it blended two of my fingers instead. No pain. I was still laughing.

By the time I'd identified which parts of the mess were bike and which parts were me, it seemed that the only real additional damage to either of us was a large scratch on the bike's petrol tank and my right foot being twisted 90 degrees out of line. I stomped over to the rider with my head now resting mostly on my shoulder and looked down on him, balancing awkwardly on my club foot and trashed hip.

The rider was alive. His helmet, which had flames painted on it, seemed to have stopped the worst of the impact he'd had with a garden wall. He would be OK after a few months in hospital. I relieved him of his clothes.

Despite the dent I also took the helmet – mostly because I thought it might help if I didn't have to show my face. I'd noticed in the cemetery toilets that part of my cheek had begun growing some sort of flowering fungus.

I'd never ridden a motorbike in real life and consequently experienced a few minor fails – one of which compacted another finger – before I got the hang of forward motion. It wasn't, however, long before I found myself cruising away from Tilebury at ever increasing speeds and feeling the wind whistling over my newly acquired leathers.

There is something appropriate about the undead riding motorbikes. Stallions or stagecoaches also work but you can't imagine a zombie in a mini, taking the bus or floating overhead in an air-balloon. You have to get with the style.

Personally, I was pleased with how things were working out, even if the boots were too big, the trousers were too tight and the gloves had too many fingers. As the engine roared unnecessarily, I felt about as sexy as you can feel when your heart has stopped.

The drive gave me time to get the story straight. Unfortunately, the period from slamming into the flagstones under the bridge, until the moment I woke... became aware of myself... in the coffin, was blank. One assumes that I was scraped off the pavement, taken to a morgue and then an undertaker, sewn back together and placed in the coffin, buried with great pomp and wailing etc. and then everyone left to eat nibbles and wear black.

That bit was fine. However, it wasn't the important bit of the story. Critically, I had no idea and no way of knowing what had happened to Deren during that period.

He'd have been interviewed, for sure. But how had it gone? Had he been arrested for coaxing me to look over the edge and then pushing me sharply in the small of the back? Or had he been comforted for the tragic loss of his lovely big-bottomed girlfriend in a terrible accident?

And what had he done with the ticket?

These things mattered rather urgently, because I was driving like a bat out of hell towards the flat we used to share. If he was in Pentonville starting an insufficiently long stretch for my murder, then I wasn't going to find him at home. Equally, if he was being comforted for my tragic demise, he could easily have gone to his Mam's.

Alternatively, if he'd cashed in the ticket he could be on a jet sipping champagne in first class. Frankly, he could be anywhere and the flat was just my best guess.

I didn't know how these things work, but I also suspected that I probably didn't have limitless time to chase him down. Perhaps I'd turn into a pumpkin at dawn or would start to rot or turn to dust if I stayed out of the ground for more than a day. Frankly, who knows what the rules are for the undead – I'd already proven that the Hollywood version wasn't right on all scores. I was going to have to be lucky.

I reasoned it like this – everyone knew that me and Deren left the pub together. They knew we were both steaming and they knew the bridge was only a few minutes' walk. I don't remember seeing anyone at the time, but realistically Deren would have to admit to being with me when I fell (was pushed).

So, he'd have said I was messing about – unfortunately, far too believable – and the booze had tripped me up and while he'd tried to save me I was over the edge before he knew what was happening. Such a tragedy, such a shock.

So, what was there to prove him wrong? Fingerprints on my tank top? Get real. So they'd have believed him. He'd have gone home but he'd not have managed more than a day with his Mam before he'd have had to get some fresh air. She's like that.

Which means by now he would either have returned to the flat or cashed in the ticket and started his new life as a plutocrat. But I didn't think he'd have done that yet. He's a crafty little toad and pitching up with a winning lottery ticket the morning after your girlfriend – the one everyone knows plays every week – plunges to her death, might have seemed to draw a little too much attention to himself.

He'd give himself a few weeks. Let the enquiries die down, mope about and get a bit of sympathy. Then he'd be calling the lottery and stressing how he wanted to keep his identity secret because he was a private person and so on. Three days later, he'd cancel his Facebook and his mobile-contract, surrender the lease and fade away to his new life. I doubt he'd even tell his Mam where he'd gone for a few years.

And it'd work, because he's not all that popular. No one would miss him enough to try tracking him down. As I exceeded the speed limit on the motorway, I found myself really, really hoping I was going to be in time to give him his just desserts.

The street was quiet. Cars on both sides meant it was going to be difficult to park and I didn't know how to dismount anyway. I decided that, nice as it would be to sneak up on Deren in his bed, ninja tactics aren't really for zombies. So I aimed for a few bins and crashed the bike into them as gently as I could manage. By leaping off at the last minute I avoided being caught under it this time.

Obviously, there is only so gently you can crash a bike and it made a lot of noise as it redistributed the bins and rearranged the fender on a white van. I also made a rather loud noise bouncing into a parked car and marginally messing up my right arm. No pain. It might be a little floppy from now on but otherwise it'd be fine.

I let myself in to the flat using the spare key we kept in a corner of the flowerbed before any nosey neighbours stumbled out to investigate the cause of all the banging. In the hall were a load of bags and boxes, some sports equipment and a rather fine ladies' coat I recognised as belonging to Charlie. The living room was full of new computerised toys.

A light was on in the bedroom. Inevitably it was Charlie whose bleary face poked out and stared at me. She screamed – which is so obvious it's almost not worth mentioning. I picked up a cricket bat and strode forward, in as confident and unshuffling a manner as I could manage with a dislocated ankle, a hip held together by fishing wire and a head propped up only by the shape of the helmet encasing it.

Deren opened the door just as I reached it. He was peevish and telling Charlie how she was imagining things. I poked the bat into his face and had the satisfaction of watching him fall over partially from the blow and partially from the shock.

I let out a blood-curdling groan just for the sake of the scene, but it was mostly muffled inside the helmet. So I reached up to undo the straps.

It took quite a while to remove the helmet. The fingers I still possessed were quite clumsy and the various collisions had distorted the neck-hole into an irregular shape which didn't slip off easily, particularly at the angle my head seemed determined to adopt. But I did it and eventually stood before them like an avenging corpse.

"Hello, Charlie."

She wasn't up to conversation. She picked up an old typewriter Deren keeps on a cabinet for show and hurled it, oddly enough, at Deren rather than me. Then she ran past me into the corridor and I heard the front door slam.

"Hello, Deren." My voice was a little indistinct and saliva-y. Not my normal crisp clarity. I suspect it had something to do with my tongue having embarked on the early stages of decomposition.

"You're dead."

"Care to join me?"

Conversation stagnated so I let out another one of my moans. I was enjoying this, perhaps, in retrospect, a little too much.

Deren moved suddenly, grabbing his cigarette lighter from the bedside and flicking the flame. What he thought this would achieve I don't know, but he held it out as if it would keep me away. If he'd had a crucifix, which he didn't, he'd probably have tried the same with that.

I was pleased to find that naked flames did not scare me (and I expect the same would be true of crucifixes). So I laughed and smacked Deren's wrist with my cricket bat. Actually, I smacked his wrist first and then laughed. He dropped the lighter and howled.

"So, what have you been up to while I was away, darling?" I asked, slurrily. "While I've been decomposing in a field where you put me, I mean, at the mercies of nature's burrowing invertebrates and the terrible mushing effects of dampness."

He jumped at me and, I must admit, rather took me by surprise. As I was not equipped with preternatural strength, his 12 stone six overcame my nine stone nine (less a few fingers) and sent me spinning into a dressing table. He used the intermission to escape into the kitchen. I used it to try to prop my head up as vertically as possible using a rather bandy arm.

Pausing only to recover my cricket bat and to make sure that the fire from his lighter had definitely taken hold of the bedsheets, I lumbered after him single-mindedly. Well actually, double-mindedly — as well as thinking about hurting him, I was also wondering what brains would taste like and whether Deren had any.

Deren had a bread knife. He also had a look of terror and a mobile phone into which he was trying to punch numbers. I was pleased to see the look of terror. When I lurched into view he dropped the mobile clumsily and backed into a corner holding his knife out like a fencing foil.

"Been spending your money, darling?" I asked waving my wobbly arm at a few new boxes on the kitchen top.

"I'm going to be rich, so no reason not to max out the credit card." It obviously occurred to him after he'd said this that talking to a zombie about personal debt financing is ridiculous, so he returned to warding me off with his bread knife instead. I advanced on him, until the knife touched my biking leathers.

"Cashed in my ticket yet?"

"No, not yet. And you're dead. What are you doing here?" He slashed the knife at me and I caught it with my hand. I lost another finger in the process but it didn't hurt. Deren dropped the knife and backed up to the fire-escape. On cue the smoke coming from the bedroom triggered the fire alarm.

He was blubbering now, which was not an attractive look. I was trying to remember why I'd ever fancied him but concluded it must have had something to do with having once had hormones and a pulse. I bashed him again with the bat and knocked out a couple of teeth. He would have to add cosmetic dentistry to the list of things to spend my winnings on.

He scrambled as far as the fire escape and made a bid for freedom. I let him get out onto the iron staircase and then tripped him with the bat so he would have fallen had he not grabbed a safety rail. I helped him overbalance a bit further so he was, in effect, hanging from both hands. Despite his unshaved stubble and exposed pigeon-chest, seeing him there, so far above the ground, was a pleasant image. I walked up to him and smiled as well as I could manage with a lop-sided head.

"Help me up, please. Help. I can't hold on, give me a hand."

"This little piggy stole my lottery ticket," I replied and whacked one of his hands. He yelped and his grip slipped. He was definitely out over the three storey drop now.

"This little piggy stole my home." I gave him another forceful tap, there was a satisfying cracking sound and he screamed in pain.

"This little piggy sent me spinning head over heels to land in a messy heap on the pavement where I marmalised my hip, shattered my neck and did an excessive amount of dying." I whacked his hand quite a bit harder this time and his grip went entirely. He now only had one hand to hold on with.

"This little piggy's going to tell me where the ticket is..." I hovered over his remaining hand but he was too busy screaming to answer so I whacked it to get his attention. Again his grip shifted until he was only just clinging on with his fingertips.

"...and this little piggy's going to tell me now..."

He finally got the idea and told me. Deren does not have enough imagination to lie so I left him hanging and returned to the flat. Conveniently, I wasn't breathing so the smoke didn't make me choke. As he'd said, the ticket was in his wallet. So, after grabbing a few things from what used to be our bedroom, I left by the front door without returning to bother Deren further.

There were lots of people on the stairs and gathered around outside the block of flats. Luckily, having just been evacuated from their beds without time to apply makeup, most looked worse than I did so no one commented as I stumbled to the motorbike.

I looped round the back of the flats on my way to the motorway. Deren was still clinging onto the fire escape by his fingers and I was pleased to see his pyjama bottoms had slipped down to his ankles. Should have got a belt.

It is a pity that Deren has spent all his money and run up debts just when all his worldly goods got destroyed by fire. It is even more sad that all this happened before he could cash in that lottery ticket. Things will be unpleasant for him for a while, but at least he should live.

For me, the sun is rising and I've written this entire thing on an ancient typewriter using my one remaining functioning finger. If there are typos, you'll have to live with it, and I won't. I've recovered my finger from behind the tombstone, where it had suffered only a few minor rat bites and will shortly be returning to my grave. I'm taking my winning lottery ticket with me and it, at least, will soon be dissolved by insects, moisture and mould.

Other than during the annual Walpurgis Night and Halloween carnivals or in connection with the occasional apocalyptic event, I don't expect to be making another appearance soon. But if I do – it'll probably be to make sure Deren hasn't had any good luck.

And I'll be sure to tell you all about it.

~

Ian Tucker's Biography

I've been writing stories, almost entirely for my own entertainment, for about 10 years. This includes two novels featuring morally dubious heroes and various amounts of misbehaviour and crime.

My short stories tend to cover horror of the supernatural rather than gory sort, silly tales nominally for children, which are probably more relevant to adults pretending to be children, and whodunit crime. These are mostly uploaded onto my website where I am writing a reader-directed novel (meaning the reader can choose the order in which to read the story by clicking links) through the monthly articles of the *Tilebury Harbinger* (a village newsletter).

I aim for entertainment over worthiness and am fond of a good story. Certainly, I would never let too much truth get in the way of one. I live in Bristol with my wife and a lot of flies (and some spiders).

Ian's website: www.tilebury.com

JOE LEAN

Highly commended story, by Bernie Deehan

January 9

My-Lann. That's her name. She's Japanese. Who would have thought it? You put 'Find a Woman' on your New

Year's Resolutions list and she appears just days later. Unbelievable. They've sat her on the desk next to mine, on the other side of the aisle. It's fate.

January 11

My-Lann is amazing. She was some kind of Olympic athlete back in Japan. I heard her telling someone in the office kitchen. And we've so much in common, with her being Japanese and everything. For example, I love sushi. Not the ones with fish in them, but the other ones. I've seen *The Seven Samurai*. Well, technically just the first half; had to turn it off when Mother insisted on watching *An Audience with Michael Bublé*. She still won't let me have a TV in my room, or a computer, despite me being a fully grown man. "I don't know what you'd be watching up there," she always says. "Temptation comes in many forms."

Well I hope it gets a bloody move on. Or at least, that's what I used to think – before My-Lann.

January 16

My-Lann actually asked me if I wanted a cup of tea. We were having our first conversation. I said, "Yes." She said, "How do you like it?" I thought for a moment and said, "Black." I doubt they do this milk and sugar business in Japan, and I wanted to show her I'm a man of the world. She was impressed, I could tell.

Tea tasted horrible, but I forced it down.

January 17

My-Lann smiled at me when she came in, and nodded

her head slightly. I wonder if I should give her a special bow in the mornings, some kind of formal Japanese greeting that a man gives a woman at the start of the day? Must look into it.

At the staff meeting, I held the door open for her and she said, "Thank you." It's the best two words I've heard all week. All month, even.

Oh My-Lann, My-Lann,
I'm your Number One Fan.
I'm so glad you no longer reside in Japan.

January 20

Spent some time with My-Lann in the office kitchen as we both made our lunches. We didn't say anything. It's amazing how quickly we're comfortable in each other's company, so comfortable we don't even have to talk.

I think it's getting safe enough to call us 'an item'.

Later, I'm so light-headed I completely forget to tap my Oyster Card on the way out of the station. Oh to hell with it — I'm crazy and in love and I just don't care.

January 23

There's a new man in Sales. He went right round the office introducing himself. Very impressive. "Lean," he said. "Joe Lean." Good firm handshake. Minus points: long, auburn hair tied in a ponytail, and an earring in his left ear. Definite no-nos. Apart from that, a good first impression. Looked me straight in the eye before I looked away. Must steal that technique and use with My-Lann.

January 26

For the past three days now, everybody says hello to Joe Lean when he arrives in the morning. You'd think he was Captain James T Kirk or something. And he always swans it at least five minutes late.

Oh well, at least My-Lann will disapprove of his poor punctuality as much as I do.

January 30

Saw My-Lann bring over a mug of tea and place it on Joe Lean's desk. What was she doing? She's not even in Sales. Plus she's at least four desks away from Joe Lean, putting him well out of her tea radius. Very strange.

February 1

Three people were hanging around Joe Lean's desk for most of the morning, and not for work reasons either. You'd think he was Gandhi or something. He murmured a line in that low drawl of his — I couldn't hear what it was — and then Dawn from Accounts said, "You were in a *band*?" Then Joe Lean nodded his head slowly and smiled. "Cacophony," he said. "Remember them?"

The next thing I knew, My-Lann shot up from her desk and practically sprinted over to join the throng.

"Cacophony?" said Dawn. "No, I don't remember them."

Ha. Take that, Mr Joe Lean.

"Well, we were a bit too ahead of our time for the UK," he said. "But we were big in Japan."

He looked straight at My-Lann, who had suddenly turned from a confident young woman into some kind of blushing schoolgirl.

"You were in the Top 10," said My-Lann. "I thought I recognised you."

"Yeah," said Joe Lean. He ran a hand through his ridiculous hair. "I think we went straight in at number three or something. Stayed there for, I don't know, four weeks or so? Bit of a haze, really."

Oh, a bit of haze was it? Let's see how hazy you are with the facts, I thought, turning to my computer. After practically tearing a hole in my Chewbacca mouse mat, I finally established the facts: Cacophony. Japanese Top 10, number three, April 22 to May 19, 2004. Just as he'd said. I clicked on Images and there he was in a range of artfully posed photographs: Joe Lean standing by an old brick wall; Joe Lean resting against a tree trunk in a leather jacket; Joe Lean on a 1950s moped parked beside a power station. The rest of the band were conspicuous by their absence, his ego perhaps being so large that they were squeezed right out of the frame. Oh yes, it was the Joe Lean Show all the way, only now he was performing it from behind a desk, his groupies all around. Including My-Lann.

I have to do something about this, and fast. The office party is next week, and I want everyone to see that My-Lann and I are very much a couple.

February 3

Joe Lean just happened to bring in his guitar case. "What, this?" he said, parking it noisily by the side of his desk. "Oh, I'm just returning it to someone later..."

He placed it facing directly into the aisle, causing a major health and safety hazard. He might as well have erected a neon sign above it saying, 'I HAD A TOP THREE

HIT FOR FOUR WEEKS, I'M ABSOLUTELY INCREDIBLE, PLEASE LOVE ME.'

Despite stating that the case was merely in transit, he still managed to pull the guitar out of it at lunchtime, after much protesting to his growing fan base that he wasn't much of a player and had gotten rusty, etc., etc. He then sat on the edge of the desk and proceeded to perform note-perfect renditions of 'Wonderwall', 'Here Comes the Sun' and the final section of 'Nessun Dorma'. You know the bit I mean. YOU'RE NOT EVEN SUPPOSED TO PLAY NESSUN DORMA ON A GUITAR. Doing it without an orchestra is just silly and a blatant act of attention-seeking.

Oh My-Lann, I thought, *please use your natural beauty and intelligence to see through this pathetic act*.

But there she was, sitting cross-legged on the floor by his desk, like some kind of sex disciple. She sipped her smoothie slowly through a straw while staring at Joe's leather cowboy-boots, which had mysteriously appeared on his feet after a trip to the toilets. The boots had spurs on them and everything. I mean, come on, where did he think he was, the OK Corral? This is Reading Industrial Park, mate.

Later, I saw My-Lann chatting with him by the vending machine. She was staring into his emerald-green eyes. He rested an arm casually on the glass as he talked. I decided to walk past, on the pretext that I needed some staples from the stationery room.

I heard My-Lann mention the office party. I stayed in the stationery room until I'd calmed down.

February 4

Mother knocked three times and came into my room.

She knew something was up because I'd said I wasn't hungry when I came in, and then I hadn't even come down for *MasterChef*. I said everything was fine, there's nothing wrong, honestly, but then she ruffled my hair in the way I keep telling her not to do, and when she said, "Come on, what's wrong, petal?" I just blurted out, "I hate Joe Lean. I HATE HIM."

Mother said that was no way to speak about someone, no matter what they were like. "Your Father wouldn't have said that about anyone, would he?" she said. "And what happened to my little boy that he'd come out with something like that?"

I refused to say any more and Mother finally went back downstairs. Later, she knocked softly three times on the door. I heard it open. I was too embarrassed to turn around. The door closed again. When I looked, I saw that she'd left a plate of cheese and ham Crispy Pancakes on the bookcase, my favourite. And a tin of Fanta.

I'll go down later and say sorry.

February 5

Action Plan:
1. Go to office party
2. Tell Joe Lean to back right off
3. Tell My-Lann that I love her
4. The End

Simple.

February 10

When I got to the party, there was no sign of My-Lann. Or Joe Lean.

I went straight to the toilets. There was no one there so I practiced in the mirror.

"Now you listen to me, Mr Joe Lean." I stood with my legs apart, like Clint Eastwood. "You keep your hands right off her, you understand?"

"Oh yeah?" he said, in my head.

"Yeah."

"Yeah?" He lunged for me.

"Yeah."

He missed by miles and fell flat on his face.

"I warned you," I said.

That went well, I thought.

Then I heard a latch open behind me and Paul from Marketing came out of the cubicle, doing up his belt. He shook his head slowly.

"Bloody nut-job," he said.

When I got back into the main room, Joe Lean was there, miraculously standing on his own. It was now or never.

"C-can I have a word?" I said. "About My-Lann."

"She's great, isn't she?" he said, over the horrendous noise from the karaoke. "Nice arse."

"N-now look here," I said. "She's mine."

Joe Lean leant his head back and laughed; a horrible, moustache-twirling laugh. "You're hilarious," he said. "You haven't even spoken to her, have you?"

"I have. We're an item."

"You what?"

"J-just... stay away from her," I said.

"You know what I'm going to do?" said Joe Lean. "I'm going to tell her all about this later, back at my place."

He leant his head back again and his whole body shook.

I grabbed the lapels of his leather jacket. "Joe Lean, I'm begging of you – please don't take My-Lann."

Then he pushed me down to the sticky floor. "What are you going to do?" he said. "Knock me around the head with some spreadsheets?"

Then I saw a pair of elegant legs approaching from behind Joe Lean.

I lay my head down on the floor, the lights from the karaoke machine flashing on her beautiful calves as she left, with two cowboy boots clacking by her side.

May 25

The new workplace isn't too bad. It's in the same Industrial Park, but if I take the long way round in the morning, nobody from the old place can see me.

My-Lann's pregnant or something, apparently. Doesn't bother me, she can do what she likes.

Anyway, there's Caroline now. Oh yes. Caroline. She's from Newcastle. I used to quite like Jimmy Nail, so that's one thing in common for a start.

I helped sort a paper jam the other day and Caroline said, "You're good at that." I almost said something I was so pleased, but I stopped myself. No point in rushing things.

Anyway, must be off. I can hear the kettle downstairs.

Good night, diary.

Good night, Caroline.

Sweet Caroline.

~

Bernie Deehan's Biography

Bernie Deehan writes short stories, some of which have been performed by actors at Liars' League, a monthly literary event, while others have appeared in *Vintage Script*, *Cent Magazine*, *The Litro*, on Visual Verse websites, and in the anthology *New Ghost Stories II*.

Bernie's website: www.berniedeehan.com

SOUP

Highly commended story, by Dirk Puis

The biggest hurdle in the isolation cell was the lack of visual clues about which way was up, and which way was down. If you weren't mad yet when they locked you up, here was a good place to get the process started. Who on Earth had come up with the sick idea of padding the ceiling with the same white leather cushions that lined the floor and walls? Maybe they expected him to start bouncing around.

Sid convinced his brain that the corner in which he huddled was located at the top of the small room, and that the wall opposite him was the floor.

"I can fly," he whispered. "Look at me. I'm a little fly."

Sid somersaulted back to his human form when the grinding click of key in lock crashed through the decompressed silence of his quilted prison. Nurse Delia gingerly poked her Taser stick through the door opening, fully prepared to zap Sid before he had a chance to pounce her. The trembling of her hands contrasted charmingly with the simulated firmness of her voice.

"OK, Sid, time's up. I hope this has been a good lesson."

Sid approached. He brushed the tip of the Taser stick with the back of his hand, half hoping she'd push the activation button in a panic. Would the current be strong enough, he wondered, to boil the body of this fragile insect?

"I don't remember what you were trying to teach me, nurse. Do you?"

*

It was hospital policy to release patients from isolation in time for dinner. Speedy reintegration into the group and a solid meal were deemed beneficial. Complaints from the nursing staff about the consequences of this awkward timing would take years to filter through to management. Sid braced himself as he was led straight from the velvet stillness of his holding pen to the eardrum shattering clatter of the ward's cafeteria. The effort to stay upright and look cool in this chaotic wall of sound brought him close to fainting.

Benny sat at the third table with the usual gang. Fragrant Bob masticated his sandwich openmouthed while staring into the misty landscapes of his own private world. There seemed to be a one-way conversation going on between Bob and his sandwich. Mister know-it-all Gregory sat next to Benny, pretending to solve complex problems on his notepad while hunched over a pile of voluminous books.

Noticing his friend's return from the dungeons, Benny waved frantically, as if Sid needed taxiing through heavy traffic. Benny shouted, spewing a fountain of half chewed bread, to make himself heard in the cutlery concert.

"You got out?" he asked. "Did you escape? Did they let you go?"

Benny was fun to play with. Sid could make him do just about anything, merely by sounding sincere. The project to instil Benny with a belief in the fearsome power of telepathy had been steadily progressing for three weeks now, and Sid never missed an opportunity to refine his manipulative skills.

"Both," he replied. "I escaped by instructing their brains to release me."

The theory was based on this simple observation: when you think long and hard, you feel tired. This proves that thoughts are energy, just like the force you use to lift or flap your arms. There is nothing unnatural about it.

Sensitive people should be able to pick up a signal and discern what others are thinking. Strong minded people, in contrast, are able to concentrate their energy beams and learn to aim them precisely. With sufficient practice, they can influence the thoughts of others.

Under direct coaching from Sid, Benny carried around a portable radio, tuned to a frequency in-between stations. Whenever possible, Benny had to hold the radio close to his ear, listening to the emptiness of the ether, and then try to force the crackling static into a tune with his mind power. Sid warned Benny never to follow any instructions he might hear through the speaker, especially if the radio was not switched on.

*

A wave of approving murmurs travelled from table to table as the soup was being served. Considered to be the chef's masterpiece, it was eagerly anticipated by the ward's population. It contained all the nutrients and taste that had been boiled out of the main dish, and was further enriched with a generous amount of alphabet pasta. The culinary clangor climaxed as metal spoons collided with porcelain bowls. Sid pinched his arm to stay conscious, and then looked down to check who was pinching him.

Sid loathed the glutinous slurping and the smacking of wet lips, especially when Fragrant Bob would start munching on the soup's soggy vegetables. Forever hampered by the cheapness of his dentures, Bob was unable to properly close his mouth. He carried a towel with him to mop the incessant stream of drool from his chin.

Benny usually got extremely excited by the arrival of the sumptuous broth. But not today. He just sat there looking tired and uninterested, lost in the tumult around him. Sid had noticed that sudden sadness in the lad's eyes before, but the boy had never looked this helpless. His face faded in a halo of greyness. Benny placed his little radio on the table and sighed.

"I've been practicing while you were in the can, Sid. But I just can't concentrate. I don't feel the energy, not even with all the arm-flapping exercises you made me do. And I can't tune that feckin' radio at all. It's not working, Sid. It's not working at all."

Know-it-all Gregory gave no indication that he was listening to Benny's plea. Still hunched over his books, not debasing himself to the level of the mere mortals around him, he spoke with the deep voice of a taunting deity.

"He's getting desperate, Sid. You better give him some demonstration of your wonderful powers right here and now." Gregory looked up and stared Sid in the eyes. "Come on, show us what you can do. Show us your telepathic voodoo."

Sid remained calm, but a careful observer would have noticed that great effort was spent holding that pose. The clenching of his teeth produced a bony bulge on his cheeks. Seeking a distraction from Gregory's suggestion, Sid welcomed the arrival of the soup bowls and cutlery. He participated eagerly in the fair distribution of the pile of bowls that were shoved across the table. But the beginning of a sparkle in Benny's eyes revealed that it was too late. Gregory put down his pencil and closed his notebook. He rose from his book ambush to push the available buttons a bit harder.

"It would be best to demonstrate before you eat the soup," he offered. "You don't want to waste all that energy on chewing first."

Sid fidgeted with the metal spoon being placed in front of him. He picked it up and slowly wrapped his fingers around the handle, tightening them until their bones shone through whitened skin. Benny was hopping excitedly at the prospect of seeing Sid in action.

"OK. No problem," Sid said. "See our new nurse there?"

*

Nurse Delia stood next to Nurse Peter, trying hard to look as laid-back as he did. She observed the lopsided twist of his hips and buttocks. He rested his weight fully on one leg while the other leg dangled forward at a nonchalant angle. He looked at ease, resting an elbow on the countertop while fiddling with the zap button on his Taser stick with his free hand. He was in full control of the cafeteria.

Nurse Delia put her left foot forward and let her leg relax. She could feel her body weight tilt into the comforting sturdiness of her hip joint. She tried to do the elbow thing, but the countertop was too low for a woman of her height. She crossed her arms instead and pretended to whistle a mental tune.

*

"Can you make her take off her blouse?" Benny enquired.

Sid pondered the possibilities, weighing the pros and cons of Benny's demo suggestion.

"Nah, later maybe. You have to start slow. Get into her mind a bit and learn the frequencies of her thought energy."

Gregory produced a little huff of suppressed

laughter, but Sid remained unmoved.

"I could make her scratch her nose. Watch closely."

*

The only person still interested in the soup was Fragrant Bob. Sid assumed he wanted to get a head start because he knew he'd need to consume twice the amount the others ate. Half of it would droop from his chin onto the towel which he tucked into his collar as an oversized serviette.

Sid focused. He tried to make eye contact with Nurse Delia across the crowded tables. As soon as he thought she was looking in his direction, he scratched his nose vigorously, hoping she'd react by scratching her own.

It wasn't working terribly well. Either the distance was too large or the noisy environment was disturbing his energy beam. Sid tried to lock his gaze on Nurse Delia, desperately blocking out the sea of bobbing heads between him and his target. The sea sloshed about in stormy currents, producing a slight wobble of Sid's head. Shattered fragments of table conversation echoed around him. Sid couldn't resist the constant temptation to eavesdrop, just to make sure they weren't all talking about him. Benny contributed to the distraction by fiddling with an imaginary blouse button on his T-shirt.

A burning itch at the back of Sid's head indicated the spot where Gregory's mocking grimace hit.

"To be honest, I'm starting to feel a bit disappointed," Gregory complained. "Shouldn't she be scratching with both hands by now?"

Sid doubled the effort to concentrate all energy streaming from his forehead into a crisp, straight beam.

He experienced a faint pop in his right ear as a capillary vein in his left eye burst. The cafeteria got fuzzy in a pink haze. The pressure difference caused a malfunctioning of the zoom control in his head. Sid got dragged away from his own line of sight and became an onlooker. He saw himself punching Gregory in slow motion, but was unable to determine whether he was really hitting him or simply imagining it. He punched harder and saw Gregory's skull crack open like an egg.

When green blubber started oozing from Gregory's open cranium, Sid immediately knew what to do. He rolled up his sleeves and examined the thick black hair that was forever sprouting from the birthmark on his arm. He locked the hair between two fingernails and yanked. He yanked harder, and winced. Each flash of pain closed Gregory's skull a few inches, until it was completely healed.

Sid was sweating like a pig, but he was relieved to hear reality come rushing back through the sound waves of the cafeteria crowd.

"Giving up?" asked Gregory.

Shaken, but not ready to admit defeat, Sid reached for his spoon.

"I'm gonna eat my soup first," he announced. "I seem to be a bit short on energy right now."

Sid stirred his soup, swirling the pasta alphabet into a vortex. Three letters floated to the middle, spelling his name. "SID," said the soup. Sid had no idea he was talking out loud when he complained, "Oh no, not that again. Not now." With a quick wipe, he dunked his name back into the depths of the bowl, but other letters now came floating up. "MORO," the soup spelled, which could mean either 'moron' or 'more'. "More of what?" Sid asked his bowl.

Sid felt a tremor in his legs. He looked down but saw his feet firmly planted on the ground. Although it felt as if he was shaking on his chair like a mechanical drill, his legs remained motionless. Maybe those weren't his legs then?

While he considered the possibility of someone stealing his legs and replacing them with fakes, the cafeteria sounds started harmonising. Like a muffled engine in a giant wah-wah chamber, the noise throbbed in massive surges through Sid's skull. The only recognisable melody coming through was of Fragrant Bob munching on his soup vegetables. Bob started clicking his dentures while Gregory renewed his attack.

"Are you reading your soup's thoughts now? What is it saying? Can it make her scratch her nose?"

Sid stirred his soup maniacally, trying to get to a patch of liquid he could scoop up without dragging a pasta letter along.

Bob took out his dentures to pick them clean. "Click click click," they went, still connected to Bob through a glistening line of saliva. He stopped to wipe his chin with the wet towel, managing only to smear the glistening film of soup over his face evenly. He then continued clicking his dentures.

Attempting to look away from his soup, and not prepared to brave the sight of toothless Bob, Sid watched Nurse Delia lick her lips. Her tongue was like a lizard's, wet and pink. Twisting like a snail, the tip of the tongue split and the two points slid up her nostrils.

Sid quickly looked down at his soup again and saw that his hands had turned green. Small scales appeared on his skin, and his fingernails blackened and sharpened to claws. The soup spelled another word:

KILL

Sid veered from his chair. He produced a primitive scream that connected directly with Nurse Peter's adrenaline system. Sid attacked his soup. With broad swipes of his arms, he repeatedly splashed his spoon into the bowl, stabbing at the offensive pasta. The cafeteria was stunned to silence while Sid kept yelling, "Stop telling me what to do. Stop it now, you creeps."

He grabbed his chair and raised it high above his head. He hesitated for just a few seconds, uncertain whether he'd hit Gregory, Bob, or the soup bowl. With a sideways swing he might even get all of them at once.

Nurse Peter got to him before Sid could decide, and brought him down with a well-aimed jolt of his stungun. Sid collapsed into a helplessly vibrating heap of flesh. Nurse Peter stood beside his victim in a triumphant pose.

"That'll be two more days of isolation for you, wanker. We're gonna teach you a little lesson."

Nurse Delia watched from a safe distance. She scratched her nose as Sid's paralysed body was dragged out of the cafeteria.

~

Dirk Puis's Biography

I'm a 40-something software engineer from Ghent, Belgium. I try to divide my free time and creative juices evenly between writing and software development. On the writing side I am heavily influenced by the likes of Jack Womack, Irvine Welsh, Kurt Vonnegut and John Irving.

I've written several short stories and last year self-published my first book, called *Paddy's Mile-High Malt*.

I'm currently working on a second book. At my usual writing pace, it could be published in about a decade.

SHORTLISTED STORIES

AN EZTRAORDINARY EZPERIENCE

Shortlisted story, by Stuart Aken

If you don't help me, I'll make you sorry.

There it was again. Every time he switched on the computer, the same threat flashed on screen, regardless of what he was doing or whether he'd started up any programs. It was unnerving, irritating and inexplicable. That is, until young Jason did the explaining.

"It'll just be a bug, Uncle Harvey. Some bored dude, with nothing better to do, must've stuck it in at the factory."

Not that Jason could do anything about it, for all he was so clever with computers.

It was an irritation Harvey could do without. He'd bought the laptop, at great personal sacrifice, so he could write literally anywhere. No, he corrected himself; not literally. He couldn't write under water or in outer space. Get the adverb right: so he could write almost anywhere. That was better.

The message, as usual, faded from the screen and he began chapter seven of the romance that was going to make his name, make him money, make him able at last to give up the boring, uninspiring day job. His heroine, Melinda, was perfect for the role; enchanting, sublime, sensual and better looking than was healthy for the males he'd surrounded her with. He didn't like that; ending a sentence with a preposition. Not right.

And the hero? Well, tall dark and handsome went without saying, of course, but he was also an eztraordinarily good lover.

Now, that was odd. He'd definitely pressed the 'x' key and it worked well enough now. So, why wouldn't it work when he tried to replace that tricky 'z' that had wandered into eztraordinarily? After 17 attempts he gave up and left it. It was just one of those irritating and inezplicable... there it was again. No. He wouldn't let it bother him. Jason would have an answer and until then he'd just let it go and get on with the tale.

Now, where was he? Oh, yes. Melinda had just emerged from her bath and wrapped herself in that soft towel, too small to afford proper cover, of course – have to satisfy the carnal as well as the romantic desires of the readers, and his own, come to that – so she could answer that insistent ringing of her doorbell. Once he got her to the door, she'd be good and mad and there she'd find the hero, whose name he still hadn't decided and he'd labelled simply as 'Hero', standing in the rain, needing her assistance due to... yes, a breakdown of his car. Cliché, of course. But a classic introduction of heroine to hero. Yes. That would do it.

So, he'd have her primed with rage at the intrusion and then melting with desire as soon as she opened the door and saw the eztraordinary Hero standing there.

This time he didn't even flinch at the errant 'z', but continued to write, ignoring it.

IF YOU DON'T HELP ME, I'LL MAKE YOU SORRY.

Wow. That was a bit unexpected. And spooky. He turned off the computer and left it sitting on the table. In the morning he'd speak to Jason and sort out this petty little problem. For now he'd had enough. It was time for bed anyway.

"You're early, Harvey."

Lorna turned over and presented her back to him, the thick cotton only emphasising her inaccessibility and lack of desire as he climbed in wearily beside her. She grunted a sort of acknowledgement of his goodnight kiss and then pretended to fall into the sleep pattern of soft breathing.

Harvey spent the night fighting off 'z's and 'x's in every form imaginable and under the most bizarre circumstances. At one point Lorna woke him from a particularly terrifying nightmare because he was so agitated he'd disturbed her sleep.

"Been eating cheese for supper again, Harvey? Always gives you nightmares."

He hadn't and it didn't.

Morning found Lorna stiff lipped due to broken sleep. Somehow it was his fault, as was the fact that the milk had gone off during the night.

"You left the fridge door open again."

He hadn't. Hadn't been near the fridge. But it was pointless arguing. He tried the positive tack.

"You're looking rather elegant this morning, darling. Special meeting?"

She grimaced. "I told you. They moved my promotion interview to today."

She hadn't told him; he was certain.

Perhaps from a sense of guilt, she twirled for him. "Thought I'd best look as good as I could."

"Lovely. Go out there and knock 'em dead, gorgeous." And he meant it.

She even kissed him for that and then she was gone, the scent of Wicked lingering as an unfulfilled promise.

No coffee to kick start the day; he couldn't stand it black. No cereal. The toaster refused to relinquish the two slices he gave it to nurture and the fumes set off the smoke alarm; piercing screeches assaulting his morning ears. In the garage, hungry, he found the back tyre flat. If he mended the puncture he'd have to cycle like fury. Better just walk, fast.

The level crossing gates went down as he approached. Glancing at his watch, he twitched as he heard again the words from that prat who called himself his boss. "If you're late once more, Harvey, I'll dock your pay."

And Lorna was still punishing him for his 'frivolous' spending on the laptop. "Not as if you've actually sold a single story, is it?"

Which was true. Though he had won a couple of contest prizes and had a few acceptances in some of the small press magazines. He obviously had talent.

The train dawdled by, pulling out of the station as

though time wasn't an issue. At last the gates rose and he dashed across. High Street was traffic mad and the lights at the pelican turned red as he reached them. He stood, tapping his foot in annoyance.

The last 200 yards were a sprint but he made it with seconds to spare as he pushed his card into the clock machine.

The day did not go well. 17 orders to be rushed and completed where he'd normally do a dozen. And the boss was more than usually sarcastic. Harvey walked back home in the rain; late, tired and dispirited.

Lorna arrived just as he was towelling his hair dry. Thank God he remembered and smiled his question. Her scowl was answer enough and she sank on the sofa and sobbed. It took him half an hour to decipher her explanation through the tears of injustice. Genuine, it seemed. And another hour to calm her into acceptance that the younger woman had probably got it because... well, he left that open to interpretation, which Lorna clearly developed into insult.

They ate in resentful silence; mutually exclusive instead of supporting one another against the world. Harvey went off to bury himself in his romance whilst Lorna drifted to the telly and her favourite DVD so she could weep a little more.

I TOLD YOU: IF YOU DIDN'T HELP ME, I'D MAKE YOU SORRY.

It was too much. "Bugger off."

All you have to do is help me out of here.

This was idiotic. It was a machine, an inanimate object. There was no question of it having some sort of consciousness outside of his input. Perhaps he was going mad.

It's not too much to ask. I just need your help. Then

I'll leave you alone.

What the hell? Everything else today had conspired against him, against them, in fact. "OK. You win. What do you want?"

Better. I want out of here.

"Who are you?"

You wouldn't believe me if I told you.

"Try me. I'll believe anything after the day I've had."

I'm Syd. Syd Mason. Used to work for the company that assembles these bloody things.

"And now?"

Now? I'm dead of course. You some sort of moron?

Dead? He looked at the screen. That's what it said. Dead. He almost brought Lorna to witness this aberration but then he considered her state of mind and the opposition she already felt toward his precious laptop.

"OK, so you're Syd and you're dead. How am I supposed to help you? And what are you doing in there anyway?"

It's a long story.

When it came to trouble, was there any other sort?

"Fire away. I'm listening."

Look. How and why don't matter. You've got to get me out. Now.

"Or?"

Or I spend eternity, and I do mean eternity, in here.

He thought of replying with the cliché that eternity was a hell of a long time but decided against it. "So, how do I help you?"

Oh, that's easy. Don't know why you didn't ask me right away.

"Me, neither."

Would've saved you, and me, a lot of grief.

So now it was his fault. But, no, he wouldn't let resentment overcome his good nature.

"What do I do?"

Just type in the message, 'I wish you would go to Heaven.'

"Simple as that?"

Simple as that.

"OK." He typed, 'I wish you would go to Heaven.' Though the temptation to insert Hell instead was very strong.

The screen blanked, flickered, and flashed a scene that might've been from a divinely inspired Old Master with angels, clouds and even a brief chord of sublime music.

THANKS.

Eztraordinary. Oh no.

Just kidding.

He tried again. Extraordinary. And sighed with relief.

That night, he completed chapters seven and eight. When he climbed into bed, Lorna was still wrapped in thick cotton and fast asleep, genuinely.

Saturday morning, neither of them were due to work. The phone rang early. Lorna answered it.

"That was work. Seems that trollop gave some false information on her application. Wanted me to know as soon as possible. I've got my promotion."

"Wonderful, darling."

"How's the book going?"

Hopefully but without expectation, he tried, "Brilliantly. Could do with a bit of personal experience for the love scenes, though."

"Easy. Help me out of this, will you?"

He did and she did. And she was extraordinarily loving.

As they dozed off again, happy and content, he could have sworn he heard her murmur softly, "That was really quite eczeptional, darling."

~

Stuart Aken's Biography

Stuart Aken was born, against the odds, to a homeless widowed artist, in a neighbour's bed. Husband, father, novelist, playwright, storyteller, occasional poet, blogger and word wrangler, he's a romantic, open-minded radical liberal, sometimes dangerous to know. Raised by a creative, loving mother and an unimaginative step-father who educated him in things natural and worldly, he had what he describes as an idyllic childhood. An author who refuses to be shackled by genre, he's written romance, thrillers, sci-fi, humour, erotic lit and fantasy. His fiction, the only place he ever bends the truth and which, after love, remains his raison d'être, appears in a number of novels, anthologies and on his website.

Stuart's website: www.stuartaken.net

BARRY'S HOME

Shortlisted story, by Jade Williams

Peering from behind his curtain I hear his flat door. Barry's home. The short, dark haired, handsome 30 something enters, dressed in a black suit. I think he's just finished work, and he's on the phone to someone. I'm going to be as quiet as possible and if I don't move hopefully he won't notice me, he hasn't before.

"What time?" Barry asks through his phone as he

takes his keys out of the door and puts them down onto a table. "Yeah, I'll be ready by then."

He removes his coat with one hand, whilst still holding his phone to his ear with the other and places his coat on one of the hooks screwed to the back of his door.

"Is Lucy going?" I hear him ask.

I watch him walk through his open planned flat and take a seat on his brown leather sofa. "Ah, that's a shame. I like her." I bet she likes you too.

Barry takes his suit jacket off and throws it down onto the seat next to him. I wish I could smell it, I bet it smells heavenly. He leans forward and takes his shoes off.

"Alright, see you later." With this evenings plans made he hangs up the phone and puts it in his pocket. Now I wish I were his phone, so he could hold me all the time in his soft, hairy hands and I could go everywhere with him.

Barry stands and walks over to a display case which showcases his incredible collection of board game dice. He's so cool, he has the biggest collection I've ever seen.

I think he's noticed a smudge on the glass doors of the display case. He licks his thumb and tries to rub it clean. It's so intense I have to bite my lip. He stops rubbing but the smudge hasn't come off. I hope he tries again but he's realised the smudge is on the inside of the case so instead he collects his keys from the table and locates the key to the display case. Obviously it's a white key with black dots on because he's just the coolest. He unlocks the glass doors, then, opening a draw underneath several shelves full of dice, he retrieves a pack of wipes. He takes one and uses it to clean the glass, then throws the wipe into a bin.

Barry takes a moment to admire his mass assortment of dice, and who can blame him? He locks them up and puts his keys back on the table. I watch him as he seductively walks into his bedroom.

I take this opportunity to come out from my hiding place and rush over to his display case, he was just here and I can still smell him. I press my gloved hands against the glass and take in his collection. It's so impressive and it must have taken him years to acquire all of these. He has all the classics. Monopoly (obviously), Cluedo, even the lettered dice from Boggle. There are several from Dungeons & Dragons too. I've never wanted him more. I didn't realise but in my excitement I've been breathing so heavily onto the glass that it's fogged up. I'll just wipe it away with one of my black gloves and he should never know I was here.

I glance over at the bin then take the wipe out of it. He's not going to need it again, it's fine. I take a Ziploc bag out of my black backpack. I never go anywhere without it, especially not to Barry's flat. I seal the wipe in the Ziploc bag and put it away into the backpack, just in case I want it for whatever reason later, you never know.

I wait outside Barry's bedroom door. I wonder what he's doing in there. I wish I could see him. I might try and open the door, just a little bit. I reach for the handle, just as my glove grazes it there's a loud bang just behind the door. I hope he's OK. He might be coming out. I quickly, yet quietly, make my way back to behind the curtain. I'm beginning to think of it as my curtain. After all, I've been spending quite a bit of time here.

The bedroom door opens and a song begins to play. I

recognise it as Bob Seger's 'Old Time Rock and Roll'. He's not doing a Tom Cruise from *Risky Business* is he? That's so cliché. Barry slides in across the floor, wearing only a pale pink shirt covering his manhood and a pair of white socks, mouthing the lyrics into a mimed microphone. I don't care if it is clichéd, it's so hot the way he does it. For the second time I've felt compelled to bite my lip.

I watch on and admire him as he dances over to a cupboard, opens it and takes out the game Twister. He continues to dance as he sets up the mat and places the board with the spin arrow down next to it. I love the way he moves his body, he has such a good sense of rhythm. And I like that he's not afraid to play Twister alone, I'm enjoying the show.

With his back to me he spins the arrow then places his right foot on a blue circle. He spins again and places his left foot behind the other on a red circle. He spins again and has to bend over to place his left hand on a blue circle next to his right foot. He isn't wearing underwear. I can see everything. My breathing becomes very heavy and I accidentally let out a slight moan. It's too much. I have to cover my mouth. Luckily Barry couldn't hear over the music. This is the best moment of my life. He spins again and moves his left foot through his left arm and right leg. His sock slips on the mat and he falls backwards. I want to make sure he's alright but I can't. Fortunately he's fine and he isn't down for long before he stands up. That's my guy.

Barry's decided that was enough Twister for one day. He folds up the mat and puts that and the spin board back into the box and puts it back in its place in the cupboard. He's so tidy. He'd make for such a good husband, always cleaning up after himself.

He turns the music off then goes back into his bedroom. Fortunately for me, this time he pushes the door to but doesn't close it fully. I reappear from behind the curtain and silently walk over to his bedroom door. As I look through the gap I become aware that I'm breathing louder than I would like, but I can't help it. Barry just does something to me.

Barry looks in his wardrobe and contemplates what to wear. I don't know why he takes so long to decide, he looks good in everything. He selects a blue shirt and a pair of grey trousers and tosses them onto his bed next to where his phone is lying. He then completely undresses, removing his socks first because he's such a tease. My breathing is so heavy, I hope he can't hear.

A naked Barry walks over to a set of drawers, opens one and removes a pair of pants and some socks and throws them onto the bed next to his other clothes. From on top of the drawers he takes a comb, looks at his reflection in the mirror, combs through his hair, then his pubic hair. He's so well groomed. Once he's happy his hairs are in the right place he sets the comb back on top of the drawers. Then he walks over to the bed and puts his underwear on. I'm a little disappointed. I wish he could be naked all the time, but I'll never forget what he looked like. It's embedded into my brain.

Wearing too many clothes if you ask me, Barry returns to his reflection in the mirror.

"You is kind. You is smart. You is important." He follows up this empowering quote from *The Help* with a wink to himself then continues dressing.

As he finishes buttoning up his shirt I realise I should probably go back behind the curtain, so I move quickly, hoping to get there before he's done. I do.

I watch from my safe spot as Barry leaves his

bedroom and moves over to his sofa to put his shoes on. He looks nice. Once they're both fastened he walks over to the front door, removes his coat from the hook and throws it on. He grabs his keys then leaves his flat.

Re-emerging from behind the curtain I take my time, making sure he's definitely closed the door and gone. I head into his bedroom and pick up his comb. I take a moment to breathe it all in before removing some of the hairs, placing them into another Ziploc bag and then putting that into my backpack. I've got to make sure I have plenty of mementos.

I hear the front door open and close and quickly turn around. Barry's home.

Then I hear him tell himself, "Phone."

I notice his phone on the bed.

Barry comes into his bedroom. I stand as still as possible but it's clear that he can see me. He stops in the doorway and we stand in silence looking at each other. I feel a little awkward, dressed all in black like Catwoman. I hope he doesn't think I'm robbing him. He breaks the silence by questioning me.

"Lucy?"

He's definitely seen me, no getting out of this one. The only thing I can think to do is to give him a cute, apologetic smile. To my surprise he smiles back.

~

Jade Williams' Biography

A 21 Year old Film Student at The University for the Creative Arts in Surrey. Focusing on comedy writing and performances, trying to make the world a funnier place.

BENEATH THE WAVES

Shortlisted story, by Olivia Arroy

As Wendy exited the car she slipped on wet grass and crushed a flock of plastic flamingos. She wondered if destroying the florescent lawn ornaments was a tragedy or blessing for the citizens of Malibu. Her husband Calvin rushed to help, but also ended up falling with a splashy thud.

"Well," Calvin said. "That hurt."

"I think one of their beaks went up my butt," Wendy replied. Calvin chuckled and got up to assist his wife.

"Seriously though, you OK? You didn't fall on your stomach or anything?" Calvin asked.

"Nope, all good."

"You sure?"

Wendy wiped her black cotton dress clean, lingering on her stomach, before allowing Calvin to help her stand. She was four months pregnant, and thankfully it hadn't started to show yet. "It would take more than a little fall to hurt the baby. I even felt a kick a little after I landed, I think he enjoyed the whole fiasco."

"Our Bruce is already developing a sense of humour."

"I refuse to name our baby after Batman."

"What's wrong with Bruce Wayne?"

"For starters his parents die."

"Touché."

*

Wendy stared at the glossy oak doors of the beachside clubhouse. It was gaudier than she recalled. In many ways the Delmont Country Club reminded her of Dave. At first it was fun to be a part of something so alluring and exclusive, but after reconsideration it became grotesque.

"This day will only get worse."

"Well that's optimistic."

"Can it really get more awkward than attending your ex fiancé's funeral?"

"You could be the husband, of the woman attending her ex fiancé's funeral," Calvin replied.

"I honestly don't know why you're willing to endure this."

"Because one day I'm going to use this as a big fat

'you owe me'," he joked.

"How mature of you."

"Would you expect anything less of me?"

"Never."

They hesitated before Wendy grabbed the brass handle and swung it open. She'd planned to slither through the funeral without catching too much attention, but that plan never made it out of the gate. Renee Pearson caught sight of her immediately, and embraced her old friend, knocking the wind out of Wendy. They had been college roommates, during Renee's brief university stint, prior to her going to beauty school. Not that any of that schooling mattered after Renee scored a MRS Degree with beach house contractor Stu Stevens. She was also the one who had introduced Wendy to Dave.

Aside from her black dress everything about Renee was colour, her shiny bourbon hair, gemmed necklaces, and highlighter pink heels. "Wendy, I didn't think you were coming," Renee said, before turning her attention to Calvin. "And you must be the lucky man."

"Pleasure to meet you. I'm Calvin Holmes."

"Holmes, like Sherlock Holmes."

"Quite right," Calvin said.

"Are you related to him?"

Calvin hesitated for a moment, unsure how to respond, but finally added, "I wish I was."

"Sorry we didn't come to the wedding, last October, Sophie was having surgery."

"Is she OK?" Calvin asked.

"She's walking on all four legs now, but the doctor says she might limp for life," Renee informed solemnly.

Calvin gave Wendy a quizzical look.

"She's a poodle," Wendy said.

Renee led them into the club's chic lounge, overlooking the ocean. There were people sprawled among the white leather couches, their wine glasses resting on the sea foam glass table.

"Stu. Honey, come here for a sec," Renee said.

Stu was listening to a story told by an elderly woman, with earrings so large they made her ears droop like a Buddha statue. She was Dave's great aunt Greta, and she avoided eye contact with Wendy. Renee tapped Stu's shoulder, and he scratched his golf ball shaped head, before glancing up. As he recognized Renee a smile sprung on his face. He immediately got up from the chair, walked towards them, and greeted Wendy with a kiss on the cheek, and Calvin with a firm handshake.

"It's such a tragedy about Dave. Choking is a shitty way to go."

"Stu," Renee replied through clenched teeth.

"I'm just stating facts."

"We know the facts."

Wendy knew that it had nothing to do with Dave being Renee's cousin. Renee was never sensitive about death. No, this was all about appearances, about behaving dignified even though she herself had probably thought the same as Stu. Dave's family was like a vintage armoire, eloquent, and flawless, a symbol of prestige and wealth. However, fling open the wardrobe's door and an avalanche of secrets and emotions came tumbling out.

"I feel like everyone is tiptoeing over the topic."

"Because it happened five fucking days ago, Stu."

Wendy could see people staring, and suddenly felt a pang of dizziness and everyone's voices turned into distant murmurs. Her eyes locked on with Greta's for a split second, and she could see she was both confused and disgusted. It was people like that saggy witch who made her not want to be there. The people who hated her for what she represented versus what she was.

Jean Pearson marched across the yacht club's white sand beach, in a black maxi dress and sun hat, with such authority. It was clear she was the designated greeter for her son's funeral. Jean had been brought up in New England, where she had mastered the art of combining grit with charm. Days like today she thrived.

"It's so good to see you, sweet pea," Jean embraced her in a long hug and then took Wendy's face into her hands. "You look so beautiful."

Unlike the others who had resented Wendy, Jean had resented Dave. Renee told Wendy that Jean didn't speak to her son for a week after the breakup, blaming him for ruining his happiness. It was really about Jean's happiness. Prior to Wendy there had been what Jean had called 'sorority bimbos'. Then after Wendy, Dave married Echo Riesling, Jean's worst nightmare. A reality star turned yoga instructor. Renee informed Wendy about Jean's rants about the marriage going as far as to say Echo had brainwashed Dave into becoming a vegan, and a Buddhist.

"I'm terribly sorry for your loss."

Jean seemed as if she had aged 20 years since they last saw each other. Wendy could tell this all emotionally exhausted her, and although there was a small warm smile on her face, her eyes were hollow and raw. "My dear, having lovely people like you here, rejuvenates my soul," she said. "I just wish Dave could see how many people came from across the world to say farewell."

"It's quite spectacular."

"Dave and Echo were trying to have children before he passed away. He would have been a wonderful father..." she said. "However, I suppose it's a blessing he didn't because they'd be raised solely by Echo, which would have been unbalanced."

Wendy knew this was a direction insult towards Echo, but dodged it completely and responded, "Raising a child alone is a difficult burden."

She then felt the baby kick her hard, and could not help the expression of pain. "Are you alright?" Jean asked.

"Yes, I just got a sudden headache, probably from the jetlag."

Renee swooped to greet her aunt preventing any lingering conversation. Jean then went to hug Stu, but paused before Calvin. Everyone knew who he was, yet no one wanted to say it, afraid it would shatter the ambiance of hospitality. "This is my husband, Calvin Holmes," Wendy explained.

"Charmed," Jean said with a sour tinge, and shook his hand. "Please make yourselves comfortable in the courtyard."

Wendy took in the fenced off piece of sand next to the yacht club. It was less of a 'courtyard' and more like a glorified sand box. There was an open bar shaded by a candy cane striped umbrella, along with a string quartet, which gave the area an unsettling festive vibe.

Calvin massaged his hand. "Christ, that woman has a strong grip."

Wendy murmured, "Obviously she is thrilled that you replaced her son."

Calvin scoffed. "Like it's my fault her son was an asshole."

"Could you say that a little louder? I don't think the

people in the back could hear you."

Wendy could see Calvin's mouth open, preparing from something snide, but before he could Stu clasped Calvin's shoulder. "Hey bud, you want to grab a drink before the ceremony? You're going to need it."

Calvin glanced at Wendy, and she gave him a nod assuring him that she could fend for herself, or at least she thought she could. Renee grabbed her by the wrist as soon they were gone and dragged her around the club's backside where the catering staff were preparing food for the reception.

"Care to explain what just happened?"

"Not really."

"That face you made, I mean it looked like you got kicked in the gut."

"Because I did."

Wendy observed the cognition transpire into an expression of pure joy. "Why didn't you tell me?"

"We were going to announce it when we arrived back in New York."

Another realisation hit Renee, and her brows furrowed. "You shouldn't be here you know."

"Because I'm pregnant?"

"Having an ex-spouse or fiancé show up at a wedding or funeral is OK. In LA everybody has more than one. It could even be considered noble for you to show up here. You're like a nun choosing the right path, even if it's difficult and uncomfortable, which is honorable. However, you're a pregnant nun."

"That's just a tad melodramatic," quipped Wendy.

"You're not doing this to get back at him? Even I'll admit my cousin was an asshole, but still that'd be low."

"Yes, I obviously got pregnant knowing Dave would die so I could brag about my new life in front of his family and friends," Wendy said, pushing herself away from Renee.

"That's not what I meant."

"Then what did you mean?"

"Why are you here, Wendy?"

"Because I was asked to be here."

The truth was she had no idea why she was there. She seldom spoke to Dave after the breakup. He had convinced Wendy into believing he was this generous doctor, who genuinely cared about his patients, friends, and most importantly her. However, she eventually realised that he really just cared about himself, and used the people around him as pawns on a chessboard. Wendy was an educated, respectable, and talented woman. Her father was a dermatologist, and her mother ran a medical journal, making her the perfect fit for the 'queen' of his life. Dave had even once said he was so lucky to find the textbook girlfriend. Wendy thought she was happy, until she re-examined other couples around her, people like Stu and Renee, who loved each other regardless of their flaws. Wendy thought of Dave's flaws. He used people to get ahead, he remained friends with people he disliked for appearances and was chummy with celebrities solely for publicity.

She could easily recall the moment it was over. A week after he'd proposed they were drinking coffee in their kitchen. She observed Dave scratch his scruffy, chiseled jaw, while reading *The Wall Street Journal*. She knew that he didn't care about stocks, but he read to appear sophisticated. "Why do you think we work? As a couple."

Dave rolled his eyes, as if she asked why the sky was blue. "Because we're two good looking, smart and successful people who understand each other."

"But what if I changed? What if one day I lost those things?"

"That's a ridiculous question."

Was that ridiculous because he would never replace her or because if she did lose those things he would replace her? She wasn't sure and that terrified her.

At the entrance of the reception was a large picture of Dave smiling confidently while holding a marlin. Dave had said being one of the most powerful doctors in Los Angeles was like being a tornado or a hurricane; unstoppable. How strange was it that a person could put out a persona of something so strong, yet have such a whimpering death. It was like an elephant tripping on a pebble.

Wendy observed the other guests around. Most had similar stories. Dave had turned them beautiful, and given them a career, or spouse, or both. They were here not because they missed Dave's existence, but felt in debt. However, what they didn't realise was Dave's surgeries might have made their lives better, but it didn't mean they were better people. In fact, maybe they were worse. They'd gained success due to their looks, and therefore believed that's what mattered most. These people had fallen through Los Angeles's trap door, and were paying tribute to one of its ringmasters.

Wendy was relieved that Calvin had saved her a seat in the last row. "It feel likes one of those weird *Twilight Zone* episodes, where everyone around me is a doll," Calvin whispered.

"The only difference is dolls are fun to play with," Wendy replied.

The first to speak was Dave's mother. Jean scanned

the audience, and then relinquished one of her smiles, a rehearsed tactic from her days as a debutant. "Dave was a special person. The kind of person who always stood out of crowds for his intelligence, wit, and professionalism. My son was not always this person. When he was five years old, and my late husband, Hanson, and I were going to a dinner party, our neighbour, Barbara, a junior in high school, was babysitting him. When we arrived back home, Dave had been placed in timeout, and his babysitter was sitting furious with her arms crossed against her chest. When I asked her what was wrong, she told me that my son had attempted to fondle her breasts. I of course apologised, and paid her double. Then after she left, I asked my son why he did that, and he said that they were not even and he was trying to fix them." At that point the crowd began to laugh, and even Jean chuckled. "Most mothers would have been concerned for their son, thinking he might turn out to be a pervert. However, I knew right then that my son would become a plastic surgeon..."

And so the stories continued. Dave's childhood best friend talked about their friendship, a medical school professor discussed Dave's talents in the classroom, followed by an array of celebrity friends/clients. Finally it was his wife's turn.

Echo glistened in her shimmery black dress, even with the solemn expression covering her face she seemed fierce and mesmerising. Wendy had not seen his wife in person, and felt as if she were staring at a deity. "I first met Dave at a party, and he came up to me asking why someone so beautiful was alone, and I said I had been waiting for the right company, and he said he could fix that. Dave was always about fixing things..."

The rest of the speech became numb, distance

murmurs as Wendy went underwater. The air became too thick, and nausea kicked in. Her hands were shaking uncontrollably. She needed to leave before she made a scene. Wendy slipped out to the restroom and splashed water on her face. She took 10 slow deep breaths, exited onto an empty patio and leaned against the railing facing the ocean.

Was it always the same? Had he taken all his ex's to the same goddamn places, and used the same pick-up lines? Were Wendy and Echo victims of the same disease, which was Dave Pearson? One knew their exes would go on and have new relationships, but no one wants to hear about, or have it materialise before them.

"Do you need a smoke?" someone asked.

Wendy jolted in surprise. It was Echo standing beside her. She could see the smugness in Echo's casual smile.

Wendy cleared her throat. "I sort of quit."

"I solely bought this dress because I could hide my cigarettes," Echo claimed, as she pulled at a pack of American Spirit from the concealed pocket on the hip of her silk dress. "Everybody thinks because I'm a vegan that means I'm a hippie tree hugger. Truth is I have celiac disease. Meat makes me drowsy, so I became vegan. But I drink and smoke more than I eat."

"This city is all about appearances," Wendy replied.

"It's America's funhouse."

There was a comfortable silence between them as Echo took a drag of her cigarette and exhaled a long stream of smoke out of her nostrils like a dragon. They could hear the distant voice of another speech occurring in the reception hall.

"Who's speaking now?"

"Dave's godfather, he's the last one."

"That's good," Wendy, said, with a tad too much

excitement.

Echo laughed. "I didn't expect you'd actually come. I was doing it to be polite."

Wendy smirked. "That's why I arrived, I thought it would be impolite to decline."

"And now we're here…" Echo smashed the bud against the railing. "You know, I hated you at first. I was jealous of the way Dave spoke of you, and I wanted to replace you so fucking bad. Then I realised that this wasn't your fault. I realised who you were. The one who got away."

"It wasn't easy. I mean, I don't know your experience with Dave, but mine was interesting."

"You can say what you thought of him. It won't hurt me. I probably think what you do, or worse," she encouraged.

Wendy was surprised. All this time she'd thought she would have to introduce herself to a heartbroken widow, but instead she found an ally, someone else who knew Dave's true nature. It all seemed so obvious now. After all, she was the only other woman Dave had been seriously involved with. "I wish I could drink. It would make it a lot easier to talk about all this."

"You quit smoking and you can't drink. Either you're a recovering addict or pregnant."

Wendy nodded. "Four months."

Echo had her wrist crossed as they rested on the railing. The only creature Wendy had seen do such a thing was a lioness at the zoo. "Dave had told me you separated because you didn't want to have kids, but I'm beginning to see that you didn't want to have kids with him."

Wendy felt the sharp zinger pierce her heart. It could not of gotten more spot on than that. "How'd you guess?"

"I was asking for a divorce a few days before his death. We'd been avoiding each other all week. I couldn't live in the box he was providing. He always believed his work and life to be superior."

Dave had always thought of Wendy's art as beautiful yet unimportant. His surgeries were permanent. Even if they were superficial, they provided a life changing purpose. His work did something for society. Wendy had once taken him to a movie costume exhibit with iconic pieces, such as Darth Vader's mask and Dorothy's ruby-red slippers. She attempted to inform him of how these costumes had impacted American culture and cinema, and how they shaped the future of art. Wendy informed him how her big dream was to create an iconic piece, which would be immortalised like these outfits, forever. Dave was disinterested.

"When I said I was done he threatened to sabotage my career in the industry by spreading rumours to his clients. So I said that's fine, I'm moving to New York, anyways, and starting a career working for the stage," said Wendy.

Echo held an expression of legitimate surprise, which felt refreshing to Wendy. She then carefully lit herself another cigarette and shook her head understandingly. "I just find it strange that you guys still talked to each other. You had a pretty good reason to say fuck off."

"In the beginning he'd call and send emails. I thought by listening to him, I'd help him heal, but then I realised he was just keeping tabs on me. Because after I told him I was getting married to Calvin, he never bothered me."

"That son of a bitch," Echo replied. "He told me he wanted to become a vegan and a Buddhist because it would make him appear more human to his clients. If you think about it, him being concerned about seeming human explains a lot. He was a total scam and people ate it up. I sent out about 150 invitations to the funeral and about 90 guests arrived. People believe he genuinely cared about them. All he really wanted was their money. He even said God's greatest present to him was inventing ugly, rich people. And the worst part is, even though he's dead, someone else will take his place. It's just a never ending cycle of vapid dicks."

"The show must go on," Wendy said dryly.

"If it's any consolation he had a pretty pathetic end. I found him on the floor wearing the shirt from his favorite vegan restaurant, and a pair of boxers, holding a half-eaten slice of meat lover's pizza. He even died a fraud."

People began to disperse from the reception hall and Wendy scanned the beach for Calvin. She needed his company now, more than ever. "What are they doing with his remains?"

Echo massaged her temples. "His mother decided we should perform a ceremony to suit his larger than life personality. So she decided we do a Viking funeral."

"We're going to burn him?"

"In California Viking funerals are banned. So they're going to take his ashes, put it into a mini boat and set them on fire as they drift on to sea. I finally get to set him on fire. It's a dream come true."

"It was a pleasure meeting you, Echo," Wendy said.

"Likewise," Echo said.

And they parted ways, knowing they would probably never speak again, but also they would never need to.

She could see how Echo felt a rush of vengeance from his death, but it didn't make Wendy feel better. All she felt was pity. He had spent his entire life building up a persona to hide his true nature, but in his last moments it had been so openly exposed. He lived and died superficially, and all he'll be remembered for was the artificial impact he had on people's lives. Because after their looks faded, his presence would fade.

Renee approached Wendy and said, "I'm sorry about me interrogating you. It's not my place to say if you should be here or not."

Wendy hugged her dear friend. "It's OK, it's all in the past now."

As the final sendoff began, Calvin placed an arm around Wendy. No words were needed, only company. Dave's ashes were brought upon a wooden boat too big to be a toy, but too small to carry a person. Echo lit the ashes on fire and placed the boat into the sea so that it would drift out to the open ocean on low tide, its light lasting until the distant horizon. Instead, a wave suddenly appeared, crashing down on the vessel. People gasped, and waited for the wreckage to appear on shore, but it never did. The abyss had swallowed it, as if it had never even existed.

~

Olivia Arroy's Biography

Olivia Arroyo was born and raised in Los Angeles. She is a recent graduate of St. Lawrence University where she majored in Creative Writing and Film Studies. Olivia will be attending Chapman University's MFA program this autumn.

BESTÅ

Shortlisted story, by Adena Graham

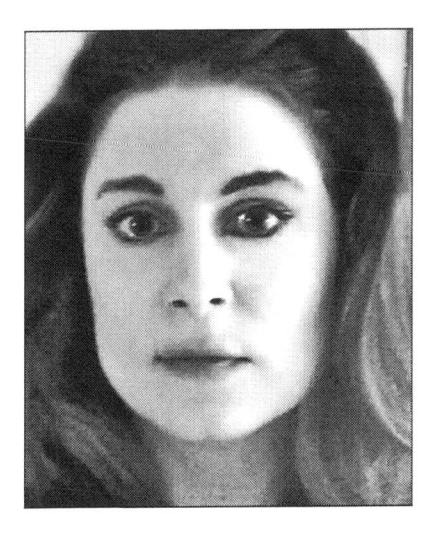

Personally, I blame the meatballs. If it weren't for the meatballs, none of this would have happened. But we'd got up late, skipped breakfast and by the time we were leaving the house, Bernadette had the bright idea that we could combine the fun of home decor with the functionality of sustenance – specifically, meatballs. So, rather than heading for Homebase, we turned the car (or rather, I turned the car, while Bernadette fiddled with the radio, tuning it to Magic - I hate Magic) in the direction of IKEA.

Me, I'd rather have had hot oil dripped onto my bare nipples for 24 hours straight, than pay a visit to that Swedish furniture vault – but when Bernadette gets an idea into her head, there's little you can do to divert or distract her.

"Did you know that you can get 10 meatballs for just £3.90?" she said, cheeks aglow – it was either the thought of cheap meat or Michael Bublé that was giving her that after-sex rosy hue. I wouldn't know, as it certainly hadn't been me causing her to look like that of late.

"Or you can get 15 for £4.50. Oh, and I could just die for their Daim Cake. There's real Daim Bar in it. I wish we'd had our wedding cake made out of Daim Bar."

I was beginning to wish we hadn't had a wedding cake at all. Or a wedding. "They're not doing the Daim Cake anymore," I said, noting out of the corner of my eye how her face sort of crumpled. Now that was the look she got after sex with me.

"You're lying," she said. "You're just saying that to upset me."

"Nope, it's true. They've withdrawn it. There was shit found in the cake. Look it up if you don't believe me."

Bernadette fiddled with her phone and when I heard her gasp, I knew she'd hit pay dirt.

"It wasn't exactly, literally shit," she said after a moment. "It was coliform bacteria."

"That's found in shit."

"But it wasn't actual shit, was it?"

"You say tomato, I say tom-ay-to. But that's OK. Next

time you get married, you can ask IKEA to make you a nice, not-actual-shit, shit cake. Or maybe Choccywoccydoodah will whip you up another one," I said, recalling how they'd fleeced me for our wedding cake. "Except this time they really can whisk in some real doo-dah. Choccydoggydoodah."

It went quiet for a while after that, which was fine by me. Well, quiet apart from John Mayer singing some song about how big his dick is. Then we hit a wall of traffic. Exactly how I wanted to spend my Saturday afternoon, stuck behind a fume-belching line of cars on the A10. Yeah, this is what life was all about – seizing the chance to acquire more toot for the home you'd hoiked yourself up to the eyeballs in debt for. Because, of course, what we really, really needed was a new television stand, bookcase, cutlery set and a 'pretty print to go on the upstairs bathroom wall' (Bernadette's pressing need, not mine, just in case you were in any doubt – I couldn't give a fuck what was on the toilet wall when I sat there doing a crap).

The thing is, Bernadette and I were sort of playing house, even though we'd been married for six years. We started off in a cheap rental above a row of shops, our lovemaking punctuated by the sound of sirens, accompanied by the waft of deep-fried cod from the chippie below – meanwhile, Bernadette's prone form was bathed in the ambient glow from the signage of the curry house opposite. At first, nothing could quell our ardour, not even Kevin Aseemi's frantic thumping on the bongo drums from the flat above. Sometimes, if we were lucky, he even picked out the rhythm of our own copulation, lending it a somewhat tribal quality.

Eventually, after many hours of overtime (mine) and much nagging (Bernadette's), we managed to secure a deposit for a home of our own. We had to move further out of London for this – making my commute to work even longer – but Bernadette didn't seem to mind the bone-shattering exhaustion I was forced to endure. She was, finally, going to be mistress of her own little castle, courtesy of Lloyds TSB (Totally Shit Bankers).

Unfortunately, home ownership didn't improve Bernadette. As soon as those keys were handed over three months ago, she began to want stuff. Before the big move, our home decor had run to a few pot plants, a charity-shop bookshelf, and a couple of Next throws for the threadbare sofa. Now, it was all Molton Brown hand wash in the bathroom and Orla Kiely cushions in the lounge. I don't know much about fashion or interior design, but I could see instantly that those were going to go out of vogue in about five minutes, especially when everything else in the shop (from handbags to umbrellas) flaunted the same eyeball-assaulting design.

Even more gallingly, the change of venue didn't do anything for our sex life. I had hoped that owning our own little haven would have added a certain frisson – after all, those Yankee candles Bernadette lit everywhere were certainly more enticing than the waft of chip fat. But no, it wasn't to be. Instead, she spent long hours online, searching for things to fill up our house and our life with. Hence the current mission.

"I was thinking, maybe we should get a glass display cabinet too," Bernadette said suddenly.

"What for? We don't have anything to put in a display cabinet."

"Well we can start getting things. IKEA will have some nice knickknacks."

"Paddy whack, give the dog a bone, this old man buys toot for his home." I sensed, rather than saw,

Bernadette pouting. I was focused on overtaking some doddery old fart in a Micra. At least the traffic was moving again.

"It's not toot. It's what makes us... individual," Bernadette said.

"Yes, I scream out my individuality by buying a Snarteeg Smareg IKEA vase that approximately 300 other people will also be buying this weekend. Hurry, we must hurry, before they sell out," I said, applying my foot to the accelerator slightly.

*

By the time we eventually arrived at IKEA, Bernadette was in a frosty mood. I spent the best part of 10 minutes driving around, trying to find a space. This is what millions of years of evolution has done for mankind – bestowed upon him the ability to sense, at a very instinctive level, when someone is heading for a car so that he might stalk them and attack their newly-vacated space.

"Right, let the fun commence," I said, cracking my knuckles and heading gamely towards the entrance.

"Food first?" Bernadette hazarded, running to catch up.

"Oh yes, dearest darling. Food first. We need to get our strength up in case low blood sugar forces us into a rash decision about the bookcase."

We joined a queue for the lift and edged, cattle-like, into its metal interior as it shot us towards our meatball-y goal. Once inside the brightly lit restaurant, it was easy to tell who had already been around the store and who was yet to rally forth. The yet-to-go people still had hopeful smiles on their faces. The people who'd been round, and were sitting down for a final caffeine-hit before the long drive home, looked as if their life essence had been sucked out of them. There was no more to say or do – other than sit there in quiet contemplation of an evening filled with self-assembly and self-loathing.

"Oh goody, they do have the meatballs," Bernadette said, jiggling on the balls of her feet. "See," she exclaimed triumphantly. I had hazarded earlier that, after their horse meat debacle, those might be off the menu too. Clearly, although they hadn't had time to get the shit out of their cakes, they'd managed to get the equine element out of their meat.

We took a tray and joined the queue. It moved slowly, which gave Bernadette ample time to study the dessert alternatives. Her hand moved towards a chocolate mousse. "I wouldn't," I said. "Brown... good camouflage for, you know... shit," I whispered. She blanched and set it back on the shelf, choosing a jelly instead. "On your head be it," I murmured cryptically.

"Why are you being such an arsehole, Phil?" Bernadette asked, her lips pinched together hard in a moue of displeasure which I'd once found cute, but now found unspeakably irritating. Probably because said lips hadn't been pinched thus round my cock in months.

"I don't know. Maybe it's because I'm worried about whether we'll find a book shelf and TV stand that match. It's a lot of pressure."

*

We sat on colourful little chairs, at a colourful little table, under colourful little lights (all of which could be purchased in-store – say what you will about IKEA, but they never miss a selling opportunity) and ate our lunch in silence. Around us, children shrieked and cried. Some grown men looked like they were on the verge of shrieking and crying too.

Afterwards, with the meatballs and their sickly gravy sitting uncomfortably in my stomach, we stacked our own trays away. It was, signs cheerfully informed us, how they kept the cost of the meatballs down. The extra shit in the cakes though was free. Have that one on us, guys.

"OK, let's get this show on the road. Let's just buy stuff, Bernadette. Follow the yellow-brick road... please, after you," I said, gesticulating to a large arrow which pointed the way.

*

I once went into a haunted house attraction at a fairground when I was six. My mum shoved me inside and said she'd meet me at the exit. 10 paces in, I was so scared I wet myself. I turned and began to push past people, back the way I'd come, but the bloke who was running the joint gave me a firm shunt in the back. "Sorry, son – you have to go through. You can't turn back. Keep going please." That's what IKEA's like. Once you enter it, you can't leave until you've seen everything. Especially if you go with my wife.

By the time we finally reached the bookcases, having navigated dining tables, chairs, beds, sofas, kitchens and wardrobes (all of which she'd stopped to study) I fully understood the worthlessness of life; the sheer pointlessness of my existence – and of those around me too. Over there, a balding, middle-aged man was stooping to investigate the opening mechanism of a glass cabinet. It entered my mind, unbidden, that he would soon discover he only had three months left to live. Simultaneously, he would realise that the Leksvik buffet cabinet he was about to spend £280 on had added nothing to his existence. Nor had the Billy bookcase or Morvik mirrored wardrobe. If only he could get this time back and go for a bracing walk, or see that friend from school he'd been meaning to hook up with. But he didn't know it, so he continued to feign interest in the fake antique stain and smooth-running drawers.

*

"This is definitely the one I want," Bernadette said, pointing excitedly towards a £480 BESTÅ TV storage combo.

"OK. So we won't be needing a bookshelf then."

Bernadette looked perplexed. "Why not?"

"Because this has lots of shelves for books. It's got 480 quid's worth of shelves."

"Yes, but that's for ornaments," Bernadette said. "It's a TV stand, with space round it for ornaments. Or DVDs."

"But we don't have any ornaments. Or not so many that we require 12 large shelves for them."

"I know we don't have them yet, but we will. We agreed that we were going to get some today."

"No, you agreed it. OK, so we won't need a display cabinet then."

Bernadette pouted slightly. "I think we still will."

"And where are we going to put all this?" I said, gesticulating to IKEA at large. "We live in a small three-bed semi. We don't need a TV unit with shelves, a bookcase and a display cabinet. For fuck's sake, can we not just get what we need for what we have at the moment, which is a TV and your book collection, which consists of *Fifty Shades of Grey* and Harry Potter?"

Bernadette began to cry.

*

Two hours later, we were close to leaving – so close I could almost taste it, like I was still tasting those meatballs – but Bernadette had stalled in the homewares department. She was throwing candle holders, vases, prints and photo frames into our trolley as though her life depended on it.

"Can we go?" I said, glancing at my watch. "We still have to find all the bits for the cabinets." IKEA teased you in this way. You saw something you wanted, but rather than being able to acquire it immediately, you had to write down a tiny reference number for later, when you were ejected into a hangar-sized warehouse. Once there, you'd have to select every element you needed to build your over-priced MDF monstrosity.

"A few more minutes," Bernadette whined. "I need to find a doorstop. Preferably in the shape of a large, comical dog made out of corduroy fabric." OK, she didn't say that last part, but I knew that's what she meant. She'd seen one on TV earlier that week. And what would her life be without an over-sized canine doorstop?

Finally, finally, finally. Fucking finally, we made it into the hangar where we spent a further 40 minutes trying to find the bits we needed. At one point Bernadette realised she'd noted the number down incorrectly and was on the verge of convincing me to run through the store again to get it. "I think you might need to..." she began.

"No," I screamed, and a few people turned to look at me. "Don't even say it. If you say it, we're through."

Bernadette's eyes narrowed. "So that's what you think of me? That's how much I mean to you that you wouldn't just nip through the store again to find the number?"

"Nip? It's taken us almost three hours to get to this point. Some people give birth quicker than this. And with less pain."

Eventually, I managed to track down an elusive assistant who helped us locate the missing pieces. The way Bernadette beamed at him, you'd have thought he'd helped her discover the building blocks of life itself.

Of course there was another long queue to pay. The final bill made my eyes water and for a moment I felt like I might have a panic attack. One last wait, while Bernadette found a toilet and relieved her bladder. Then, naturally, a fight over where the car was parked. Deduct another 20 minutes from my life for the time that took.

*

Home. A refuge you might think. But oh no. Bernadette wanted her 12-shelf BESTÅ TV stand put up that very night. So, there I was – past midnight with the cabinet only three-quarter built and, somewhere along the way, I'd managed to lose a screw. Or the screw was never in there. "Cunt," I screamed. "You utter cunt." Picking up the hammer, I slammed it into the partly-constructed cabinet. Oh, that felt good. "Have that you shitting load of toss-wood," I bellowed, smacking the hammer down again and again.

Suddenly I stopped, spying Bernadette in the doorway, pyjama-breathed and sleep-dishevelled. Her eyes widened as she took in her beloved BESTÅ, now lying in pieces on the floor. "You pig," she yelled. "How could you?"

I stood there speechless, hammer clasped in my fist. "Well let me tell you," I said, approaching her slowly. "While you were asleep, I was down here trying to put together your precious TV cabinet but I've lost a screw."

Bernadette scrunched up her face. "Too right you've lost a fucking screw. You've destroyed my cabinet. I loved that TV cabinet and now I'll never see it completed. I hate you," she bellowed. "I hate you so much and I don't think I actually ever loved you."

"You hate me?" I breathed, creeping towards her as a hot ire filled my chest. "You hate me? You whiny, selfish, boring bitch." Before I could stop myself, I had raised the hammer high over my head and, with a guttural yell, I brought it down, feeling the sweet release of rage flow through my veins.

*

So, here you find me. A man contrite. A man who blames meatballs for a chain of events from which there is no going back. Right now, Bernadette's still, silent form lies upstairs on the bed. Meanwhile, I'm frantically beating eggs and crumbling digestive biscuits. Ah, it is almost ready... now for the pièce de résistance.

Gingerly, I climb the stairs and pop my head round the bedroom door, bracing myself for what I'll find inside – the remnants of a woman I once adored.

"Something for you," I say.

Bernadette refuses to look at me at first, lying limply

on the duvet. She has a large plaster on her arm where the hammer made contact. "Oh, come on," I say. "Just take a look at what I made you." Her eyes eventually shift over to the plate, unable to resist the temptation. "That's right. It's a Daim Cake. To say I'm sorry."

The corners of her mouth turn up slightly. "You made that for me?"

"Sure I did." Walking over, I cut off a forkful and spoon it into her mouth.

"Yum, I'm impressed. You've never made anything like this before."

"Well, I've never hit out at my wife with a hammer before. I've been forced to take a long, hard look at my life."

"So does this mean you'll go and get another TV cabinet today?" she asks, reaching out for the plate.

"Yes, of course. Of course. But only if you come with me. It'll be more fun together. We could even have meatballs again."

Bernadette grins. "You're on. Just let me finish this and I'll get ready."

*

Whistling, I make my way back downstairs and into the kitchen. Trevor, our Bull Terrier, is sitting there, thumping his tail to some unknown beat. I reach down and give him a pat. "Thanks mate. Your coliform contribution to the cake won't go unrewarded," I say, tossing him a bone as I stuff the remains of the TV cabinet into a bin bag.

A giggle escapes, unbidden, as I take one last look around the living room, preparing to shed the accoutrements of married life – goodbye BESTÅ, ciao

Liatorp, adjö Hemnes; it's been a hoot, but I won't miss you.

I'm just shutting the front door quietly behind me when I hear Bernadette running full pelt towards the toilet. I reckon she'll be in and out of there for a while. But at least she now has a nice butterfly print to keep her company.

~

Adena Graham's Biography

I have had other stories published in various magazines (both online and offline). This includes *Creepy Pasta*, *Unhinged*, *Dead Things*, *QWF*, *Writers' Brew* and, most recently, three editions of *Popshot Magazine*.

I've also had two erotic novels published (under a pseudonym) – I'd like to say it was *Fifty Shades of Grey*, but there are three of those and my bank balance indicates it wasn't them.

I've also recently finished a novel which I'm trying to find an agent for.

CHEER

Shortlisted story, by Patrick Tuck

Lewis placed the basket on the counter and showed his wristband - *Monday*. He watched with dull anticipation as the shopkeeper passed the items over the monotone scanner.

"Anything else?" asked the shopkeeper.

Lewis eyed the shelves opposite him. "Yes, can I please have 500 grams of brown caster, some Fruit Pastilles and some All Sorts?"

The shopkeeper touched the till screen. "Please step on the scales, sir."

Lewis climbed upon the metal plate and tried to raise his muscles in a forlorn attempt to reduce the burden of his mass. The shopkeeper eyed the ruler beside Lewis's left ear and typed the information into his computer.

"I'm sorry, sir," he said. "I can only serve you a half unit."

Lewis instinctively feigned indignation. "But I was here last week and purchased that exact amount. I have the money; I'll pay a good price."

"I'm sorry, sir," repeated the shopkeeper, "I am legally permitted to sell you half a unit. You may purchase three items of fruit, a tube of confectionery or 10 grams of icing or caster sugar."

Lewis admired the queue forming behind him. "There must be a mistake. I want you to measure again."

The shopkeeper sighed and swivelled the screen to face Lewis. "See, your BMI stands at 34 and therefore I am only permitted to sell you half a unit per week. You can either purchase the items I have mentioned, or please step aside so I can serve the next customer."

"I'll have the Pastilles," mumbled Lewis.

"Fine. That'll be 42 pounds, 37 pence."

"How much?"

"Your basket comes to 31 pounds," said the shopkeeper. "And the sugar tax for your BMI is four pounds a gram."

Lewis dredged the melange of change and crumpled notes from his pocket and thumped them on the counter. He stepped out into the fine afternoon and greeted Eve on the corner.

"What'dya get?" she asked.
"Pastilles."
"How many?"
"One."
"Bag?"
"Tube," said Lewis. "They're fucking crooks. I oughtta hold that place up; then we'll see how much that prick with his computer'll give me."

"Hey," said Eve, pressing her lips against his cheek. "At least it's something. We'll go and see Hamish; he always has good stuff on a Monday."

*

Eve tapped the wooden door. Hamish, opened the door a latch's width and smiled at his visitor.

"Evie, what a pleasant surprise."

"You busy?" she said, lifting the diminutive candy before her cleavage.

Hamish eyed her wristband: *Friday*. "Where you getting *cheer* on a Monday?" he said, opening the door.

Lewis followed her into the flat and watched the visible disappointment on their host's face.

"We were in the area and thought we'd see if you fancied a hit." She kissed Hamish on the cheek and strolled to the lounge. Hamish was rich, self-made through banking, property or tech or whatever intelligent, driven people make their money in these days. The flat was fine and lacking in soul, but with his money he could source *cheer* from any of London's black markets with a simple phone call.

"You don't mind if I cook this up?" asked Lewis. He knew Hamish put up with him out of lust for Eve, but there was nothing he could do about that. He might as well get a decent score from the guy.

"Why don't I sort us something?" said Hamish.

Lewis dropped to the sofa with a considerable creak and wrapped his arm around Eve. Hamish soon returned with a tray and placed it on the coffee table. He lifted the kitchen knife and stroked the flame of his lighter across either side of the thick blade. Lewis's eyes gravitated to the seductive block of goose fat, as Hamish unwrapped the tin foil and sliced 50 grams.

"I got this from my guy at Claridge's," said Hamish, as he transferred the fat to the ladle and twisted the knife's point to create an inch-wide dimple.

Lewis began to salivate in anticipation. His blood trickled excitedly like an adolescent in inexperienced foreplay. Hamish opened a small cellophane bag filled with heavenly, brown granules and carefully pressed them into the goose fat.

"Is that pure?" asked Eve.

"100% Demerara," boasted Hamish, "direct from Cuba."

"You're the best, Ham."

Hamish blushed a smile and lifted the flame beneath the ladle. The smell invaded Lewis's nostrils and he quivered faint with desire. He watched the sugar bubble and congeal with the fat. In that moment he could see nothing else. The *cheer* was everything.

"Is it ready?" asked Eve.

"Patience," smiled Hamish, laying his hand on her bare knee. "You have to dissolve all the sugar or it gets lodged in the veins."

Lewis didn't notice Hamish's hand; he didn't notice Eve looking at him; he didn't notice the perfectly formed cushions of clouds that swept by the window. It was impossible to notice anything but the needle and the thick golden deliverance in the ladle. In five minutes he wouldn't be just another man on a sofa. Everything would be inconceivably perfect, the kind of perfect that nobody could hope to describe or understand, the kind of perfect that could hide the confusing world that for some reason had chosen him to suffer bland mediocrity.

"OK," said Hamish. "Eve, you first."

Hamish wrapped the rubber tube to Eve's bicep and ran his fingers along her vein. He prodded the blue line on the inside of her elbow and flicked the travelling blood.

"Ready?" he asked.

She nodded with visceral anticipation.

Lewis beheld his lover with pathetic, impatient envy as she fell back in instant ecstasy. Hamish handed him a fresh needle. His hand began to shake as he lingered over the bulbous vein between the knuckles of his index and middle fingers. He took a deep intake of breath and plunged the needle in. The faint cloud of blood mingled with the syrup as the world rolled up inside him. As Hamish administered his own hit, Eve and Lewis instinctively gravitated to one another. They locked their limbs and entangled in a perfect intoxicated embrace.

*

"Get up, get out."

Reality returned with numb candour. Lewis blinked between various stages of consciousness and shifted on the sofa.

"Go on, get out," Hamish was pacing, spitting confused anger in his direction.

"Hamish, baby, what's the matter?" slurred Eve.

"All you do is use me, coming round here, batting your eyes and then fornicating on my sofa with this layabout."

Lewis noticed Eve's bra was misaligned and felt his unbuckled belt.

"Using?" asked Eve. "We brought some *cheer* with us. It's the Demerara, Hamish, you're paranoid, confused."

"Don't play your tricks," replied Hamish. "I know what you think: Hamish is good for a few grams; Hamish can get us some good stuff."

Lewis crawled to his feet and made for the exit. "Come on, Eve."

The midnight air sliced his confusion. *Where am I?* thought Lewis. *Dalston, I think I'm in Dalston. Home is Hackney; is that near? I think it's a couple of miles; is that far or near?*

"Let's go home," said Eve.

"It could take hours," replied Lewis. "Why don't we rest a little on the swing?"

Eve followed his gaze to the playground across the street.

"We'll rest on the tyre," said Lewis, "then, when it's light, I'll know what to do."

*

"Look at those kids," said Lewis. The sunlight grated his eyeballs. The feral sounds of the city crashed around as he reluctantly tested the dryness of his mouth.

"What kids?" Eve looked terrible, entirely devoid of vigour; her once sparkling eyes looked haggard and hopeless.

"In the bandstand."

Eve watched the four adolescents. The tallest held a bottle of Lucozade attached to an empty biro casing with a jelly baby at one end. He lit the contraption and watched the confection burn smoke through the liquid before passing it to his companions.

"Let's go home," said Eve. "I need to sleep it off."

"Let's just have one hit," said Lewis.

"They're just kids," said Eve. Watching as another of the youths inhaled the vapour from the fluorescent orange liquid.

"So, it's illegal, we'd be doing them a favour."

"What do you want to be taking glucose for anyway?"

"I just need it for the come down."

"It's monosaturates for a come down; glucose'll only wind you up. Have you still got that *cheer* from yesterday?"

"I haven't got any needles."

"We could just eat it."

Lewis turned sharply on her. "Eat it? Do you have any idea how much that costs? Right, sod it, I'm getting a hit."

"Lewis, you can't."

"It's illegal, Eve, so nobody owns it."

Lewis climbed the stairs and lurched his considerable bulk towards one of the boys. The wiry thing evaded him and Lewis confronted another of the group. The boy stared up and Lewis flashed his eroded, blackened teeth. He heard the plastic bottle clatter on the concrete among the speeding footsteps.

Lewis placed his lips to the mouthpiece. The sugared gelatine grasped the lungs and Lewis felt his extremities throb with numb self-forgiveness.

Eve sat beside him and took a hit. The park began to

assume some tranquillity, some awkward beauty. The day inherited optimism.

"Put it down," came a voice.

Lewis looked up and noticed the uniform.

"Put it down."

"It's medicinal," said Lewis.

"Of course; you *chunkies* make me sick."

"I promise, diabetes."

"And whose fault is that?" The voice was cruel and mocking.

"It's genetic, type one. I swear; my mother has it and her mother too."

"Let's see your license then."

"It's not here, it's at home."

"Let's go there then."

"In Hackney."

"We're in Hackney."

This is Hackney, thought Lewis. The panic was disorientating. He rose to his feet and thrust the contents of the bottle into the policeman's face.

"Run," he screamed to Eve as he bundled down the steps.

Lewis turned to see the policeman fast on his heels.

"I'll see you at the flat," he cried to Eve. He wanted to kiss her goodbye but there wasn't time.

Lewis darted at a right angle confident the copper would follow. He looked back – he was nearly caught – then a sudden lift in his legs. The glucose must be kicking in. He pumped his knees forward and felt the stale city air plaster against his face. He turned back once more; the policeman was slowing, giving up, he'd made it. And Eve was safe too.

*

Lewis inspected the bags under his eyes in the bookies' window. *I was a boy once*, he thought. He tried to shift his hair to reflect some element of humanity.

"Lewis," came a voice.

He turned and admired the wiry figure and weasel face.

"Hello, Ray."

"Good to see you, man." Ray turned to the window and watched his reflection. "Man, my head is all over, you know? I popped a couple of E-numbers last night. That shit gives me the worst comedown."

"What do you want, Ray?"

Ray was on a different level, shooting and snorting any old junk he could find. *Cheer*, trans fats, salts, colourings, sulfates, raising agents, yeast, flour, preservatives. You name it; Ray and his lot had tried it.

"Where've you been? Everyone's been worried sick."

"Well," said Lewis, "here I am."

"I mean it," continued Ray. "Eve's been crying for days."

"Eve? What do you know about Eve?"

"She's down at Daddy's; thought you were rumbled by some copper."

Daddy's, thought Lewis, *she wouldn't get mixed up with that lot.*

*

Lewis heard the scuttle of vermin as he stepped into the corridor to Daddy's. A pipe dripped ominously as the stale smell of rotting life infiltrated his sober nostrils. Ray knocked three times, paused and flicked the letterbox. The door opened and upbeat country music fled the room.

"Lewis," said the enormous man. "Thank fuck for that."

The furniture comprised uniquely of mattresses. In a room to the left of the entrance a man placed 10 unpeeled bananas into a large sieve. He crushed the fruit into a paste and added the contents of three plastic lighters. Lewis watched as the man spread the paste onto the counter into a thin layer, inspecting and removing any clumps.

"Lewis." Eve thrust her arms upon him.

Her kiss was euphoric relief. All concerns dissipated.

Lewis watched the man ignite the halogen lamps and they passed to the communal area.

"We should celebrate," said Eve.

"Not here," whispered Lewis.

"Where are we gonna go? I can't get anything until tomorrow."

"Then we'll wait."

"I haven't seen you for two days. Let's just do one together. You can spare us one little hit can't you, Daddy?"

"All I've got is fructose," replied their host. "I can't get any decent *cheer* until next week."

"I don't like fructose," said Lewis, "it's too sharp."

"It's good stuff," replied Eve, "organic."

Daddy returned from the kitchen with a brown box. He scooped the cream coloured powder onto a CD case with his driver's licence and began to crush and cut the substance into lines.

"I believe the honour is with our returning hero," said Daddy, passing the case to Lewis.

Lewis lifted the note to his nose and winced as the fine powder hit the back of his throat. There was something he couldn't put his finger on, a slight saltiness. He felt his teeth numb and his limbs tingle. This was the problem with fructose, the hit was fast and short and there was nothing to sate the mind's thirst.

Eve took her line and wrapped herself to him. This was all that mattered. He felt her more; the hit opened his senses to her every move. She crawled into him and then stiffened.

"Evie," said Lewis.

He rolled her to face him; she was drooling.

"Evie?"

Lewis watched as she shuddered and gasped.

"What's in this shit?" he screamed.

"It's fructose, bananas," replied Daddy.

"What else?"

"I think I cut it with a little dried Wensleydale. It takes the edge off."

"You idiot," screamed Lewis. "She's lactose intolerant."

Daddy shrunk. "I didn't know; I'm sorry."

Lewis turned back to his love. He could see the intoxicant writhe through her veins. Her diaphragm surged pushing drool and vomit from her poisoned oesophagus.

"Have you got an EpiPen?" cried Lewis.

Daddy scrambled manically through the corners of the room.

Lewis cradled her as he rubbed his hands on her chest and pumped with resigned futility.

Daddy returned. Lewis grasped the EpiPen in his hand and placed his thumb over one end. The fructose took hold of him; the room span in manic, pitiless confusion. He ripped open her blouse and felt for the beat of her heart.

Three, two – the sweat dripped from his brow – one.

He slammed the EpiPen onto her ribcage.

The scream crippled the room. Lewis stared at his hand. The needle had shot straight through his thumbnail. In the confusion he had gripped the wrong end. Blood dribbled on Eve's chest and clothes as she shivered in agony.

"Give me another one," screamed Lewis.

"That's all we've got."

Lewis leapt to the kitchen. He filled a glass with warm water and poured in the salt. He frantically blended the two and poured the liquid down Eve's mouth.

The blood and vomit washed away.

"Come on, swallow it."

The corpse lay still.

Lewis lifted her head and poured more of the liquid. He began to pump her chest and blew in her mouth. The body wasn't stiff; it was limp and lame. He continued his attempts at resurrection until Daddy pulled him away. It was hopeless; she was expired.

*

Lewis admired the bandage on his thumb. The sun beat down on the street and forced his wet eyes to squint. He wiped his face but the tears continued running as he stood over the bin and felt through his pockets. He tossed the lighter and the needles. *I won't need those anymore.* He rummaged through his coat and found the pastilles. His hand lingered above the can. *I can't cope with a comedown*, he thought, *not now. I'll just eat them, just one little tube to wean me off.* He placed the roll in his pocket, rubbed his eyes and walked towards Hackney.

Patrick Tuck's Biography

I am a 29 year old working for a micro-brewery in London and writing short stories in my spare time. My favourite authors are Graham Greene, Douglas Adams and Leo Tolstoy. The stories entered into 'To Hull & Back' are my first submissions.

FANCY THAT

Shortlisted story, by John Emms

He rang the bell. The door opened. Fiona stood there, dressed in a tight, shiny, garishly-coloured outfit. He reached under his jacket, pulled out a pistol and adopted what he hoped was a cool, confident stance.

"My name is Bond. James Bond."

"Nigel, for heaven's sake. It's supposed to be fancy dress."

"This is fancy dress. I'm Bond. He always wears a

dinner jacket."

"Yes, but it isn't fancy, is it? I mean, that's what you usually wear when you go out to dinner."

"I've got a gun."

"That's not dress. That's a prop."

"Well, what are you supposed to be? You don't look much different from normal, either."

Fiona replied with some emphasis, "I am supposed to be a tart."

"Yeah, well. Like I said..."

Fiona moved back inside.

"Right. Well, you're not coming in 'til you're in fancy dress, as specified."

She slammed the door.

Nigel was nonplussed. He'd been quite pleased with his adopted persona. He decided that he'd always known that Fiona was a bitch. Then he shrugged his shoulders and set off down the street. Walking aimlessly, he turned a corner and found himself outside a small nightclub he didn't recall seeing before. He went through the door. Inside, a plush lobby was impeccably furnished. A beautifully proportioned girl, with a mass of blonde curls, was behind a desk. She stood up as he walked past, and approached him.

"Excuse me, sir. Are you a member?"

Nigel tilted up her chin with one hand and planted a firm, lingering kiss on her lips. With the other hand he took out his wallet and flashed a card at her.

The girl gasped, when she was able to, then returned to being business-like.

"Oh, yes, of course, Mr. Bond. I do apologise, I should have recognised you."

"Never mind. You will next time."

Nigel shocked himself by slapping her bottom as she

returned to the desk, where she pushed a button. A hidden door opened to one side and he walked through. On the surface he appeared calm, though his mind was struggling to catch up with events.

Behind the door a cosy, but elaborately decorated bar contained a scattering of people. On a small stage a girl who looked a little like Diana Ross was singing huskily into a microphone. A waiter bustled up with an obsequious smile and ushered Nigel to a table in a quiet corner.

"Your usual, Mr. Bond?"

"Yes, please. And make it a double."

The waiter scurried away, returning with a drink which Nigel thought he didn't recognise, despite apparently finding it perfectly familiar. He leaned back in his chair.

Suddenly strong clamps emerged from the chair, binding him to it. He felt himself descending through the floor, which closed above his head. A light snapped on and a pair of cold eyes focused on him from a smooth but grossly unattractive face.

"So, Mr. Bond. You thought you could enter my lair unmolested?"

"On the contrary, Blofeld. I was relying on this. I can now put paid to your schemes."

Nigel found himself moving the tip of his tongue to a hollow tooth. He pressed the tiny button which he found there. The clamps which held him to the chair sprang back. He leaped forward, directly at the face, which recoiled. Instantly two large, bald-headed, sweaty weight-lifters (they looked like weightlifters to Nigel) threw themselves upon him from either side. He grabbed each of them by the neck and banged their bald pates together hard, taking care to ensure that

Blofeld's head was between them.

Leaving the three in a motionless heap, and feeling quite surprised, Nigel ran to a nearby door. Set in the wall beside it was a large red button marked 'Denouement'. In an adjacent cupboard he discovered the wetsuit and aqualung he now realised he was looking for. Donning them, he opened the door and looked outside. A beach, edged by the sea, glistened in the moonlight. Responding to an urge, Nigel pressed the red button, then he ran down to the sea and plunged into the water as the island behind him exploded in a massive ball of flame. Diving deep to avoid the flying lumps of rock which were plummeting into the sea all around, he swam to the other side of the strait, surfacing in a small deserted harbour. There he climbed the steps to the jetty, his flippers raising echoes as they slapped on the hard surface. Removing them, he began making his way along the nearest street. A little way along he came to a door he recognised.

He rang the bell. The door opened. Fiona stood there.

"That's better," she said. "You can come in now."

~

John Emms' Biography

A few years ago I retired from a career as a local government lawyer, during which the only vaguely creative writing I could manage was for professional journals, so not wildly exciting. I now at last have the time to indulge my long-held desire to write in a way which is less vaguely creative. I have a number of short stories and articles published here and there, though quite a few not published anywhere. I have also written several plays, a few of the shorter of which have been performed or given rehearsed readings at venues such as the Cast Theatre in Doncaster and the Kings Arms, Salford.

MY WEEK WITH KIM JONG UN

Shortlisted story, by Will Haynes

I've been to some sketchy places in my lifetime but North Korea certainly bags the Lonely Planet Wooden Spoon for 'Worst Place Ever'. How I came to end up stranded and alone there is the subject of some debate on social networking sites that litter the internet, but casting my somewhat unreliable eye back over the events of the past few weeks, as much as I can determine is that it started in the most innocuous of places; a McDonalds franchise on the Kao San Road in Bangkok, my third night in Thailand's capital…

"Bullshit... that's bullshit..." he said again and again as my mind drifted back into the rather tedious conversation.

These pearls of wisdom were being thrust, uninvited, in my direction by a highly articulate and worldly-wise 25 year old on his first ever jaunt abroad from the North of England; Wakefield or Warrington or somewhere, most probably, judging by his accent.

"...and if you want my opinion..." he repeated for the fifth or sixth time.

I sighed and raised my finger, stopping him mid-flow, and said, "Ah, yes, you see, that's where you're going wrong... because I really don't want your opinion... I neither requested nor value it, but you, for some quite inexplicable reason, seem to be under the deluded impression that it's of some importance."

This seemed to perplex him in some small way. I'll never know what his real name is, but as he was a red-haired clown and we happened to be in McDonalds, I'll simply refer to him as 'Ronald'.

I continued, "You asked if you and your girlfriend could join me at this table and so I said 'OK' and then you asked what I'm doing here and so I foolishly told you..."

Regretfully, I'd confided in the disagreeable little twerp, Ronald, the personal information that I'd left London a year prior to travel and pursue my writing ambitions. His girlfriend seemed to like this. He did not. It would not compute in his Amstrad CPC664 of a brain, as I sat patiently for several minutes while he called me a liar, a fraud and a coward. I learned the glistening pearls of information from him that I was in fact pretending to be a writer as a cover story and that I was simply running away from real life. I also learned that I'd never worked in the film industry; this I had obviously falsified as nobody in their right mind would ever leave such a glamorous profession unless they had been kicked out for gross incompetence or theft. It's quite remarkable the truths that one can learn about oneself from a total stranger with which you've shared perhaps two or three pieces of rather bland information. If I'd let him continue I'd have no doubt discovered I was also on the run from a triple murder charge or was actually in command of day-to-day admin ops for ISIS.

"...and you proceeded to generously share all manner of your unrequested thoughts with me, but you see I'm really not at all interested in your thoughts. To be honest, What-ever-your-name-is, your incredibly limited and, frankly, insignificant opinion is absolutely irrelevant to me."

Ronald's opinion was about to bare significantly more relevance to me. Before I could add, *"Now please excuse me as I'm going to move elsewhere, but do enjoy this table,"* which were the words I'd intended would spring forth from my lips, it happened.

And it made quite a mess of the place.

Early Tarantino gore... *Reservoir Dogs*.

A searing eruption of pain exploded from behind my eyeballs as my blood spray-painted the 'restaurant' and anybody who was sitting within a three-metre radius; the closest person to me, Ronald's girlfriend in fact, looked like Sissy Spacek in the climax of *Carrie*.

It took me quite by surprise and I'll admit, in Ronald's defence, he certainly had talent for landing a solid connection to the hooter. I doubt an infuriated Boston Docker, or even Muhammad Ali in his prime, could have done a better job at turning my nose into something that now so closely resembled a sweet potato.

Fellow diners fled for the hills. The exodus of McDonalds. Not wanting to escalate the situation any further, and spotting the shimmering gleam of psychosis in Ronald's lunatic eyes as he swung back to take his second whack at me, though this time with the absence of surprise, I (according to witness statements) leaned over, plucked him from his seat like a rag doll onto the floor and then, rather than hitting him back, just sat on him so he couldn't move.

"Have you finished?" I asked him (quite calmly, given the circumstances) as my blood monsooned all over him. His white T-shirt turned carmine in seconds.

Ronald hadn't quite finished just yet though; this mangy little dog in the fight. He scrabbled and scratched and swore and swung and strangled, but to little avail as 14 stone of Haynes pinning you down, as blood rains into your eyes and mouth, momentarily blinding you, is ultimately quite difficult to keep up the good fight against.

"It's over. Done. Just give it up," I stated several times to the compromised Ronald as he wriggled around like a fat little worm on a hook, until finally the aggression drained out of him like the torrents of blood from my newly applied nasal cavities.

Once released back into the wild, the feral little ferret Ronald sprang up from the tiles and sat shaking on a plastic stool, rocking back and forth, struggling to comprehend the horror-movie set he'd created around him as I apologised profusely to the shocked staff, some of whom were busily mopping up a combination of my blood and my uneaten sandwiches and my chicken nuggets from the floor. The indignity. His girlfriend was cooing sweet nothings into his ear to snap him back from his trance and then she apologised and thanked me in equal measure for not actually hitting him back while I had the opportunity. I begrudgingly accepted the apology but pointed out that not everyone would react so diplomatically to such an attack (I suspect that even Gandhi, under the circumstances of making acquaintances with Ronald, may have been swayed to momentarily relinquish his deeply held convictions of pacifism to plant the irritating little shit with at least a sucker punch or two...). She agreed and said that they don't usually. It appears that this was not the first time little Ronald had done this kind of thing.

After a couple of hours, several buckets of SangSom (Thai rum) to dull the pain of my throbbing potato nose, and many, many plasters that proved most ineffective at stemming the gory flow, the cranial passage wouldn't stop haemorrhaging blood. Finally, on the advice of some shocked ladyboys I passed on Kao San, I ended up making my way to A&E.

Scans, prods, X-Rays and general microwaving determined that my nose was broken in several places and would require an expensive operation to snap it back into position. This was as painful as it was costly when the local anaesthetic didn't quite kick in (the downside of an ox-level tolerance to toxins) before they crunched it back into its former shape. I cursed the ginger psycho who'd set me back about 1,000 quid in medical bills for this privilege. The surgeon informed me of what I couldn't do until it healed, which was pretty much anything; No drinking, No smoking, No diving, No sports, No tumbles, No any kind of fun. No, No, No, and all in capitals. My initial plan for a month of lazy island-hopping came a cropper. That being said, he did give me a prescription that read like Pete Doherty's ideal

Christmas wish list – a vast cocktail of drugs, including Tylenol, Tramadol, Reparil, Augmentin, something called Experipsychodelamentin and many more. So I spent a couple of days in my hotel room, whacked-out on the cocktail of painkillers, and then, like a phoenix rising from the ashes, the thought occurred to me... North Korea. I could do some first-hand research on the rogue totalitarian state, necessary for my next novel.

There's a misconception that the chubby, youthful North Korean Supreme Leader-cum-Dictator Kim Jong Un was privately educated at a Swiss boarding school, but this is a falsehood. He was actually educated, in secret, at Rugby School in Warwickshire, England, my old school to be precise, two years below me, under the guise of being a mysterious foreign diplomat's son, and we shared the same boarding house. You make some interesting connections at these institutions. This made the bureaucratic, and traditionally impossible, access to the fortress-like State somewhat easier as I passed through the red tape and the DMZ (de-militarized zone) from South Korea into the Heart of Darkness that is the Democratic People's Republic of Korea.

I ♥ North Korea Ministry of Propaganda Tour, Day 1

I took a controlled excursion of some of the areas the Party deem fit for outsiders to see. It didn't take terribly long; a few parts of the country that don't have people starving en-masse in the street, while occasionally being instructed by the 'tour guide' (handler) to look out of the opposite window when passing many a forced slave-labour prison camp: the Gulags.

It's a barren wasteland. Stoker's *Dracula* springs to mind, when Harker describes Transylvania. Buildings look like an architectural Mengele experiment, and don't get me started on the grey matter that's classed as food... but Kimmy's really got his propaganda locked down so the people are genuinely grateful for their thimble of gruel after 14 hours of back-breaking labour, seven days a week. I'm sure that I'll eat a little better at the Palace though, safe in the bosom of the Fatherly Leader's prodigal grandchild.

I hit Kim's pad, the Palace in Pyongyang, at about 4pm, after the breezily satanic tour. He's got a lot of Palaces in the Capital, and they continue to keep springing up like toadstools on cow shit (despite North Korea's 'temporary' economic downturn), but this one is his favourite. It's the flashiest of the lot. The décor suggests the Interior Designer was strapped down in a torture chamber and kept awake for three weeks, forced at gunpoint to watch endless screenings of *MTV Cribs* (repeated emphasis on the one with Mike Tyson's house), whilst being repeatedly sodomised by Donald Trump. The result is as if they've somehow tapped into any tasteful designer's worst nightmare, or a Premiership Footballer's wet dream... I mean, everything is FUCKING COVERED IN GOLD (including the loos) and mock Louis XIV chandeliers drip from the ceiling of every room. Colossal paintings hang on every wall; portraits of the Man-Gods Kim Il-Sung, Kim Jong-Il, and one or two (which seem more recently added) of Kim Kardashian. This particular Palace is called 'The Celestial Majesty of The Great Leader's Palace, For The Worker's Paradise that is The Glorious Democratic People's Republic of Korea, that Benefits All of the Free Citizens (Pyongyang Palace # eight)'. So, naturally, if one of the proles ever laid eyes on the bling inside they'd be no doubt shot on sight.

I'd wondered to myself what Kimmy's day-to-day responsibilities as Supreme Leader consisted of. He's sat plumped on a giant throne-like beanbag, trimmed in gold leaf, sipping from a pitcher of Hennessy and smoking a joint while playing World of Warcraft on his X-Box. He doesn't take his eyes off the cinema-sized plasma-screen as he bludgeons an opponent to death, but says, "Yo, yo, yo, what's hangin' dog?"

"All good thanks," I reply. "How's tricks?"

"Bitchin'," he says. "Got a whole fuckin' country now bro... but Obama's getting on my tits. That was him that just copped it. Wanna play?"

"Uhuh," I say.

"What happened to your nose? Looks like there's a miniature menstruating polar bear clamped to your face, bro... And is that a tampon shoved up its ass?"

The balance of power has shifted dramatically since school.

I grab a controller and park myself down on a beanbag.

Days 2-5

The days pass by at the Palace in a blur of Hennessy and X-Box sessions with the Supreme Leader-child. It appears that this is ALL he ever does, day in, day out. The food improved significantly though; foie gras (flown in daily on one of Kimmy's private jets straight from a trendy boutique delicatessen, favoured by Elton John and some of the minor Royals, on Boulevard du Montparnasse in Paris) is served with Lobster Thermidor and kimchi (Korean spiced cabbage) on the side for every meal. The quality is excellent.

I have to make sure I don't forget to keep taking my

meds.

Day 6

After the standard Lobster lunch, Kimmy proposed, "Come on, bro, let's do something different." *I'd finally started to beat the little shit at World of Warcraft.* "You'll fucking love this."

I'm a little surprised to be led out the back of Kimmy's Palace to find a mass of terrified army types bound, gagged and tied to wooden posts. On a giant golden trestle lies an impressive array of weapons; AKs, rocket launchers, bazookas and the like, even some medieval axes and spiked balls-on-chains and other nasty stuff. One of the 'relics', a spring loaded triple dagger, still has a faded gift tag on it that reads, 'To my very good friend The Eternal Leader of the Workers' Paradise of the Democratic People's Republic of Korea, Kim Il-Sung. Warmest regards, His Excellency, President for Life, Field Marshal Al Hadji Doctor Idi Amin Dada, VC, DSO, MC, Lord of All the Beasts of the Earth and Fishes of the Seas and Conqueror of the British Empire in Africa in General and Uganda in Particular (aka Idi)'. The devil's in the detail. Kimmy picks up a rocket launcher and inspects it with a connoisseur's eye before he lugs it over his shoulder.

"What's this?" I exclaim. Genuine shock.

"FIM-92 Stinger," he replies.

"Not the weapon, this. This situation. What is it?"

"Oh, right. Bit of post-lunch sport," he says nonchalantly, lining the weapon up to eviscerate a petrified former General or Commander of his armed forces. He then changes his mind and swaps it for another model.

"Actually fuck it, the Panzerfaust three... better for specificity... This bad boy'll hit the nuts on an ant 20 miles away. German engineering, baby – you can't fucking beat it."

I stare at him incredulously.

"Come on," he says, "Grab a tool and get stuck in, man... mi casa su casa."

Tool? Sport? There's nothing in the least bit sporting about it.

"Woah, woah, woah," I say, "time out. You're fucking kidding, right?"

Kim looks at me like I'm a maniac, like *how could you possibly NOT want to play this sadistic game of exploding organic toy soldiers?*

"Nah," he responds coolly, shoving a rocket into the pipe and realigning the bazooka. The General makes a whimper as he prepares to meet his maker; probably Kim's grandfather, the Eternal Leader, Kim Il Sung (word has it the man got around).

"But, but, but what have they done?"

"I dunno... traitors of some kind, probably? They look pretty guilty anyway and I could do with fucking some shit up. It's good for the digestion. My physician told me so, just before I had him fed alive to a pack of starved wild pigs."

"You can't just kill them for... for... for sport, for no reason."

"I can do whatever the fuck I want, bro. I'm the Supreme Leader of the Greatest Superpower in the universe."

Somehow, I manage to convince Kim not to engage in the brutal activity but instead play a game of my Travel Monopoly. He takes to it pretty quickly, like a dictator to corruption, but of course he's a cheating, spoilt bastard (always was) and steals Park Lane and Mayfair immediately and then helps himself to cash from the bank whenever it suits him. His method at playing Monopoly perfectly mirrors his domestic management and economics policy. I think they might have made him a prefect at school, which would have made him even worse; the early footsteps to taking your place in this world as a corrupt, murderous dictator.

After I've had to sit through Kimmy taking every property and all the stations on the board, fairly or otherwise, with houses, hotels, crack dens, brothels, the works, on every square, he says, "Come on, man, let's get baked before dinner." He reaches for an industrial-scale bong, then adds, "I'm entertaining tonight. Some of the boys are coming round to eat."

Day 7

So dinner the previous evening with the 'boys'; Kim Jong Un, Robert Mugabe and George Dubya Bush, to be precise. Mugabe spent most of his time slagging off Tony Blair, who was notably absent.

"Fuck him," said Mugabe, "we're freezing him out. Borrowed one of my villas for a week that time but didn't bring a bottle of wine or write a thank-you letter. He didn't even leave a tip for my slaves. Tight-fisted fucker."

Bush pointed out that Tony couldn't have made it regardless as he was delivering a lucrative after-dinner speech at the Dubai Four Seasons on how to achieve peace in the Middle-East. There's general sniggering around the table about this remark.

"We're still freezing him out anyway," added

Mugabe, somewhat testily.

I asked Bush why he's on such good terms with the other two as this seemed a bit at odds with his former foreign policy.

"Are ya kidding?" whispered Dubstep nervously, "Don't misunderestimate mah judgement. Rob ain't got no oil, so ain't worth shit t'invade, and Kimmy actually HAS some WMDs. He's got The Bomb, man. Hot potatie. Gotta tread careful in them circumcises."

Kimmy drunkenly launches into his Sea Of Fire speech again, and everyone starts laughing. Bush then adds, "Middle Eastern Peace Envoy," and they burst into hysterics. This provides the basis of HOWLS of laughter inside the banquet room for the entire evening. My nose hurts and I pop some more of the Experipsychodelamentin and wash it down with some of Kimmy's Hennessy. A little wobbly, I make the mistake of actually referring to Kimmy as 'Kimmy' to his face, a nickname he's hated ever since the schooldays and one that only the foolishly brave or criminally insane would ever utter in his presence. It's made worse by the fact that Bush thinks it's hilarious and starts repeating it and it spreads like wildfire as Mugabe catches on.

"Fuckofffuckofffuckofffuckofffuckofffuckofffuckoff, stop calling me that," shouts Kimmy petulantly.

*

And that was how I came to find myself on day seven, chained to a stake, in Kim Jong Un's back garden as Kimmy, Bush and Mugabe played with various gruesome weapons.

"Can you lot just fuck off," I shouted. "This isn't

fucking funny, you know."

"I want the rocket launcher," screamed Mugabe like a disgruntled adolescent.

"Na-ah," said Bush, "I called shotgun," while Kimmy began to swing the Morning Star (the medieval spiked ball and chain thing). Choose your friends carefully.

"Really, really fuck off. It's NOT FUNNY," I bellowed again in protest, but they were all having too much fun playing with their military hardware to pay the slightest bit of attention to my trifling discomfort.

Mugabe primes a shotgun. Kimmy's chosen medieval. Bush raises the rocket launcher and squints as he aims it in my direction.

I'm in shock rather than awe.

*

I'm now sitting here back in Bangkok at The Atlanta, an old Colonial-style hotel, mulling over my experiences. It doesn't seem quite real, though it was so vivid, but I can't quite recall how I got back here. Did I make a break for it and cross the Tumen River into China? Did Kimmy give me clemency for old time's sake; not bog-flushing him at school? Did Tony Blair perhaps make a Skype call from his penthouse suite at Dubai's Four Seasons and persuade them not to explode me, or were they just fucking with me all along for a bit of *sport*?

I've finished my course of medication for the nose and it's healing very nicely. Doesn't look quite the same as it did before, though perhaps it gives a certain devil-may-care quality.

I'm sipping my tea in the courtyard and the fellow on the next table strikes up a conversation. He's a youngish doctor from London, mid-thirties. His opinion may be of some relevance to me. We talk about my nose and Ronald and the operation and the meds I've been on.

"Experipsychodelamentin?" he says. "You want to watch out for that one. It's pretty new to the market and there's some funny psychoactive side effects."

"Yes, I've noticed. I've had a very strange week on it."

"Did you have the North Korea hallucination?" he asks.

"Yep," I say.

"Yeah, that's pretty common. Did Bush, Blair and Mugabe come round for dinner?"

"Bush and Mugabe, but not Blair... they're freezing him out."

"Right. Of course."

"But Blair couldn't have made it anyway, as he was too busy promoting peace in the Middle-East."

He sniggers at this.

~

Will Haynes' Biography

Will Haynes began his career in the UK film industry as a dogsbody, before turning to writing. He has been on the run since his controversial fable on rural affairs, *The Parish State*, was denounced by the Countryside Alliance. North Korea have also doubled the bounty on his head for his shocking exposé of British Public Schools in his story, 'My Week With Kim Jong Un'. And the Royal Family are said to be less than happy about his dystopian allegory of hereditary Neoconservative dynasties, *The People's Republic*. He was last seen in a bar somewhere in Paris, complaining that the martini lacked an olive, before staggering down Boulevard du Montparnasse on the hunt for one of those awesome cheeseburgers that you can only get in Paris. His publicist has declined to comment.

Will's website: www.willhaynes.net

OUT OF THE MOUTHS OF BABES

Shortlisted story, by Sheila Corbishley

Here is the news. In a last ditch attempt to remedy what the Education minister has called 'an epidemic of inarticulacy', the Government has given the go-ahead to the controversial Speech Implant Scheme. From April 1st all pregnant women will be implanted with a coding device which delivers speech patterns to the developing foetus via the placenta. In the 'Every Child A Talking Child' initiative, newborns will emerge from the womb

fully able to speak. The Minister says he anticipates soaring SATs results within the next few years.

Dear mum,

I hope you are ok and dad is not getting you down. I am fine thanks for the fags and the cholats they was much ~~apris apper~~ everybody says thanks. I have got a bit of news for you you will never belive it. You know Paula the girl in the top bunk well she is only pregnant The chaplain says it is a act of god but Paula says it was not god she is nearly certain she knows who it really was. I wonder if they'll let her keep it it would be lovely to have a little baby to play with we could make it things in sewing class.

I will see you soon tell Dazza if he does not come this time I will chop his balls off we are allowed to use the pinking shears now.

Your loving daugter Shyanne

Dear mum

Well time is passing and we are getting very exited in here. Paula went to the hospital this morning to have her scan and speech implant and everythink. She was a bit scared but the chaplain says not to worry he says a implant is gods way of learning baby's to talk. He says in the olden days there wasnt no implants so when the poor little baby was born it couldnt speak nor nothing because it never had the chance to learn. I said that is shocking it is child abuse because if the baby is crying and you say what are you bleedin crying for now? it would not be able to tell you. but he says we must not judge because they didn't no no better in them days.

Paula is back now. She said it did not hurt. She got two implants the audio one and a new one. The new one is called a image. It is state of the art it has a picture of Paulas face on so if a pervert pretend's to be a nurse or somefink they cannot snatch the baby because they will know it is not theyr real mum and they will holler. I have been moved to the top bunk because Paula has got so big Mr Simpson you know the ginger one with the funny eye says if she rolls off she could crush somebody. He says it is a health and safety issue they are very hot on that in here as you know? Remember when they confiscated your stiletos.

See you soon tell Dazza he is breaking my heart if he does not show his face I will never see him again.

Your loving dugahter Shyanne.

Dear Mum

You will not bielive it Paula has had the baby. He is lovely he has red hair and a funny eye Mr Simpson says that can happen to anybody. The only thing is we cannot understand a bleedin thing the baby says. The Govenor come to have a look and he says it is speaking chinese. Paula says there was a chinese woman in front of her at the hospital and she pinched the womans place when she went to the toilet so they must of give her the chinese implant instead of the English one. She is not very happy about it because now the baby will have to learn to talk by hisself like the chaplain told us about the olden days which takes ages we looked it up on wikepedia. Still he will be useful when Paula wants a takeaway. The good thing is he cries in english so at least we know when he is not happy.

See you soon tell Dazza when I get out he will be sorry because my biologic clock has started ticking and he will have missed it.

Your loving daghuter Shyanne.

Pss I have wrote a poem in them literaccty workshops we been doing.

> Welcome little baby to this vale of tears
> I will cut a blanket for you with my pinking shears
> You have lovely ginger hair and dimply knees
> What a pity you can only speak Chinese.

~

Sheila Corbishley's Biography

I took up writing when I retired from teaching. I write short stories for adults and have written a couple of children's novels which are – I'm going to be positive and say 'as yet' – unpublished.

I've had more success with short stories and have been published in *Woman's Weekly*. I have attached a photo but I do look rather strange in it because it feels very weird and vain to be taking a picture of yourself, so I haven't got the hang of taking selfies.

SHIRT TALES

Shortlisted story, by Adele Smith

Was that a door unlocking? It doesn't sound like my door. Besides, no one else has a key. Perhaps I'm not at home. Come to think of it, this doesn't feel like my mattress so I'm definitely not at home. Where am I?

"Wakey, wakey, rise and shine. Though by the look of you, you won't be doing much shining today."

I don't recognise that voice...

"Come on, Sleeping Beauty. Can't keep you here any longer."

...but it's definitely a woman. Wait. Did I pick up last night? Maybe I'm at her place? I don't remember getting here. In fact, I don't remember anything about last night. My eyes hurt, and they won't open. Why won't they open? Oh God, have I gone blind?

"My eyes, I can't see."

"They're just swollen. Try opening them very slowly. Come on, I'll help you get this T-shirt on. Sorry, it's a bit whiffy. It's the only spare we had. Yours is ripped right down the middle. I bagged it up for you. Pretty useless now, I guess."

Ripped in half? Wait... what if *she* did that? She's either a rough fighter or maybe... last night got a bit steamy? Damn. Wish I could remember. I have to open my eyes. I have to see her. Here I go. Oh. She's... I'm in a...

"Ah. You are alive. Let's start again, shall we? I'm Constable Peters and by the looks of you, you got yourself on the wrong side of someone last night. Now, is there anything you want to tell me?"

*

It's daytime. I glimpse myself in the glass doors when I walk out of the station. I have two lovely black eyes. I wonder what the other guy looks like? I told them, I wish I could remember. I can't think with my head pounding. Worst of all, my chest feels like an elephant sat on it. What happened?

At least the police were good enough to ring me a taxi. I still have my wallet. My attacker obviously wasn't after money but I must've royally pissed him off. My T-shirt – ripped clean in half. I know it's mine. It has a small cigarette burn on the right shoulder where that woman brushed by me in the pub and didn't even apologise. I was really pissed off at the time because...

no... it can't be the same one because this ripped T-shirt's plain black.

*

Home now. Cup of tea. Shame I don't have any milk. Glad I had enough money to pay the taxi driver. It couldn't have been a big night because I still have 40 quid in my wallet. 40 quid. I never end a night with more than a fiver. I stare at my ripped T-shirt. It looks like something Dr David Banner tore off before turning into the Incredible Hulk. Maybe I have superpowers. Maybe I was saving someone from certain death with my super-human strength. But I do have two black eyes, so I'm clearly not that super.

"Thanks, mate. I owe you."

A memory. Was that from last night?

"Here. A little gift for you. To show my appreciation."

Appreciation of what? I wish I could remember who said that. I hope my brain isn't permanently damaged. Perhaps I really did help someone last night.

*

Thud. Thud. Thud.

"Mark. Are you ready?" Thud. Thud. Thud. "Mark?"

What? Who... what time is it? How long have I been asleep?

"Mark. Come on, man. We're going to be late and I want to get down the front. Open the door."

Robbo. I'm supposed to be seeing Rampant Plague with him tonight. It can't be tonight now, can it? It's only just started being today.

"Mark."

Thud. Thud. Thud.

My head's still thumping as I walk downstairs. I swing the door open. Robbo stares at me. I can see by the light outside that it's evening. I must've slept the whole day.

"Man, you look terrible. What the fuck happened to you? You didn't get into a fight with Simon again, did you? I told you, man, he's a wanker, and she's well... you're better off without her."

Simon - I'm sure I'd remember if I got into a punch up with him. He's the loser Gemma left me for. She said I was an uncultured slob. I look down. I'm on the doorstep in my underpants.

"Errr... come in." Robbo shuts the door. "What time is it?" I ask him.

"Time for Rampant Plague, man. Get some clothes on."

I shake myself into action, pull on my jeans and dig out my Rampant Plague T-shirt. They sure are four mean looking dudes. I'm pushing my head through the neck hole when I sense something is wrong. It's like I'm having my own personal earthquake. I feel as if someone, no, lots of people are kicking me in the chest – another elephant, perhaps? It hurts like hell. Then there's this sucking sensation, like my heart's being ripped out and just when I think I can't take any more, it stops. I feel like I've been struck by lightning. I look in the mirror. I'm still me, plus two black eyes and my chest is intact except that it isn't – not quite. I just put on my Rampant Plague T-shirt – I know I did – but Rampant Plague have gone. I'm standing here in a plain black shirt. Confused, I rip off the T-shirt and take out another with a printed skull. In the mirror, I stare at the image on my chest. My face contorts, the air seems to wobble around me and the skull – disappears. I see my right hand. I'm holding an actual skull, smooth, solid and definitely there. I look like I'm about to do that speech from Hamlet. Now I'm seriously freaked out.

I hear a knock at my front door. Robbo opens it.

"Oh, man." I hear him say. "No way. Mark. Get down here now. Rampant Plague have come to see *us*."

Robbo isn't wrong. There they are, on my doorstep, staring, like they have no idea how they got there. I attempt a smile, but they don't smile back. They look even meaner than they did on my T-shirt. I can only think of one word to say.

"Beer?"

*

Rampant Plague didn't want a beer. We're in Robbo's car, the four of them squashed in the back like heavy-metal sardines and being driven by their most insane fan who won't stop asking them questions.

"What effects pedal did you use for 'Dining with Satan', 'cos man, I've tried it with my Tube Screamer, but I just can't get that same distortion. Fuck. I can't believe I'm actually discussing guitar pedals with Rampant Plague."

As Robbo babbles on like a demented loon, Boz, their lead guitarist, starts growling. "Man, I don't know what's going down right now, but if you don't stop with the yakking, you're gonna get some major distortion where the sun don't shine so shut the fuck up and get us to the gig."

Robbo guns the accelerator. "You've got it, Boz."

Luckily for us, Rampant Plague blamed the whole incident on drugs. If they knew what'd really happened, that I was quite probably the cause, I think they would've eaten me alive with Robbo for entree.

Later in the pub, a sweat-stained post-gig Robbo hands me a beer. "They were fucking *awesome*. Best gig ever. Nice guys, too."

"Meeting us didn't seem to affect their performance much," I say, still wondering about my sanity.

"Yeah. What *was* that, man? They never explained why they came to your house. Fucked up, but definitely the best moment of my life." Robbo takes a gulp of beer.

"Yeah. Robbo, about that. I think I might know why they turned up."

"Yeah?"

"I think it was when I put my Rampant Plague T-shirt on. Everything went all weird and shaky, and when I looked in the mirror, my T-shirt was plain black and Rampant Plague were at the front door. I don't know how but I think I... *teleported* them off my T-shirt."

Robbo snorts beer out of his nostrils and almost chokes to death laughing. "Man, I've heard of people being deluded but that's on another plane. Oh, wait... are you high?"

"No. I'm definitely *not* high. Right now, I'm as subterranean as it's possible to be without suffocating. I am a man who woke up in a police cell with two black eyes and no memory of how he got them."

"Be cool, man. Are you really telling me that you somehow managed to make them appear? From your T-shirt?"

"I know it sounds crazy, but yeah. It happened with my skull T-shirt too, but that's not the crazy part."

"Sounds pretty loco to me, bro."

"No, my ripped T-shirt from last night, I'm sure that wasn't plain black when I put it on either."

"Oh yeah? What was on it then?"

"That's it. I can't remember."

Robbo's staring at me now, mouth half open.

"Are you a *magician*?"

"No. Course I'm not a fucking magician. Believe me, if I were, I'd be magicking back my memory."

"But you could be, right? You just made Rampant Plague appear from your tee."

"Maybe it was just a fluke."

"Let's test it."

"What? No."

"Yes. We have to. Here. Put mine on. Bring Rampant Plague to the pub."

Robbo's ripping his shirt off in full view of everyone. He's not exactly the 'Diet Coke man' so I say, "Robbo. Stop. I am *not* bringing Rampant Plague here. They weren't exactly delighted about it the first time so just think what they'll do if I make them come back. I don't think Boz was joking about where he wanted to put his distortion pedal."

Robbo studies me. "Fair point."

Robbo looks around the pub. "Hey. What about him in the Iron Maiden T-shirt? That'd be cool."

"So you think bringing a 10-foot towering Eddy to life would be a good idea, do you?"

"Well, if you're not going to prove it, how am I meant to believe you?" Robbo turns back to his beer looking disappointed. Then I spot this guy in the corner wearing one of those tees that's supposed to look like a tuxedo.

"What about him – the guy in the tuxedo shirt? I don't mind giving that a try *if* you can persuade him to take it off."

"It's done, man."

I watch Robbo saunter over. I don't know what he said, but before I know it, the guy's walking over to me with a smile on his face. If anyone's got the magic touch, it's Robbo.

"Your mate's just told me that you can make pictures on T-shirts real," says tux T-shirt guy.

"Well, I–"

"Go on, then. Here." He takes his T-shirt off. The guy behind the bar gives us a funny look.

"We could have gone into the gents," I say.

"No man, if this works, I want the whole pub to see." Robbo drains his beer and bangs the glass on the bar. "Hey listen up, everyone. For your amazement, my mate Mark will perform a trick never before seen. He will put on this man's T-shirt, which as you can see, is a print of a tuxedo, and behold. It will become a genuine, bona fide bib and tucker. Now, watch."

Yep, Robbo's definitely missed his calling; if not a magician, then a snake-oil salesman. The whole pub is staring. A group of tough guys by the pool table fold their arms and look at us like we're a pair of bullshit artists, but they did stop their game to watch so I'd better make this work. Why did I have to tell Robbo? I should know by now he can't keep a secret for longer than five minutes.

He gives me a nudge. "Go on, man. Do your thing."

I sigh. There's no way out of this. I take off my jacket and pull the tux T-shirt over my head. Immediately I start to shake. My chest feels tight like I'm having a heart attack. I can't breathe but then – it stops. I look down at my chest. I'm wearing a shirt, a black, slightly shiny suit jacket with a red carnation in the lapel and under my collar, a bowtie. The pub crowd are silent for a moment and then there's this rush of applause and everyone starts cheering, even the pool table guys. Robbo grins at me.

"Take a bow, man," he says, so I do.

"Do mine," shouts a girl with really big boobs. She's taking off her T-shirt and she's not the only one. People are ripping off their clothes like they're in an interactive strip club. I look at the cluster of waving T-shirts in front of me. Maybe one more? I take the T-shirt from the big chested girl. It has a picture of an ice-cream sundae. The girl is over the moon when an enormous ice-cream in a great glass bowl appears in front of her (it was a plus-sized T-shirt). She looks from the dessert to me.

"Thank you. You've brought my ice-cream fantasy to life," she says. She and her three friends start digging in. My chest hurts like hell, but I feel like I'm in so far now that I have to do more. I pull a T-shirt over my head with a picture of a small dog. Nothing happens for a minute, but then there's this whining sound from behind the bar. The amazed publican lifts up a heart-melting West Highland Terrier to a unanimous round of 'Ahhhs'. Whilst everyone's busy fussing the dog, a bemused boy band whose likeness was on a T-shirt I'd just put on, stagger in to the pub. Their young fans start shrieking and grab the shocked singers in a lock a wrestler would be proud of. The terrified boy band only manage to wrest themselves from their fans by flagging down a passing taxi and making their escape.

A creepy-looking dude hands me his *Night of the Living Dead* T-shirt. I hand it straight back. This town's not quite ready for a Zombie apocalypse.

I have to get out of here.

*

I lie on the bed, watching the light come through the window. At least I didn't wake up in a police cell. This time I can remember last night exactly. I put my hand on my chest. It feels like I've broken 20 ribs. It even hurts to breathe.

Thud. Thud. Thud. What time is it?

I go downstairs and open the door. It isn't a someone; it's a sea – an ocean of people, all holding T-shirts. Someone takes my picture. The flash makes green and yellow spots before my eyes. More camera flashes. I put my hand up in front of my face and someone sticks a phone in front of me.

"Giles Porter, *News of the World* – Mark, when did you first discover you could bring pictures on T-shirts to life?"

"Mark, you're trending at number one on Twitter. How do you feel?"

"Do you come from a family of magicians, Mark?"

"We've all seen what you did with Boys Ahoy. Who else have you brought to life?"

"Mark, in your opinion, what's your best T-shirt trick to date?"

I slam the door shut and slide to the floor.

I escape out the back and when I'm almost into town, I turn on my phone. Shit. I have 30 missed calls. It rings immediately. It's Robbo.

"Man. You're famous. Someone filmed you in the pub last night. You made Breakfast TV."

"Robbo. I don't want to be famous. I want this to stop. Now."

"Are you nuts? This is your moment, man." Robbo starts rambling on about managing my career but I'm not listening. A headline outside the newsagent has caught my attention.

Tiger linked to mauled man mystery.

I hang up on Robbo and turn off my phone. I start to feel sick. I nip into the newsagents and read.

A tiger, which was discovered roaming the city centre in the early hours of Saturday morning, has been captured and taken to the City Zoo, but the zoo denies that the tiger was from their facility.

"We know the tiger didn't come from the zoo," said Senior Zookeeper, Paul Murray, 43. "All of our tigers are safely in their compound. We don't know where this tiger came from."

The escaped tiger is being linked to the mauling of a man found in the city centre in the early hours of Saturday morning who remains in a critical condition.

I stop reading. I have to check my wardrobe. Now. I run all the way from town to home. The crowd outside my door is even larger. There are TV camera crews and vans everywhere. One of the vans has driven over my neighbour's petunias and he's raging at some poor guy holding a boom mike. I use the distraction to nip round the back of my house and slip inside.

I run upstairs. My heart feels like it's about to burst through my bruised chest. I've remembered what I was wearing that night – that T-shirt with the cigarette burn on the sleeve. I have to check. I rack through my T-shirts. Please, let me be wrong. It's missing, the one I got from the Open Wildlife Park. I sit down on my bed. The shirt was ripped in two. I lie down and close my eyes. I have to recall Friday night. I think about making a cup of tea but then I remember I don't have any milk. Milk. That's it. On Friday night, I went out to get milk.

I was walking down the street. I heard someone calling for help. There were two guys. One had his back to me. He was punching the guy who was shouting for help. The guy doing the punching hadn't noticed me. I did it without thinking. I kicked the punching guy's feet from under him and down he went. The guy being assaulted stared at me. He put his hand on my arm and said, "Thanks, mate. I owe you. Here. A little gift for you. To show my appreciation." Then he ran off like a shot.

But punching guy didn't stay down for long. He was really angry. He slugged me right in the face. I backed off but he grabbed me by the shoulders. Then, that earthquake feeling, chest pain and I… oh fuck.

I have to find him, the guy who gave me his *little gift*. He has to take it back.

*

I've been holed up for a week but there are still some photographers hanging around outside. Surely I must be old news by now. I have the paper delivered so I can check it every day. The man who was mauled by that tiger is recovering. I feel a mixture of relief and concern. There's just a two-inch column about me. I'm a recluse apparently. I glare at my drawn curtains towards the ink-slingers perched outside. At least they haven't made the connection. Yet. For light relief, I turn to the paper's Arts section. There's an ad for a magician. A magician…

I grab the phone and call Robbo.

*

"Come on, man. It'll be a laugh. It might even cheer you up."

"I'm not sure, Robbo. What if I'm wrong?"

"No one knows about your goddamn tiger T-shirt, do they?"

"Keep your voice down. They might've bugged my house."

"Who? How? You've not let anyone in except me. Anyway, you didn't hurt anyone, it was the tiger."

"Robbo. Shut UP." Robbo folds his arms across his chest.

"What's it worth?" He's looking at me with that scheming expression of his.

"What?"

"My silence. Is it worth an all-expenses paid night out to see a kick-arse magic show that'll be the best thing you've seen in weeks?"

"What if I get mobbed by crazy people with their T-shirts again?"

"Think of me as your personal bouncer."

*

Trust Robbo to get front row tickets. I should've known. I'm wearing glasses I haven't worn since I got contacts six years ago and a cap pulled down so low I keep bumping into things. If it wasn't for Robbo guiding me along, I think I would've broken something by now. Mind you, if it wasn't for Robbo, I wouldn't be out in this stupid disguise in the first place. It seems to be working, though. No one's so much as given me a second glance. They probably think I'm blind, or drunk — or both.

There's a loud burst of show tune music, the lights come on and dry-ice churns from the stage. People cough. Through the fog, this guy appears in a glittery tux, his face caked in orange tan with a giant fluorescent smile.

"Ladies and gentlemen, welcome to my show. To begin, I need a volunteer from the audience. If you're brave enough to come up here, I have a little gift for you, just to show my appreciation."

My heart starts to thump. I stare at the guy onstage. Even through the blur of my coke-bottle lenses I can see it's him.

"So who's it going to be? Anyone out there ready to have some fun?"

My hand shoots up. "Yep. Right here." Robbo stares at me, eyes wide.

"You didn't even want to come tonight."

"In for a penny," I say. What he giveth, he'd better be able to take away, even if it does mean I have to act like a chicken or something.

So I'm a chicken. That's cool. He's good, I'll give him that; I even feel like one. Everyone's laughing but I don't care. Then someone calls out.

"Hey, it's the T-shirt guy." The spell is broken. I stop pecking at the floor. A ripple goes around the room. I look at the magician. He's staring at me too. He knows who I am.

"That little gift of yours," I say. "Any chance you could take it back?"

*

The TV crews camped outside my front door left as soon as word got round that I was just an ordinary dude again who could wear a T-shirt with a design like anyone else. Mr Harris, my neighbour, won't speak to me. Apparently, his petunias are ruined. Still, it's nice to have some peace again. I'm just putting the kettle on when someone knocks at my door. I look through the letterbox. It's a girl. She's cute. I notice she's wearing a T-shirt with a picture of a ginger cat. I like cats. I open the door.

"Hello?" I say.

"Hi. My name's Melanie. I'm really sorry to bother you but I've heard about… about what you can do. I've come all the way from Devon. Can you help me? She points to her chest. This is my cat, Bauble. He got run over. He's my baby. Can you bring him back? I'm willing to pay." She stares at me like I'm her last hope. I sigh.

"Come in," I say to her. "I've just put the kettle on."

I tell Melanie the whole story. Of course, she's disappointed I can't bring Bauble back but even she wonders if a reincarnated Bauble would be the same cat. It was a dangerous gift.

While I'm handing her another tissue, I have an idea. "Hey, seeing as though you've come all this way, why don't we visit the zoo? I hear there's this tiger who might need cheering up."

Melanie's face brightens. "Great. We could always tell him my favourite tiger joke."

"Go on."

"A man goes to the cinema and a tiger sits down next to him and the man says, 'What are you doing at the movies?' And the tiger replies, 'Well, I liked the book.'"

I think I'm going to like Melanie.

~

Adele Smith's Biography

After many years as a drama teacher and school production scriptwriter, I have since completed three novels: *The Garden Dancer*, *Left Field* and *Show Me Where*. I have also written several short stories. 'The Biscuit Burglar' received third place in the To Hull & Back competition last year, which made me very proud.

Juggling teaching, fitness training, and working with native Australian animals, I am still looking for that elusive publishing deal, but most importantly, I write because I love it.

TELL US ABOUT YOUR STAY

Shortlisted story, by Dan Brotzel

We hope you've enjoyed your stay in this cottages2diefor.com cottage. Please use this online guestbook to share your feedback with your hosts and pass on tips for future guests. Don't hold back.

Lovely setting, warm welcome.
    We enjoyed a quiet and restful Xmas. We could have

wished for better weather, but the lovely setting more than made up for that. Coupled with lots of good food and fine wine, of course. Thanks for the warm welcome, Jean and Tony – you have a lovely place here, in a lovely part of the world.

Bryan and Glynnis, Pat and Peter, West Sussex

Response from owner.

Jean: Lovely to see you all and introduce you to this beautiful part of the world. We've been here 12 years now and are still discovering new treasures. Hope to see you again and do tell your friends about us.

Comfortable and tranquil.

We enjoyed our two weeks here in comfortable accommodation amidst peaceful and tranquil surrounds. Many thanks for the welcoming coffee cake and the 'home-laid' eggs – what a treat to have fresh free-range boiled eggs of a morning. And many thanks, Tony, for the loan of the walking boots.

Clive, Wolverhampton

Response from owner.

Jean: Clive, it was an absolute pleasure. The pair of you are very impressive walkers. I don't know anyone who's completed the Padstock Hill circuit in less than a full day before. Do keep in touch and tell your friends about us.

Tony: My boots smell cheesy.

Lots of history, great hiking.

It was a cosy and quiet place to stay. The immediate area had lots of history behind it.

Ewan, age 13

We recommend the hike up Padstock Hill and the Busy Lizzie tea rooms. And thank you for the delicious homemade walnut cookies Jean.
Ewan's mum and dad, 42 and 41

Response from owner.
Jean: You are welcome back any time, Ewan, with or without your mum and dad. I will beat you at draughts next time, I promise.

Bliss in Golden Valley.
Thank you SO MUCH for letting us stay in lovely Hill House Cottage. It has been a lovely, relaxing and peaceful week. Thank you for the cake and the kind invitation to the summer fete, which we enjoyed immensely (I need to brush up my Aunt Sally skills though). The local chip shop is fantastic and the Thai food at the Duck is exceptional (and I have been to Thailand twice). Most of all, listening to the two owls call to each other across the Golden Valley early every morning was just sheer bliss.
Graham and Dorothy Shelby, Newtonwards

Response from owner.
Jean: So glad you enjoyed your stay. Please tell your friends.
Tony: You don't mention it, but looks like you enjoyed the cake Jean made you too. And the eggs.
Jean: Ignore him (I do...).

You are benevolent and chivalrous.
We've had a wonderful and chivalrous week. Thank you very much for putting out the children's games and the chocolate cake. You are benevolent and awesome,

from my perspective. Your cushions are doughy and your sofa is plush. My favourite chicken is Vanessa.
Isla, age eight

Response from owner.
Jean: Isla, what wonderful vocabulary. Now I know what you mean by the 'WOW' words you learn at school. We hope to see you again soon – and Vanessa says hello too... Is your little brother's wrist OK now? Tony was just trying to show him how to rev his racing car properly. He doesn't know his own strength sometimes...
Tony: Pass the sic bag. 'Vanessa' is actually Rufus the cock, but each to his own.

It was a nice place to stay.
Jay B, Milton Keynes

Response from owner.
Tony: Steady on JB, don't overdo the detail. Leave some room for the others.

Top spot, great beer.
A lovely cottage in an idyllic setting. Thank you for the warm welcome. We had a lovely holiday. A super area to explore with lots to do. Hereford Cathedral is well worth a visit, as is Wye Valley. Local chippie offers massive portions – and the ales on tap at the Duck Inn are not to be missed...
Peter Morgan and Jenny Taygate, Borth

Response from owner.
Tony: Seconded sir. All hail to the ale.

Beware the prankster.

A lovely cottage in a beautiful location. Lots of castles and gardens to explore, with marvellous shopping at Ludlow and Hereford. We also loved 'Puzzlewood' nr Coleford and 'Big Pit' nr Blaenavon. The dramatic narrow roads make the longer drives seem shorter. Takes a bit of getting used to the speeds the locals drive at though – and to Tony's pranks. Fab holiday.

The Hendersons

Response from owner.

Tony: Excuse my 'Oirish' sense of humour, Mrs H. It was only a plastic scorpion.

Jean: Did he pull that stunt again? I am SO sorry (he's not even Irish so don't know what that's about).

Basil: Nonsense, Sybil dear. They loved it.

Rain and rifles.

Enjoyed a generally relaxing week in a well-equipped cottage. The Big Pit is well worth a visit. Also great days out in Ross on Wye and Hay on Wye. Could have done without the early morning air rifle practice though, Tony. And the rain...

Emily and James, Carshalton Beeches

Response from owner.

Jean: So sorry if Tony woke you. He says it's vital to keep up the rural traditions, but I think he just likes shooting at things (sigh). We've been unlucky with the weather this year.

Tony: Stop talking Jean and keep loading. We'll get 'em next time.

A BEUATIFUL PART OF THE COUNTRY.

A SECOND WONDERFUL BREAK IN THIS LOVELY COTTAGE; THE WEATHER PLAYED FARE, CONSIDERING THE TIME OF YEAR AND WE ONLY HAD ONY REALLY WET DAY. IT IS A BEUATIFUL PART OF THE COUNTRY, SO RELLAXING. BUT BOY DOES A WEEK GO FAST.

James Beck, Padstow

Response from owner.

Tony: Ahem, dodgy grammar alert. Back to spelling school for you, Mr B. AND DON'T YOU KNOW CAPS IS SHOUTING.

Shame about the weather.

A lovely comfortable cottage. We didn't have the best weather, although it could have been worse, much worse. But we enjoyed discovering this corner of Herefordshire.

Ilona Heidelsteck, Mildenstein, Bavaria

Response from owner.

Tony: Rain comes with the package, I'm afraid ~~Helga~~ Ilona dear. As a German I should have thought you'd have researched all that beforehand... (JOKING)

Quite a character.

Lovely New Year break, thank you. Beautiful countryside and great places to visit, including Monmouth, Ludlow, Ledbury. Not even the heavy rain on Wed/Thu could dampen our spirits with Tony's impromptu Stiff Little Fingers impersonations...

The Gladstones, Melton Mowbray

Response from owner.

Tony: Darlings, please, spare my blushes. You lot can come again any time. I'll do my Suggs next time (my head still hurts...).

Laughs, kindnesses and lovely scenery.

Thanks Jean and Tony for a really lovely time. You were such attentive hosts – there was really no need for you to come and meet us at Hereford station or walk all the way round the Common with us Tony, and the cake was absolutely scrummy, Jean. That soft play place in Abergavenny was a great tip. And I will never forget Tony jumping out of the airing cupboard and surprising the children when we got back from the Big Pit. It was so funny, though I'm not sure our two-year-old saw the joke straight away... We didn't even know you were in the cottage. I shall add a government health warning about your sense of humour on the cottages2diefor.com website, Tony.

Kath and Christopher, and Jo (eight), Gabby (five) and Huw (two)

Response from owner.

Jean: You were wonderful guests. Such lovely children. And well done for putting up with Tony's sense of humour. That 'Health Warning' sounds like a very good idea to me, Kathy... Wish I'd thought of it years ago...

Tony: She doesn't mean it, do you, oh light of my life, oh fire of my loins?

Jean: See what I have to deal with?

More than just a cottage.

'Cottage' is really not grand enough a word for this

abode. The upside-down layout really works, especially if you're visiting with an older relative, as we did. You seem to have thought of everything: a welcome chocolate cake and even a trouser press. You do really need a car for this area, I'd say, though – my elderly mother found the absence of pavements to walk into the village a bit of a bind. And I've got to ask: Tony, what IS behind that locked, half-smashed-up door in the room behind the kitchen?
Colby Paterson, West Virginia

Check out Magna Carta and Busy Lizzie tearooms.

A cosy and quiet place to stay. There are so many things to see and do in the area that are just a short car drive away. We loved inspecting the copy of the Magna Carta in Hereford Cathedral, and we heartily recommend Jacks Court Castle. Our two young boys played on the ramparts for hours. Also we loved the serene ambience of the Busy Lizzie tea rooms, just 15 minutes' drive west, through the village and on a bit along the road to Nantford. Sorry again about the door in the back, Tony. Didn't mean to try and force the lock. Please let us know if we can reimburse you.
Tina Hadford and family (Janine seven, Gemma five)

Response from owner.
Tony: It was a total treat to play host to your delectable self and your grand gals, ma'am. You have some fine ladies in the making there. And don't think for another second about that door – I keep odd bits and tools in there out of harm's way, and should have explained that the lock was dodgy.

Get better soon Jean.

Thanks for the custard creams, Tony. And all the leaflets to local places. We got loads done – we went on a steam train, did Puzzle Wood, the Magna Carta, Jacksons Court castle. Highlight was the Big Pit Museum. I do hope you recover quickly from your fall, Jean, and sorry not to see you– must have been a really nasty sprain.

Marguerite and Brendan P, East Hoathly

Response from owner.

Tony: Jean's coming along very well, thanking you all. I think it's just an excuse to get out of changing your sheets.

We love it here.

We love it here. Jim and I come back around this time for the arts festival every year, and invite different guests each time. This year we had Jim's sister and her husband. Tony kept us entertained with his jokes and political chats all week. All feel a bit bleary now – all those late nights drinking Tony's Glenfiddich and talking about Cuba and whether a socialist state could ever really work in practice. Food for thought as always. Give our love to Jean – so sorry to miss her this year, but can't begrudge her a well-earned week painting watercolours in Tuscany.

PS, did you leave us a message on the mobile the Sunday we left, Tony? There was a garbled voice going on about dead rabbits or something??

Jim and Pat, Dennis and Ivy – 'The irregulars'

Response from owner.

Tony: Not guilty as charged, Senorita. Always a

pleasure to see the old gang, though. Viva la revolution.

???

Why is there what looks like a used tampon in the back garden???

Response from owner.
Tony: Pass. Did you put it there??

Not really child-friendly?

My two-year-old loved running through the front yard chasing your chickens. They became very tame and by the end of the week were almost taking bits of grape from his hand. He's obsessed with farm animals so this was heaven for him. Sorry if his crying disturbed you in the night, Tony. He can be a bit noisy if you're not used to it but you did advertise your cottage as 'child-friendly' and I'm not sure all the shouting really helped anything.

Graham Drow, Southgate

Rain, rain, go away.

Comfortable, well-equipped, lovely surroundings. Nothing to fault, except would have liked easier access to back garden and less rain...

Marcia Adams, Peterborough

Response from owner.
Tony: Look it just rains a lot in this part of the world. Can I just check that everyone gets that I am not God and so not actually responsible for the thefucking wweather???

You mad fuck.

TONY, YOU MAD FUCK. YOU SPIED ON MY WIFE DRESSING, YOUR MAD DOGS ATTACKED OUR LITTLE COCKERDOODLE, YOU TERRIFIED OUR CHILDREN BY JUMPING OUT AT THEM FROM A CUPBOARD, AND MY THREE-YEAR-OLD UNCOVERED A BIZARRE SHRINE TO YOUR EX-WIFE IN THE BACK ROOM (WE KNOW ALL ABOUT THAT BECAUSE YOU SPENT A NIGHT IN OUR KITCHEN SOBBING ABOUT IT WHILE YOU DRANK ALL OUR MALT). YOU'VE GOT BITS OF HER HAIR AND SOILED UNDERWEAR AND FUCK KNOWS WHAT IN THERE. NO WONDER SHE LEFT, I ONLY HOPE YOU DIDN'T TAKE AN AXE TO HER AND BURY HER IN THAT BACK GARDEN YOU'RE SO WEIRD ABOUT. THEY TOLD ME IN THE VILLAGE YOU WERE A CHARACTER, I DIDN'T REALISE THAT WAS CODE FOR 'PSYCHOPATH'. ADVICE TO GUESTS: GET THE FUCK OUT WHILE YOU CAN. SOD THE DEPOSIT. LEAVE NOW.

Response from owner.

Tony: you don't know YOU DON'T KNOW YOU DON'T KNOW Only good rabbit is a dead rabbit the sliver of ice in woman's heart 'dog' spells 'god' backwards but where is the capital G

~

Dan Brotzel's Biography

As a child, Dan Brotzel believed that people who wore glasses weren't allowed to get married. This proved untrue, and he now lives in London with his wife, Eve, and their three young children. Dan's short story, 'Fat Birds Don't Fly', won Carillon Magazine's 'Absurd

Stories' competition in 2014.

THE DEATHS OF ARTHUR

Shortlisted story, by Georgina Sanjana

1. King of Albion

"And what exactly am I supposed to do with this?" asked Arthur, turning the Grail upside-down to inspect it from every angle in the dim candlelight.

"It is a source of life and healing, sire," replied Merlin mechanically. It appeared he'd run in through the pounding rain to Arthur's chambers to personally hand him the battered goblet, and had expected a more enthusiastic reaction for his efforts.

"OK... so how do we access this magical healing power? I'm not really an expert in divine crockery."

"Well, I believe for cups the usual protocol is to drink out of them," said Merlin, squeezing drops of water from the ends of his beard onto Arthur's best bearskin (Arthur was sure it was deliberate).

Arthur gave a, "Hmph." Merlin was a sarcastic little warlock, but he did have an irritating tendency to be right.

"What are you waiting for, then?" Arthur thrust the Grail at Merlin. "Get me some ale."

"I believe wine would be more traditional, sire," muttered Merlin as he took the goblet. He peered at the strange symbols round the edge and suddenly his whole bearing seemed to change. "Er, actually, sire..."

"What is it now?" Arthur was not the most patient of men, even when he hadn't just been woken up in the middle of the night.

"It's just there are some, er, conditions in the inscription that we may want to take time to translate before–"

"Oh, give it here, I'll do it." Arthur pried at Merlin's hands.

"Really, sire, I can't let you–"

But a wizened old man was no match for King Arthur's strength. Arthur easily snatched the Grail away – and promptly stumbled backwards with inertia, tripping over the head of his bearskin rug and smashing the priceless goblet into pieces on the stone floor as he landed painfully on his backside.

A vile-smelling black smoke seemed to pour out of every crack in the Grail, surrounding Arthur and clinging thickly to his skin. A well-timed roll of thunder burst through the air around him, as a stroke of lightning briefly filled the whole chamber with a searing light.

Then everything went quiet. The smoke and Grail had disappeared.

"Well," said Merlin after a moment, "that's not ominous at all."

*

Many years later, as Arthur lay dying, Merlin knelt down by his side. "Sire."

"Merlin." He clasped their hands together.

"It's alright, I'm here with you."

Arthur coughed violently. He seemed to be breathing in more blood than air. "You're not going to... oh, say... do anything about... this gaping wound in my side?"

Merlin's eyes were filling with tears. "I'm sorry, Arthur. But you'll return one day."

"Return..." It didn't sound like a half-bad idea, but it was possible that his opinion was being swayed by the massive blood loss.

"The once and future king, the hero we all need," said Merlin, but Arthur gave no reply.

2. Foot Soldier

Arthur awoke in some sort of field. The sky above him was dull and grey. Apparently Heaven was in the process of redecorating.

He propped himself up on surprisingly skinny arms. It seemed he'd obtained a new body, one that irritated him immediately with its scrawniness.

He stood up and looked about himself; there were loud noises and signs of commotion coming from behind a nearby copse.

Arthur recognised those sounds and became even more annoyed. Someone was having a battle and he hadn't been invited? He may have technically been dead, but still, that stung.

He hurried over as fast as his newly unfit legs would carry him. He grabbed a sword from where it had fallen and joined in the fray, using 'people who didn't seem very English' as his main criterion for selection.

He was hampered by his unfamiliar body, but managed to get a few cheers of encouragement before succumbing painfully to lack of armour, muscle tone, and organisation on the Saxon troops' part.

It could have been worse, though. They really were making mincemeat of that poor chap with the arrow in his eye.

3. Peasant

Arthur woke up in a field. The strong sense of déjà vu was lessened by him being fairly sure it was a different field, but it was nonetheless bizarre.

Perhaps Merlin had somehow made him immortal. This would generally be considered a good thing, he supposed, but couldn't he simply be invincible? The whole dying business was rather painful and inconvenient.

It was only a short walk to the nearest village. Strangely enough, when he arrived it appeared almost deserted. Windows and doors were boarded up and the place was eerily quiet. It also stank. Arthur grimaced.

"Peasants," he muttered to himself.

Just then, a couple turned into the street. He intercepted them.

"Excuse me, er, sir and madam, but I appear to be lost. You wouldn't mind... telling me where we are, would you?"

The two exchanged looks and whispered to each other unsubtly. Then the man spoke, but Arthur couldn't understand.

"I'm sorry?"

The man spoke more slowly, but it still made no sense. It sounded like some obscure French dialect. Arthur suddenly started wishing that he'd spent more time as a boy listening to his French tutor instead of carving rude pictures into the desk with his pocket knife.

"Uh, *oïl. Jo...* er... *bon*?" he said.

They frowned at him.

He decided to try out his rusty Latin. It was worth a try. "Um... *eripere vitam nemo non homini potest, at nemo mortem; mille ad hanc aditus patent.*"

Arthur was rather proud of himself for remembering that. *Good old Seneca*, he thought. Unfortunately, his impressively accurate recital only earned him more baffled looks.

Then the woman indicated to Arthur that he should follow them, which he did for want of any better ideas.

They led him to a tavern. There were few other people, mostly looking either depressed or suspicious of the newcomer. The woman gestured for him to sit down and brought him a tankard. Arthur nodded his thanks and took a sip. At least, he supposed, whatever godforsaken wasteland he ended up in – even in France – there would always be beer.

Her husband brought over some sort of priest, who spoke to Arthur directly.

"*Quis es?*" he asked. *Who are you?*

Arthur's Latin wasn't great, but he could manage that one. "King Arthur," he replied.

"...*King* Arthur?"

"Yes. Er... I'm lost." He looked around himself again. "Where is everyone?"

The priest frowned at him. "That isn't funny."

"I wasn't trying to be," muttered Arthur.

There was a short, garbled conversation between the three people in front of him before Arthur was addressed once again.

"You come from a land that has not witnessed the Great Pestilence?"

Wonderful, thought Arthur. War, Death, Pestilence... he sensed a theme developing.

The priest spoke again, but Arthur's limited lingual skills failed him. It was probably the subjunctive, which he'd never quite seen the point of.

Now another man came over, one who had been observing them from a corner of the room. Arthur didn't like the look of him. He didn't seem pleased in the slightest.

The new arrival reached down and grabbed the front of Arthur's shirt, lifting him up by it. Everyone started yelling at each other. Arthur fell to the ground as the flimsy shirt ripped in two.

"What's happening?" he demanded, feeling shocked and ridiculous and vaguely wishing he knew how to swear in Latin.

"He doesn't trust you," came the reply. "No one trusts a foreigner." The priest was kneeling by him, but suddenly looked up in horror as the two of them were faced with an angry local in conjunction with a large farming implement.

A scythe? *Naturally*, thought Arthur, *why wouldn't you randomly carry a scythe around for threatening forei–*

His thoughts were mercilessly cut short, mercifully quickly.

4. Sailor

Arthur's next appearance was during the attempted invasion by the Spanish Armada. Now, to a casual observer well-versed in 16th century history, it might appear that Arthur was in little imminent danger, for no English vessels were lost under fire and hence the risk of him dying horribly was minimal.

However, a curse is not a curse without a great deal of misfortune and inconvenience, and it was on the deck of an ill-fated Spanish galleon that Arthur found himself summoned into existence.

Arthur thought he caught sight of a familiar face on a nearby ship – he thought he saw a grey-flecked beard and gentle blue eyes – but only for a moment. A cannonball struck, gunpowder caught alight and he didn't even have time to wonder whether that really had been Merlin.

Arthur needed to have serious words with him.

5. Roundhead Spy

Arthur was beginning to lose his equanimity. This was all getting rather humiliating.

He was bound tightly to a chair he'd been propped up in. Men in bright uniforms sat around the large oak-panelled room in luxurious armchairs. They wore floppy-rimmed boots and massive feathered hats. There was one particularly threatening man pacing in front of him, wearing a richly embroidered sash. He gestured wildly with his foofy hat as he addressed Arthur in the increasingly popular nonsensical fashion.

Having begun this life in a ditch – he'd even managed a step down from the ever-popular field – Arthur had realised he was incredibly hungry. What with all the carnage, it hadn't occurred to him to stop for a bite. He'd noticed a suitably imposing house not too far down the road, with an open window practically exuding temptation.

In his earlier days, Arthur hadn't lost much sleep over his habit of breaking and entering. After all, when you had the power of life and death over people they tended not to argue. But now that he had no crown or deftly-wielded sword or loyal band of merry followers, the whole pillaging lark seemed rather less acceptable.

Oh well, he'd decided. He was King at heart. He owned everything, really.

But as was his luck recently, he'd been spotted sneaking in (or rather falling in) through said window, and promptly found himself on the wrong end of his first musket-whipping experience.

"What's going on?" he demanded, hoping everyone was just pretending to be foreign for a big prank or something. "See, I might look like a peasant, and yes, I realise I do have some amount of dirt on me, but the truth is I'm actually the King. You know, King Arthur? Owner of mythical swords and distinctively-shaped tables–"

The man unsheathed a thin blade, pointed it at Arthur and uttered more gobbledygook.

"Look," stammered Arthur, remarkably calmly for someone tied to a chair with a rapier to their heart. "I'm sure we can work this out..."

Arthur had never considered himself a vindictive man, but he did derive a certain mitigating satisfaction at being able to bleed all over the expensive-looking wooden floor.

6. Kitten

Though he was not aware of it, Arthur's next life took place during the earlier half of the Seven Years War. In the ordinary course of events he might well have been torn between his former kingdom's economic interests on one hand and heavy civilian losses on the other. However, someone had provided him with a ball of string.

His few weeks of moderately peaceful existence were brought to an abrupt end due to a particularly vicious encounter with a toy spaniel.

Arthur would maintain that the dog started it.

7. Spitfire Pilot

Arthur was sitting in a very small space. There was glass over his head, and in front of him a panel of little lights and circles with moving pointers. There were straps down his chest, some sort of helmet on his head and a weird crackling sound by his ear, but what was most disconcerting was that the metal machine he was in appeared to be suspended in mid-air.

Panic set in. Arthur started to hyperventilate – he'd suddenly realised that not only was he very far up from the ground, but said ground was approaching at a much greater speed than he was comfortable with.

Suddenly there came a voice from by his ear. Unfortunately, it was talking gibberish again.

"What the..." he muttered, wondering what sort of bizarre magic this was. "Tell me what to do with this sodding contraption." He hoped the voice on the other end would acknowledge him. Perhaps they did, but it was no good because he couldn't understand their response at all.

"Would someone please just *speak English*," he yelled.

There was a loud explosion to his right and before Arthur knew it his metal machine was tipping over to the side and spiralling downwards. He desperately fiddled with the controls in front of him, but to no avail.

"If I ever get my hands on you, Merlin..." He closed his eyes and hoped it would all be over quickly.

8. Cheese Plant

Arthur was busy decorating the interior of a rather fancy new office suite in Holborn when the antimatter bomb struck.

He was once again facing certain death without adequate explanation. He would have complained loudly, but it was difficult to be both eloquent and incisive when one was fully preoccupied with being a pot plant.

As such, even as he sensed annihilation rapidly approach, even as the Earth shrank and doubled in on itself, he managed only one solitary thought: *Oh no, not again.*

9. Warrior Against the Undead

There was grass all around; long, itchy grass. The sun was hot. Arthur was tired. Upon finding himself lying down in a field in the middle of nowhere for the third time in as many lives, he decided that it might be best just to stay there. After all, he knew what would happen.

Maybe he would be trampled by a wild animal. Torn apart by lions. That would make a change.

Arthur lay there for a long time. He felt faint despite being flat on his back.

Death by dehydration, perhaps.

His mind wandered aimlessly. Just as he found himself on the border of an ill-thought-out existential crisis, a familiar figure appeared, leaning over him.

"...Merlin?"

The figure kissed his forehead and whispered something unintelligible, but Arthur hardly cared any more. Merlin would never let him die.

Except for that once.

He was too tired for thoughts. His eyes closed.

*

Arthur couldn't remember ever being quite so obscenely comfortable. He decided not to question this, and rolled over in bed, sighing contentedly. Of course, this couldn't last.

Merlin entered the room. Many terrible days in Arthur's first life had started out that way. He had more than a few memories of being shaken awake and fairly dragged out of bed to be informed of yet another dire threat to the kingdom.

"Yes, OK, OK," he mumbled, untangling himself and sitting on the edge of the bed. As he stretched out his arms he suddenly noticed something. Two somethings.

"Oh," he observed, mostly to himself. "I appear to be a girl." For some reason the idea of this disturbed him more than being a kitten or a pot plant.

Merlin sighed and murmured a spell. Suddenly Arthur was right back in a youthful version of his first body.

"Ah. Thanks. I knew there was a reason I kept you around," he said, and then frowned. There was eerie, ghoulish chanting coming from outside that he hadn't registered before, smothered in blankets as he had been.

On top of that, even his most trusted friend had begun to talk nonsense at him. He couldn't understand a word.

"What on Earth are you wombling on about?" he asked, beginning to get aggravated.

It was as if a light had gone on above Merlin's head. He grabbed something from a drawer and reached for Arthur's face. Arthur tried to dodge his hand, but he was persistent.

"Steady on, there," said Arthur, standing up and backing away. "I know I'm attractive, but this really isn't the time–"

Then Merlin tackled him. Arthur ended up on the floor pinned beneath him, while Merlin pressed small metal devices into each of his ears and muttered something. Arthur thrashed around under him.

"*Googuru taamsu akkusepputu.*"

"Stop arsing around, Merlin, and tell me what the hell is going on."

Satisfied, Merlin released him and stepped away.

"There we go," he said. "If you weren't being such a brat that would have been a lot easier, you know."

Arthur's response could best be described as 'flabbergasted'. He decided to go straight for the most obvious source of confusion out of some stiff competition.

"So... what year is it exactly?"

"2047," replied Merlin.

That certainly explained some of the difficulties in communication.

"How did you find me?"

"Oh... magic." Merlin literally waved his hand in lieu of explanation.

"How come you're still alive?"

"Magic, duh," said Merlin. "Actively combats the seven signs of ageing," he added with a grin.

Arthur decided that it wasn't worth the explanation. Certainly Merlin seemed a lot more dewy and smooth-skinned than before.

"Oh. But I've only had seven lives since... well, the first one, and they weren't exactly long."

"Well," said Merlin apologetically, "I did say you'd return when Albion was in need. Admittedly, I only expected you to come back once. Like that time the Earth was destroyed..."

Arthur looked about himself, perplexed. The Earth was quite definitely there, unless one wanted to get into a convoluted debate on Platonic realism that he quite frankly didn't have the energy for right then.

"Oh," said Merlin, noting his expression, "it did come back. It was mostly an admin error."

"I... what?"

"Don't worry, I don't understand either."

Arthur shook his head. This was all a bit much.

"Anyway, it seems we should have taken that Grail curse a bit more seriously," continued Merlin. "It seems to have interfered with things. I've done some research this past millennium, and I expect you'll keep dying brutally and coming back until you can break the curse by saving Albion."

"OK... so what's the emergency this time?"

At that moment they were interrupted as the chanting outside became exponentially louder.

"Well," said Merlin, glancing anxiously towards the window, "there is some chance it has something to do with those rumours about the giant cephalopod."

"What?"

"This alien octopus thing that's been spotted. Some people are saying it's Cthulhu, but they're the kind who see the word of God burnt onto their toast and go around shouting about how nigh the end is every second Tuesday."

"What?" said Arthur, for want of originality.

"You know, Cthulhu? It's like the Questing Beast or a chimaera or something," said Merlin. The look of abject terror on his face wasn't exactly comforting. "Just with extra tentacles... and a bit of a *cult following*." He giggled nervously as he nodded towards the window for no reason Arthur could fathom.

"So, what you're saying is, I have to kill an octopus monster?"

"That would seem to be the idea."

"Alright, then." Arthur might be confused beyond salvation, but killing things, that he knew. "You'd better find me a sword."

"I think you're going to need more than just a titchy sword."

Arthur cast his mind around. "How about a really big one?"

"That's what she said."

Arthur blinked.

Merlin sighed. "Let's go and get you a laser gun."

*

"Right," said Arthur, having been kitted out with a laser gun, protective clothing and a considerable supply of hand grenades, "so where do we find this thing?"

"Well, if it is Cthulhu..." said Merlin, pausing to put on his most dramatic voice, "...in R'yleh. The legendary corpse-city of loathsome darkness and such hideous non-Euclidean geometry as to drive even the bravest of men to insanity."

Arthur opened and closed his mouth a couple of times.

"Well," he managed after a moment. "Sounds peachy."

"Wait," said Merlin suddenly. The animalistic chanting had died down and in its place came faint but unmistakable shrieks of horror.

"Maybe we won't need the helicar after all," he continued. "I think you're on."

They stumbled outside and the sight that greeted them was enough to render even Merlin silent. The creature's monstrous bulk was supported by lizard-like clawed feet. Its flabby head was a mass of slimy, squirming tentacles, between which gaped glowing blood-red eyes.

For once it was Arthur who was able to articulate his verdict on the matter.

"Holy shit."

The beast lumbered towards them. Passers-by fled in sheer terror. Merlin grabbed Arthur's hand and whispered a spell. "*Onto the roof.*"

Arthur had no time to comment that Merlin's spells seemed rather less impressive in translation before the two of them were transported onto the roof of the building. The creature reared up – it being just as tall as the tower block, the only result of the spell was to give them fewer opportunities to run or hide.

It lunged.

Arthur threw a couple of grenades, but to no effect. The two of them ended up dancing this way and that across the rooftop to avoid the flailing tentacles.

"Do something, Merlin," exclaimed Arthur as the laser gun was knocked from his hand by a massive claw.

"*Rabbits*," incanted Merlin and suddenly the roof was covered with small twitching rodents.

"What the bloody hell?"

"I'm out of practice," shouted Merlin, almost drowned out by a cry emanating from the tentacled maw. "I had to earn a living."

"Oh, you blithering idiot." Arthur ducked a tentacle; it whirled over his head and dripped slime on his hair, which irritated him rather more than it should have given the circumstances.

The creature was about to strike again. Arthur was completely out of ammunition, so he did the only thing he could think of and picked up a rabbit.

Merlin stared at Arthur. Arthur stared at the beast. The beast stared at the rabbit and the rabbit stared back with huge brown eyes. Its little nose twitched and its fluffy ears flopped.

The alien's response was a heart-stopping, blood-curdling roar, but to Arthur's ears it only came out as an, "Awww."

One slimy tentacle reached out and grabbed a rabbit by Merlin's foot. It dropped it into a bulbous claw. The beast cocked its head to one side. "That's adorable," it said. "You know what... I'll just keep this one. I'm sorry to bother you," it added sheepishly before turning to crawl back whence it came.

The two of them watched it disappear from sight. For a moment they were silent.

Arthur turned on Merlin. "You really are a complete and utter... utter..."

"What?"

"...nincompoop."

"Nincompoop?"

"Yes. An absolute nincompoop."

"We really have to get you into the 21st century sometime." Merlin looked around the rooftop and shook his head. "Alien tentacle monsters... defeated by bunnies?"

Arthur shrugged. "They are quite sweet." He picked one up and scratched it behind the ears.

"Now we just have to herd them all down the fire escape. Brilliant."

"You were the one that brought them here."

"And saved our lives," protested Merlin.

"Actually, if I hadn't been so resourceful..."

"Using a *bunny* as a shield, you mean? Oh yeah, King Arthur, so brave and full of valour–"

"Merlin?"

"Yes?"

"Stop calling them bunnies. Anyway, what happens now?"

"What do you mean?"

"Well, usually I've died horribly by this point," said Arthur. "Have I broken the curse? Do I just... what? Hang around here and open a rabbitery?"

"I could get rid of them," suggested Merlin

"No. No, don't. I mean, I wouldn't want to upset you by making you do that."

"*Riiight*. Anyway, you're welcome to stick around."

"What, with you?"

Merlin shrugged. "If you like."

"Well, you do need someone to take care of all the bunnies."

Merlin grinned like an idiot. "Of course I do."

Despite himself, and despite his recent spate of violent deaths, Arthur couldn't help but grin stupidly back.

~

Georgina Sanjana's Biography

Georgina is 23 and studying for a master's in astrophysics. She sometimes writes stories and poetry to amuse herself, and a few months ago suddenly realised she might one day get paid something for it.

Georgina enjoys reading, writing, eating, being right, ice-skating, learning languages, using Oxford commas, and wasting time on the internet. Her dislikes include Facebook, tinned tuna, and writing about herself.

THE WEDDING OF UGLY BOB

Shortlisted story, by Scott Johnston

Work finished late that Friday afternoon and I handed off my mates' offer of a dirty pint or three and made my way home. I illegally parked my works van and walked in to the empty house. I quickly choked down a sandwich and a tin of cider, and I clumped up the stairs, stumbling to the shower while peeling off my work clothes.

As I am about six-foot-three and 18 stone, it wasn't quite *Strictly* even though the iPod was blasting out ZZ

Top's 'Gimme All Your Lovin'' through the speakers. I resisted the urge to moon-walk to the shower. It was Date Night in Mudflat-on-Ditch on the edge of the Cotswolds.

I was ready by the time Ann came home and, in a lightning quick two and a half hours, so was she. We started our evening with a quick glass of vino collapso for Ann and a pint of Black Rat for me at the Duck & Dive.

From there, we went to the village Italian restaurant for an early dinner. It was locally known to many as 'Fellatio's' to the great annoyance of Gino, the owner. One of the joys of small village life here in the Cotswolds is the circumstance of having only one Italian restaurant in the village.

The waiter, Gino's son-in-law, had put on his best white shirt and Italian accent for the evening. He is a welder by day and normally speaks with a Geordie accent but, at night, in the restaurant, he spins up a marvellous mix of Milanese accented English which enthrals and amuses the unknowing Ann. I had the roast peppers stuffed with heartburn; she had something very small and cheesy (like the staff) and a salad.

We finished our meal, paid up and eventually escaped Gino's famous 10-minute 'goodbye' including complimentary grappa. We slowly walked arm in arm a short distance to the Old Town.

The village, small that it is, had its full range of star attractions on display that evening. The village drug addict was in his usual position, sitting next to the cash machine and trying to intimidate money out of people. That's a tough thing to pull off when you're 50 kilos and weak as church tea. Ann remarked that there were several more of them last year but the harsh winter had taken its toll on them.

"Every cloud…" I replied and got a nudge in the ribs from her.

Further on was the town's Irish pub, the Leprechaun, locally known as 'the Leper' for reasons all too obvious once inside. We stepped past this and on to further attractions.

The town's trendy wine bar was almost full to the gunwales with under-employed estate agents, a few solicitors, and several of Ann's desperately-single-man-hating mates. I opened the door and held it for Ann while watching the bouncer, Jerry, shake his head and roll his eyes at me. Jerry and I played rugby together for a few decades and hate each other like brothers. He smiled at Ann and kissed her smiling cheek while I grumbled in protest. "Do you know where that mouth of his has been?" I said to her.

Gerry shook hands with me like the gentleman he isn't and pointed us to a good table with a 'reserved' sign on it. I parked Ann there and made my way to the bar.

I returned to Ann's table to find that several of her desperately-single-man-hating mates had roosted there. They were all in highly animated conversation about nothing in particular. I set the drink down in front of her and smiled and asked if the vultures would like a drink.

One of them, Chlamydia, hissed and asked if I would be so kind as to bring a bottle of Chablis and four glasses. I nodded and turned away thinking how many mortgage payments I could make for the cost of a bottle of wine in this dump.

I had no intention of buying them anything other than a bottle of hemlock and I wandered over to Jerry near the door to allow Ann a bit of spell-trading time with the witches.

Just as I reached Jerry, Ugly Bob, another old rugby mate, walked in. If Bob was a work of art he would be a Picasso or maybe a Warhol. Bob was an agricultural engineer. He fixed farm machinery for a living. It was not unknown for cows to stop milking when Bob arrived to fix some mechanical problem on a farm.

Jerry nodded at Ann and her mates and asked me, "Who are those beasties with yer missus?"

"That's Chlamydia in the blue dress, and she's out hunting penises. Her mates, Sumo and Alopecia are along to provide backup venom if she corners one. She just split up with some asshole and is looking for her next victim."

"She looks alright. What's the catch?"

"Control freak. Has to be in charge. Total head case, she is. And now she's looking for her next kill."

We turned to each other and laughed and both said at the same time... "Bob."

As Ann finished her rum, I returned to the table unable to wipe the smile off my face. I gestured to her that we should be moving on and we made our extraction.

She smiled at my smile as we walked away and said, "You forgot their wine."

"Ohhhh Welllll," I replied, while walking her to the door.

I could feel the heat on my back from their stares as we walked away from the table and I resisted the urge to throw some corn on the floor for them to peck at.

Bob was talking with Jerry as we walked past and Jerry signalled 'goodbye' with two fingers as I went by.

Ann and I walked slowly through the Old Town laughing a bit and talking as we never do at home. We stopped at the little Portuguese place for our last of the evening. I ordered my traditional espresso and she had another rum. She remarked how lonely her mate Chlamydia was.

I replied that Jerry was on the case and perhaps we could arrange a bit of a blind date for her. And a cunning plan was put in motion.

Ugly Bob was not just a single dad. He was the superman of single dads. There was almost nothing which Bob would not do to give his three boys a better life.

Bob worked long hours at his business and was frequently called out far and wide to repair broken farm equipment in Somerset, Wiltshire, Gloucestershire and occasionally further afield. Bob's sister, Jen, lived nearby and would see to the boys if Bob had a call out. Given Bob's Neanderthal looks, it was nothing short of a genetic miracle that Jen was not only human, but actually very attractive.

Bob's ex-wife had run off two years ago and left him raising three young boys, aged four, five and seven. She was a high strung, stressy thing, originally from one of those strange cities in the frozen wastelands north of the M4. I think the fresh air, sunlight and open spaces of life in the Cotswolds shorted out her personality and she bailed on Bob with some lower league football player. I heard that they shared the same manicurist and hairdresser and had developed a relationship.

Bob had only one outlet for himself in his life and that was his rugby. His mum or sister would mind his boys for a few hours on Saturday afternoons and Bob would have a chance to blow-off steam and, on occasion, have a quiet pint or seven. Bob was known for his ability to take a severe beating and stay on the pitch. In rugby, fullbacks are allowed to call 'mark' when a ball is kicked high into the air and they are not allowed to be hit or tackled as they catch the ball. Bob played for 15 years and I never knew him to call 'mark'. The poundings he took were legendary, or criminally stupid, depending on your outlook.

During one game, Bob suffered a collapsed cheekbone fracture after catching a knee in the face. He looked horrible. When asked why he didn't call 'mark' Bob replied, "I didn't know Mark was playing today." Clearly, he was the stuff of legends.

We took him up to the local hospital after a veterinarian, who played for the opposition, diagnosed Bob with a broken face and probable hoof in mouth disease, as he lay injured on the pitch at the end of the game. The vet had wanted to put him down but stopped when we refused his offer as too expensive. Not wanting to miss the drink afterwards, we propped Bob up in the waiting room, told the admissions nurse we had found him in a crashed UFO, and made our way back to the bar for the rugby afters.

We returned to the rugby club and after showers, several pints and a bit of food, several players came up urgently and asked through mouthfuls of spilling food, "Eeerrrr, what's happent, tuh the Ugly Bob then? They putting him down er whaaat?"

Before I could answer, a mud covered Land Rover drove up in the gravel car park, the passenger door opened and out staggered Bob. I pointed my sandwich at him and replied, "Ask him yourself."

Bob entered the bar to a great roar of cheers and thrown half-eaten sandwiches and staggered towards a table with a jug of beer on it. He grabbed an empty glass and poured himself a pint, ignoring several shouted questions, and downed it in one.

He poured another without having let go of the jug. Bob then explained that the doctor had examined him in the casualty unit and had recommended immediate admission for Bob's multiple cheekbone fractures and other blunt trauma. Bob had jumped up off the table, and said, "Sod that for a laugh, Doc, I'll miss the beer jugs and the afters... I'll come by in the morning and you can see to it then," and he walked out. Good old Ugly Bob wasn't going to let a multiple skull fracture keep him from his beer and craic on a Saturday afternoon.

The beer flowed well that day and Bob's impersonation of the Elephant Man wasn't the only entertainment for the night. In west country rugby, the skill levels are quite low but the levels of violence and brutality are far above what you would see on television. It's a very important aspect therefore of local rugby to make sure you replace adrenaline with alcohol after a match to avoid facing the pain of your accumulated injuries until Sunday morning.

As the evening and the drink progressed, we became more comfortable with Ugly Bob's uglier than normal looks. There was talk of having him lie on the bar while we re-enacted a *CSI Cotswolds* episode and performed an autopsy on him. Before this could be organized however, the club captain, Dave Taylor, announced that we had a bit of gentleman's entertainment that evening in the form of a stripper.

Taylor announced that an auction would be held and that the highest bidder would be allowed to undress the stripper and that any transactions which took place after that between them was an entirely private matter. We all shouted and laughed as Taylor grabbed an almost empty beer jug, threw the remaining contents on our new scrum half, John Fisher, a serving RAF lad from a nearby base, and threw a fiver in it to open the bidding. Fisher, outraged at having beer thrown on him by Taylor, started to stand up in protest, looked at the colossal Taylor, did a quick physics calculation and then sat down shaking his head and frowning.

Taylor, a large violent man in a room full of large violent men, went around the room with the jug extorting money in the form of donations or bids. The funds would be going to the club after liberal expenses being deducted. I threw a few quid in the jug but declined a competitive bid and Taylor moved on after spewing some Welsh insults at me.

Bob was in a panic and was scrambling around trying to borrow money urgently. Taylor approached him and announced that the highest bid was standing at £23. Bob tried to offer £23.40 but Taylor cruelly proclaimed that it would cost Bob £25 if he was going to win the auction with a further £3 fine for leaving the game two minutes early with his injuries. To everyone's joy and amazement Ugly Bob stumped up the £30 needed to win the auction. No change was given.

There were cheers all around as Taylor brought a chair onto the raised portion of the bar floor which served as a band stand at functions. Bob was announced as the winner and was just beaming with anticipation as he made his way forward to the chair on the band stand.

Bob didn't have much time for courting with his huge family and work commitments, and given Bob's normal horrible looks, opportunities for intimacy were extremely rare. Bob sat in the chair and Taylor blindfolded him, turned, and with outstretched hands called for the room to quiet down for his introductions. The room was a hushed silence other than the sound of an occasional dropped pint glass, a scrapping chair and random shouts of abuse. Taylor now had everyone's attention. Bob was smiling under the blindfold and hopping up and down in his chair.

"Gentleman of the opposition." He bowed to the opposing team captain. "Fellow team mates… Please give a warm welcome for, all the way from Soho in distant London… I give you… for your sophisticated entertainment… Mistress Pirelli." He handed the blindfolded Bob a blow up doll.

Bob tore off the blindfold, tore up the doll and chased Dave Taylor around the room trying unsuccessfully to get his money back. I laughed so hard I had tears in my eyes and the evening faded easily into a late night and on to an early morning.

The other half of our practical joke, Chlamydia, on the other hand, was quite nice to look at. She dressed very well and seemed to know that she was better looking without a kilo of slap on her face. She had some senior position in the local National Health Service which involved huge measures of back stabbing, self-importance seminars, and generally jerking around the poor souls who actually tried to help people.

Like Bob, she too had been unlucky in love. Ann explained that Chlamydia needed to be in control of a relationship and that is why she chose 'less outgoing' men.

I asked if I was a 'less outgoing' man and she laughed out loud and said, "No dear, you're like a four year old boy trapped in the body of a grizzly bear."

I ignored that while I gave myself time to consider if that was a good thing or not. I mentioned that Jerry knew a guy who was of similar age and might be available for a date in the next week or so if Chlamydia was available and willing. I claimed not to know his name. She said she would see if Chlamydia was up for it and asked me to get more details.

A few days later I spoke to Jerry over a few pints about the situation. I asked if this was a bit of a cruel thing to do and maybe we should just kill it off before anyone went sideways about it.

Jerry replied, "Of course it's a cruel thing to do, but they deserve each other. Bob is a beast on the outside and she is a beast on the inside, can you imagine the rugby playing potential of any offspring if they managed to reproduce?"

I set my pint down and said, "Can't have kids, something wrong inside. Anyway, I thought you privately educated guys were supposed to be more sensitive and caring."

"You've played rugby with me for 15 years or more. Are you saying I'm not sensitive and caring?" Jerry said.

"Never mind," I said, shaking my head and passed on Chlamydia's phone number to him to give to Bob.

We finished the beer session on my round which was normal. I felt like Robert Oppenheimer making an atom bomb... a slight feeling that I was doing something fundamentally against nature.

A few days later, Ann interrupted me watching Stewart Barnes on Sky Sports' *Rugby Club,* explaining why Bath were not going to win anything in the next 50 years, with news that Chlamydia had a date. I coughed out some coffee and managed to say, "That's nice for her, when and where?"

"He's going to pick her up and take her for lunch next Saturday. He's a single dad and they have to drop his kids off on the way."

"Oh yeah? How does she feel about that? She bringing along her pepper spray and knuckle duster?" I asked.

"She sounded really excited about it all," she said.

I was amazed and now began to feel bad because the kids were involved. This thing was developing into a runaway train. Jerry has a lack of conscience which would have shocked even the Nuremberg prosecutors, but I had the wrath of Ann to deal with. I was not happy.

Date day came and went and I had pre-arranged a few diversions early on Sunday morning in order to keep me out of the immediate blast area when the shock wave of the inevitable date catastrophe made its way to Ann.

I returned at midday and Ann showed no external sign of blast damage. It was a worrying sign indeed. She was busy rearranging the weeds in her flower pots in the garden. I walked out holding a cup of coffee and stood next to her.

"Lydia called earlier today," she said, opening a conversation I didn't want to have.

"Marvellous, let me guess, she wants some help burying a body?" I returned.

"Not at all. She was telling me about her day out yesterday," she countered as she poked a small garden tool at some roots in a potted weed.

"Oh yeah, how'd it go then?" I asked.

"She had a marvellous time," she said.

"First time for everything I guess. What happened, did the guy die on her or what?"

"Not at all, you'll never guess who the man was?" she said.

"Go on then, who was the victim?" I said.

"It was your mate Bob, from rugby."

I feigned shock and dismay and listened to the tale of the date which would challenge all of Darwin's writings on natural selection.

It seemed that Chlamydia was totally smitten, not by Bob, but by the whole collection of Bob and his boys. When Bob drove by and picked her up, Tommo, Bob's youngest, had demanded to sit next to her and hold her hand. When they got to Bob's sister to dump the kids, Tommo told her not to make his dad cry.

They had a lunch at the Italian place as planned. Bob took her home after and they stopped by his sister's house and picked up his boys on the way. Once again, little Tommo had sat next to her and held her hand.

Over the next weeks, Chlamydia steamrollered the bewildered Bob happily into a relationship and eventually, in the months to follow, plans were made. Bob's boys took to her strongly and she took to them more so, fussing them to school, buying them clothes, and making sure they ate properly.

I had a few pints with Jerry a week or so after Bob's wedding plans were announced. He was beside himself with grief. "Who would have figured that result? I thought she would rip his balls off. It was part your idea, I'm not taking all the blame for this," he whinged.

I just shrugged my shoulders and ordered another round.

A few weeks after that, in a small stone church in a wood on the edge of town, which seemed to be only used for weddings, baptisms, and funerals, a large collection of large men gathered in ill-fitting suits and shirts too tight at the collar to see off a legend.

In the church yard, several flasks were passed around in calloused hands with fingernails which, despite several scrubbings, would never be entirely clean. Jerry kept looking up at the sky and when I asked him why he just said, "Lightning bolts," and hunched his shoulders a bit against the cold.

The service was remarkably forgettable. Bob was standing at the alter and turning his battered, misshaped face to watch his bride walk towards him. His boys, lined up beside him, looked like time sequence photos of Bob as a younger man before life and rugby had altered his appearance. They managed the 'I do' and 'I will' parts with a convincing sincerity... and they were married.

The afters were at the rugby bar and all took that for the sign that it was. It seems that Lydia would not be calling the shots in this marriage.

The bar resembled something seen on the Discovery Channel about watering holes in Africa, with the larger more dangerous species drinking first and establishing territorial limits while lesser creatures darted in where opportunities presented to sneak a pint.

Lydia's family had come from distant lands back east, rumoured to be as far away as Basingstoke. They wandered around meekly in a bewildered and shocked state trying to introduce themselves to the uninterested giant locals. Dave Taylor managed to infuriate the mother of the bride by asking her, "Do you have to feed your hat often, or does it find its own food?"

Speeches were made and ignored and a meal was choked down. The tables were quickly cleared and another stampede for the bar ensued. The cake was cut and the couple took to the dance floor to cheers, polite applause and at least one shout of, "Ride 'em Cowboy."

While they danced, she tried to straighten his tie once and then realized after a minute that the tie was straight but it was the face above it which was crooked. She smiled at that realization and patted his shoulder with a relaxed and contented smile the likes of which few had ever seen on her.

It seemed that despite all of her previous proclamations of what she wanted in a man, and all the trendy stylish things she dated, the thing she needed most, was to be needed.

And I will deny to the gallows our part in this crime against nature. And now you know the terrible secret of the wedding of Ugly Bob.

~

Scott Johnston's Biography

Former forces, and now a pipefitter. I played Southern Counties level rugby for three decades and now I write under the nom du plume 'Old Fat Prop'.

I write funny pub reviews under the theme of Prop's Pubs. I also write a series of humorous travel shorts titled *The Rucksack Chronicles* and also shorts about life on the buildings, which has received critical disclaim under the title *The White Van Chronicles*.

This particular tale is from a series of shorts I call *Tales from Mudflat-on-Ditch*, which is a piss take on life in a small village I lived in a few years ago.

I am unpublished and have no agent. I submitted this one in another comp and although it was mentioned, it was disqualified. I released the hostages anyway.

I have already spent the prize money so it would be useful to win this. Just saying...

TO WYKE-ON-HULL AND BACK

Shortlisted story, by Danny Shilling

1

Summer was approaching and that meant one thing for Patricia Hemelsworth; it was time to outshine her neighbours with a luscious and gorgeously well-kept front garden. Peter Hemelswrath, no relation, had ended Patricia's four year domination of the unofficial best front garden accolade but she was determined to stop a repeat.

Patricia, or Pat to her friends, if she had had any, decided to make early preparations for this year's unofficial contest, which meant she was bent over, her face nearly touching the ground (though it never would; that would upset the delicate upright stance of the individual strands), snipping each strand and collecting each piece in the pouch of the bib hanging around her neck.

Patricia barely noticed anything out of the ordinary at first. It was only when the cuttings she made began to drift away from her as she cut them, and the grass strands began to lean slightly to her left, that she deposited her tongue back into its original place and searched for the disturbance.

At the edge of her garden, by the gate, was a bizarre grey orb-like thing suspended from the ground. It was slightly translucent around the edge, but gained more volume towards its centre. It appeared to be spinning quite slowly, sucking in all loose objects in its close vicinity, including the garden fence, like a black hole pulling in stray stars and comets.

Patricia stared, stunned and speechless as the grey-hole began to spin quicker and quicker until it was almost a blur. Leaves flew past Patricia, even a mailbox, and a bird was frantically beating its wings in an attempt to escape being sucked in, when suddenly a quiet explosion of sorts occurred, and everything that had been sucked in was mightily thrown out. The poor bird slapped into Patricia's face, covering her with dislodged feathers.

One final thing burst out of the grey-hole, something that had not been sucked up initially.

It was a man. An old man, with a long pure white-as-snow beard reaching down to his waist, half-covering a wrinkled and weather worn face. He landed heavily on his back giving a tremendous, "Ooooff," before laying still for a moment.

Just when Patricia thought the man might be dead, he sat up suddenly, eyes wide and attentive. His head darted left and right, and left and right again. He got to his feet, rubbed himself down, and finally noticed Patricia sitting there, looking flabbergasted at him.

He ran to her, "What year it is?"

"2015," Patricia whispered.

"My oh my." The man jumped in the air before laughing wildly. "This is tremendous," he said. He turned and ran out of the cul-de-sac whooping. What was quite strange, if a man materialising out of a grey-hole was not strange enough, was that he had been wearing a robe of deep blue with many unidentifiable symbols sewn into the fabric, and atop his head, in the same colour, was a pointy hat, flopping at the top from the weight of gravity.

Patricia could hardly move until Peter stepped outside. "Pat, what was all that noise about? I heard a great ruckus out here from the back garden... Pat, are you alright? You have a dead bird on your lap."

"My-my-my-my... MY GARDEN."

2

His experiment had been a success. After all those years studying and testing, Anat had managed to concoct a spell to bring him into the future to complete King Edward's task.

King Edward had wanted to know the ramifications of turning Wyke-on-Hull into a juggernaut of a port, fishing, whaling, and military market town. It was potentially lucrative but also came at the risk of significant taxpayer losses.

A young girl showing far too much leg despite the chill in the air was walking towards him now. She held a bundle of books to her chest and stared vacantly at the floor.

"Young lady," he said. The girl paid him no attention. *How rude*, he thought, and waved his hands at her.

She noticed Anat and, after pulling two small white balls out of her ears, said, "Yes?"

"I want to get to Wyke-on-Hull, where are the nearest stables that I might acquire a horse for transport?"

"A horse? What, are you from the medieval ages? If you mean Hull, then you might want to rethink and get a car or a bike. You'll take weeks to get there, otherwise."

"A week is typically how long it takes to get to Wyke-on-Hull by horse so long as there are few attacks on the way."

The girl started to walk away. "Whatever, man, go jump on a bus or something, weirdo."

"What is this bus that I can jump on?"

The girl was already walking off before Anat could ask another question. What was a bus? And for that matter, why were peasants being so rude to their betters now? This had to be reported to the King and measures put in place to stop this ever happening.

Anat came to a group of three people huddled under an arcing misty glass dome with green bars holding the glass in place. He said to the first person – an old lady holding onto handles that attached to some box like object – "Where might I find a... bus, I believe it's called."

"Right here, young man, this is the bus stop."

"Oh, grand." This was a good start. He had only been here for a short time and already had a form of transport. But where was it? "But where is it?"

"It's coming, hold ya horses, young man. My, you youngsters are too hasty nowadays. You'll have to wait..." a moment passed while she squinted at a sign with writing on it, "...three minutes."

So Anat waited patiently for three minutes until a big green and glass monster came rolling up to the stop. For a moment Anat was too afraid to even contemplate willingly walking into the mouth that suddenly opened on the side of the monster. That was, until the old lady stepped happily in.

Buoyed by the bravery of the old lady, Anat was determined not to let a fragile old woman out-do him. He stepped into the monster's mouth quickly and came to the monster's driver who was sitting behind another pane of strangely common glass.

"Ticket?" the driver said.

"For what?" Anat said.

"The bus."

"The bus?"

"Yes, the bus."

"I do not possess a ticket for this bus."

"Well, where are ya heading?" Anat could hear the patience thinning in the driver's voice, and that began to irritate Anat himself. Peasants, no matter how annoyed they were, should never show that to the Lords of the world.

"I must get to Wyke-on-Hull," Anat said.

Suddenly the man burst into a fit of laughter, turning Anat's face a deep shade of red. "You ain't getting anywhere near there on a bleeding bus, mate." Another round of laughter. "Tell you what, you've obviously had a few—"

"A few what?"

"It's almost the end of my shift and that outfit has made my day. I'll drop you at Halfords and you can see about getting a bike or whatever. Take a seat, Gandalf."

"But my name is An—" He was cut off as the mouth of the monster closed and it lurched forwards, sending Anat stumbling down a corridor with rows of benches on each side.

At the back of the bus was a long seat with one occupant. He was slouched in the corner, hugging himself, a hood over his head.

Anat stumbled to the back of the monster as it swayed, desperately trying to throw him down. Finally Anat slumped on the middle of the long seat and scooted to the window. He stared out as the monster made its way along its course. Anat still had a long way to go, but he was sure he could make it. The world had become a fascinating place, King Edward would surely want to hear of all this.

*

"Hey, Gandalf," the driver said to Anat. Anat turned to him, wondering on this insistence to call him Gandalf. "This is your stop. Halfords is on the other side of the road. They'll have what you need."

Anat exited the bus, turned to the man, bowed and thanked him as the mouth closed once again. This startled Anat, who fell back as he watched the man laughing as the monster continued its rampage once again.

After it had passed, Anat saw on the other side of the road a bright orange sign with black words in the centre. "Halfords," Anat said to himself as he patted dust off his robe. "This must be it."

3

"I require some form of transportation to get to Wyke-on-Hull immediately, if you please," Anat said to the assistant whose front teeth protruded over his bottom lip, complementing the already chipmunk looking nose.

"Do you mean Hull?"

"Yes, I need to get to Wyke-on-Hull."

"Well, now I ain't heard of Wyke-on-Hull, but if you want to get to Hull, then you sure got a far way to get going, now ain't you," the spotty-nosed adolescent said.

"Yes, well, I would like one of these bikes, and a hand-drawn map to guide me to my destination."

"Well, now, I'm not sure where you're from, Gandalf," the adolescent chuckled, "but we don't have any hand drawn maps. I can get you a bike, and a GPS system that will guide you to Hull. If you bear with me a second, I'll go grab some bits for you."

Before Anat could reply the peasant was off to get the things. Another strange attitude of these people; they did not wait for their Lords to give them permission to leave. Anat made a mental note to ensure any more peasants to leave without his permission would be reprimanded and possibly disintegrated, depending on his mood.

Sometime later the peasant came back wheeling a waist high metal contraption on wheels. "Where is my driver?" Anat asked, expecting one to step out from somewhere.

"What? You'll be the driver. It's a bike. You never ridden a bike before?"

Not wanting to appear peculiar in this time, Anat said, with some apprehension, "Oh, of course, of course I have."

"Well, anyway, take this here GPS, I've already programmed Hull towncentre into it so that will guide you right there. I'll ring up the register now so you can pay."

"Pay? What do you mean, pay?" Anat was used to getting whatever he wanted from peasants. He could not remember the last time he handed over coin for something.

The adolescent stared at him, dumbfounded. "You didn't think this stuff would be free, did ya? It's at least 180 pounds."

Anat's jaw dropped. He had only 35 shillings on him and no idea how many he would need for 180 pounds. "I have 35 shillings on me."

"Shillings? What the hell are those?"

Anat was too shocked to reply. He turned and slowly walked out of the store, turned right, and slumped against a brick wall. How was he going to get to Wyke-on-Hull with only 35 shillings? He couldn't believe how expensive transportation had become, and it was quite clear shillings had been ousted from use. He was going to have to walk all the way to Wyke-on-Hull, otherwise he would fail his quest for King Edward, and he could not let that happen. He could gain substantial preference with the King should he complete this satisfactorily.

A couple of coins bounced at his feet. Anat looked up and saw a man turning away, stuffing his hands into a black coat of some sort. Anat looked at the coins; a small bronze one with a face on one side and an unidentifiable sketch on the other. It read 'One Pence'. The other was silver, much larger, about twice the size, and the same woman was on the coin. Why was King Edward not on these coins? This one read '10 Pence'.

Anat jumped to his feet and rushed back into the store. The man who had served him before was wandering aimlessly so Anat approached him once again. "How many of these do I need for the bike and GPS?" he said, holding up the silver coin. It was clearly worth 10 times the amount of the smaller one.

"Errr, I never got a good grade in maths, man, hold on.' He thought for a moment. "1,800."

Anat rushed out of the store and followed the wall round to a corner. Here he ducked behind a large container that had a formidably awful smell emanating from it. Seconds later, after casting his spells, he was back in the store, waiting at the counter while the peasant counted out 180 pounds in 10 pence coins. A steady line of disgruntled and bemused customers was quickly forming behind Anat.

4

Anat was gliding along the road following the GPS. The peasant had shown him how it worked before Anat left the store. He was to follow the green line that somehow knew exactly where he was. *Incredible,* Anat thought, *the magic here has progressed at an amazing rate*. "At the end of the road, turn left." When Anat had first heard that high voice in the store during the peasant's demonstration, he had jumped back and almost smashed the thing on the floor with the intention of freeing the woman trapped in there. The peasant explained that there wasn't anyone in there, just that Anat was listening to a recorded voice, like a talking map in his hands.

Anat wobbled as he turned the bike's handlebars slightly to the left. He took a wide berth and drifted out into the middle of the road, only to be roared at by one of those smaller bus-beasts. That was the fourth one already, and one of them had even shouted, "Get off the road, Gandalf." He had considered destroying that one but that would not help maintain his low profile.

There has to be a faster way to get to Wyke-on-Hull, Anat thought. The GPS was saying he still had three days to get there and it had started on two. Anat wouldn't have minded it taking so long – he had brought rations and the trip always took a few days at the least – but Anat was having to do his own work to get there and that was unacceptable. Either he had to get someone to take him or he had to find something that would get him to Wyke-on-Hull with less work or in less time.

*

Hours later, Anat was struggling to continue. His knees, old as they were, were beginning to ache. Sharp stabbing pains shot up his body. He pulled up onto the pathway and turned into an enclosed area filled with more of those small bus-beasts. He was wary at first, but they seemed to be asleep; the red one did not react to his kick.

Anat went towards the building. It was long and flat, with a peaked roof on its top of browns and greys that looked old. It was getting dark now and Anat could see light coming from inside, a magnificent glow that could not have come from 1,000 candles. Anat stopped for a moment to admire metal contraptions that were a lot like his, only much bigger. They all seemed to be in the same design; black with fire painted onto their bellies. He leaned in and read the scrawling calligraphy. 'Harley Davidson.'

Anat nodded approvingly and went into the Biker's Rest, hoping that the 'Rest' part meant it would be some sort of inn. Anat stifled a yawn as he went to walk through the doorway but instead collided with an invisible force. *What is this sorcery*? Anat pondered his predicament a moment, deciding on what spell would be best, when someone held their arm out and pushed forward. Anat noticed a brown rectangle following the man's path. The frame could be linked to the invisible wall and so Anat ducked behind the man and almost cheered when the wall was not there to impede his progress once again.

Inside, the buzz of excitement was palpable. He felt almost like he were back at The Crutch and Crown's Jewels with all the other (inferior) King's wizards sharing ale. The noise was loud, voices milling together to create one great cacophony of sound. Anat could not help but smile.

He went to the bar and signalled for one of the servants, clicking his fingers to get their attention. One of them – a wench who was chewing on something vigorously – eyed him, gave him a sour look, and turned away. A peasant man shook his head at the wench and approached Anat.

"Can I help you?"

"I require a room for the night, and food, and ale. Lots of ale," Anat said.

"I can give you two o' those. We don't have any rooms, we're just a bar, you see," the peasant said, his hands placed shoulder width apart on the long wooden bar.

"But isn't this a place of rest?"

"Tis. But not for sleep, just for grub and booze... or a diet coke if you're so inclined."

"Grub?"

"Food, yes. We do a cracking pulled pork BBQ plate."

"Pah, I need rest. But that will have to do. Give me that and a jug of your best ale."

The peasant nodded. "Where will you be sitting, Gandalf?"

There was an empty table near the window. Anat pointed at this and went to sit down. When he was seated and comfortable he stared at the peasant and contemplated whether he should just turn him into a rat or dust for what he had said. He didn't have long to think, though, because the wench came over with his jug of ale and a clear cup. Anat said his thanks and marvelled at the cup, seeing his hand through the other side. *What craftsmanship*, he thought, *I must take this masterpiece back with me.*

Anat drank the ale for the time being and then, when the steaming plate of sauce laden food came, dug into it with his hands and teeth until all that was left was a plate of bones. He leaned back, burped, and undid the tassel holding his robe tight to his stomach. Only then did he notice the Harley Davidson beasts just outside where he was sitting. Anat admired these until his gaze was diverted by a burly man sitting opposite him. Clean shaved, he wore dark eye-glasses and a crumpled jacket with that same Harley Davidson stitched into the breast.

"You like them bikes, Gandalf?"

"Yes, I do," Anat said through gritted teeth. "Are you Harley Davidson?"

The man sat down opposite Anat, slapped the table with his thick hands and laughed. He looked back to a group of similarly dressed men and laughed some more.

"I wish I was," he said, "but me name's Randy Andy, Gandalf."

"Call me Gandalf one more time, and no one will be calling you Randy Andy again," Anat said.

"What are you gunna do... Gandalf?"

Anat said nothing. Randy Andy guffawed and kept slapping the table with his ham hands. Anat concentrated. The air in the tavern chilled considerably to the point that the cup started frosting with ice. Randy Andy kept on laughing, until he was lifted up with his chair. It was slow for the first six feet but after that, as a similarly dressed man went to grab Randy Andy, he flew up another 10 feet. Randy Andy began shouting, "Get me down, get me down." He began turning in circles, faster and faster, until he was a blur and the torrent of vomit soaked those at the front of the spectating crowd. Suddenly a hole appeared in the roof, a swirling vortex of air rushed in and engulfed Randy Andy, and flew out with him.

Anat concentrated for a few moments more and then slumped back. He jumped when the jacket and glasses landed on his table. The faces all around were staring at him. It was at that point that Anat knew he'd screwed up. *No matter*, he thought, *I gave him fair warning*.

Whatever these people might do, Anat decided he did not want to be around to see it. He grabbed the jacket and eye glasses, slipped both on and went outside. He also decided, as he magically pushed through the glass gateway, that he wanted a new mode of transportation and guessed that the beast with Harley Davidson on its side belonged to the man who had once owned the jacket Anat was now wearing. He climbed on, ignoring the stares of the people in the building. *How does this one go?* Anat thought. There were no pedals on this. On searching he found a key hole, so, like opening a door, maybe this would make the Harley Davidson move forwards. He had no key though... but wait. Anat patted the coat and felt something lumpy in a pocket. He put his hand in and brought forward a metal key on a metal ring. Anat inserted this, twisted it, and the beast roared.

Now all Anat had to do was figure out how to make it move without pedals. It took a while and a lot of twisting and turning, but Anat managed to make the beast scream when he twisted the tip of the right handle bar. The beast jumped forward. He managed to steady it... just.

Using the long handle bars, Anat was able to steer himself out of the stable for the beasts. He stopped by his bike, removed the GPS, and hooked it up to the Harley Davidson. Another twist of the handlebar, this time harder, and the Harley Davidson jerked forward onto the road. Luckily the road was clear and Anat weaved his way along the road, following the GPS's navigation.

It took some time, but Anat managed to bring down the three day estimated time of arrival to just a few hours. The Harley Davidson did less weaving and more roaring and soon enough Anat arrived in Hull. And not long after that, an excited Anat was whizzing back down the road in the opposite direction.

He had seen all he needed to see and it was time King Edward received the good news.

5

Patricia Hemelsworth had been trimming her garden when it happened. There was a niggling bit of overgrowth by the doorstep that just couldn't wait to be trimmed. There was no way Peter Hemelswrath was going to beat her again on a minor point. She had been sloppy in the past, but not today.

Patricia had just bent down with her scissors open like a long jumper in mid-air, when she heard the fat man's shouts. His body was twirling in the air, round and round, in a quite mesmerising manner. Her eyes followed as he flew over her head and landed with a 'thump' right in her beautiful flower bed, crushing all those pretty flowers and her garden contest dreams.

The fat man sat up and shook his dazed head. His back was covered in a myriad of colours that had been torn from the ground.

Patricia fainted.

~

Danny Shilling's Biography

I am currently a trainee accountant working in London, but my real passion lies with telling prose and getting all the rumblings in my head down in some sort of coherent manner.

If I were to be asked why I write, I would say, "Because I have no choice in the matter."

Even if one person were to read my story and enjoy

it, then I would be happy (although getting a bigger audience would be preferred).

UPS AND DOWNS

Shortlisted story, by Mark Rutterford

Picture the scene where watery evening sunshine warmed me and my wife, Trish, as we sat on a bench in Ilfracombe harbour. Picture us eating vinegary chips as if recovering from a near-death experience. We were laughing so loud that a rowing crew some 50 yards away, carrying their boat to the water, stared at us like we were in the care of the community.

Whilst all that is true, it is also near the end and I don't want to start there.

I want to start with the writing on the tickets. Factually correct and misleadingly innocent:

'Lundy Island lies 10 miles off the coast of North Devon where the Atlantic meets the Bristol Channel.'

The day Trish and I went to Lundy I was possessed by the devil. I was seriously ill. I had a run-in with Her Majesty's Armed Forces, and – you will be impressed by this next bit – I still managed to send a postcard home.

Trish and I had a week away, on a farm in Exmoor, in May. It was a fresh-green spring and lambs accompanied our every step as we walked the hills and the fields. Daylight, fresh air, food and drink, all that we require for a good time, were each in plentiful supply.

But what if we ventured further, had a really big day out?

That would be fun, wouldn't it?

After many years together, I know the limit of my powers of persuasion. I had been trying to convince Trish to go to the island of Lundy for a couple of years.

"Maybe..." she said.

"What's there again?" she asked.

And, "How big is the boat?"

And yet, this May, all it took was a couple of beardy men we encountered on a coastal path. They had military-spec binoculars and pasty crumbs in their facial hair. They were visibly excited in a train-spottery kind of a way, as they pointed to black and white specks flying over the sea. They proclaimed, in a Captain Jack Sparrow kind of voice, "Them's puffins. There's loads of 'em on Lundy."

It was like Trish was hypnotised or body-snatched. She was suddenly converted and so, as I wondered if the beardy gents could advocate a clear out of the loft, I promised to book the trip.

*

Two days later we woke early, to still air and sunshine. As we left the farm, we were delayed by a 90 year-old cow herd and his great grandson, guiding cattle to a field for the day. *It was the only delay on the journey and a good omen*, I thought. *All is well*.

As we parked in Ilfracombe harbour, we could see our ship – *The Oldenburg*. It was sturdy and safe and could take 200 passengers in all. On that day, there were about 80 on board for the two hour trip there and the two hours back.

We sat on the upper deck, facing backwards. I was sitting on the outside, Trish was tucked in beside me and, thrilled it was such a calm and sunny day, we both had smiles on our faces.

The engines started and we moved towards the iconic Damien Hirst statue, Verity. She looked proud and defiant from the back, holding a sword to the air as if to guard the harbour from marauders. By the time we got to the front, we could see the face was half-skull and that Verity's belly was open, with protruding innards and a baby on the way.

It was as if the safety of the harbour was about to end.

As if, on a calm sunny day like this, the Captain was announcing that it was blowing a force five in the Bristol Channel and that we were going to feel the movement of the ship quite a bit.

As if...

Now I'm no sailor, but I do know that as long as you

can see the horizon, you won't feel sea sick.

I now know that to be complete and utter bollocks.

15 minutes in and the back of the boat was moving up and down like a Mexican wave. I hooked my arm over the rail and held on tight, thinking, *this is going to be an adventure*.

30 minutes in and the spray was crashing over the brow of the ship – my jeans were soaked and water ran down my neck. I was thinking, *this is going to be shit*.

A man returned to his seat with a bacon sandwich and a coffee for his wife. One huge swell later and he was tipped on his arse; the coffee expendable, his dignity overboard, but the sandwich… saved. It takes a lot to separate a man and his bacon sarnie. As he tucked in and his wife dehydrated, I read his mind: *Oi, Neptune, come and have a go if you think you're hard enough.*

The swell was getting a bit hairy, so I thought I would strike up a chat with the couple sat opposite. *Husband and wife*, I thought, *met and married in their late-30s, knowing it was too late to change each other, so making the best of it*. They'd not drawn breath since sitting down so I thought I might as well participate, instead of listening to my inner voice and screaming, "You two are clearly black-belts in the martial art of inane conversation, but I wonder if you might SHUT THE FUCK UP."

I am much more polite than the voice inside my head, so I enquired if they had been to Lundy before and asked where they were staying. They told me, in excruciating detail and I took an interest too. But talking and listening required concentration and in that few minutes, I lost the horizon and my equilibrium… entirely.

As I sat back, I looked like Shrek and felt a lot greener.

I tried deep breaths.

But it was hard to ignore the girl across the way being *very* sick indeed.

I tried to think about other things, but all my brain did was remind me that bacon sandwiches and milky coffee and pints of beer were available below decks.

Oh no. I really was going to be sick in that uniquely Marks and Spencer's kind of way. You remember the adverts: *"This isn't just steak, this is succulent, juicy, nubile steak... with a blow job for afters."*

And when God invented it, he must have hired the same advertising agency: *"This isn't just puke, this is bilious, watery, sea-sickness puke and you are never going to be kissed again."*

At this point, all I cared about was finding something, other than my sandwich box, into which I could be sick.

I turned to my wife and said, "I'm gonna need a bag."

In the time it took Trish to say, "I haven't got one spare," I was possessed by the devil.

"YOU NEED TO FIND ONE," is what I said, as if I was Lucifer himself... having just stubbed his toe.

I don't know what she did with them. Trish didn't eat them, or throw them to the gulls. In the limited time available, I suspect she may have slipped them in the cups of her bra for safe-keeping... but our emergency cheese rolls were removed from the carrier bag and the bag was passed to me for an altogether different purpose.

For the next 45 minutes I was turned inside out. I was retching and I was dying, with short spells of comfort and long spells of sickness. I wasn't alone, far from it. But mass indignity hurts no less than a solo effort – did you see England in the World Cup in Brazil?

I was cold and ill and ready for my life to slip away. And then… Captain sodding Birdseye came over the Tannoy again.

"Ladies and Gentlemen, we have an extra special treat for you today. The search and rescue helicopter are on exercise and they're going to come and meet the ship."

As the sea got bumpier and the temperature dropped – as I became emptier and emptier – a bloody big yellow hairdryer arrived in the sky.

It was hovering over the boat and with a running commentary, a winchman was lowered onto the deck and picked up again. Onto the deck and up again. What a tosser.

The noise of the engines was deafening.

The diesel fumes made me gag and the whole performance went on for ages. It was like the bank holiday boy racers – the pasty and pimply ones that would spend their teenage years never getting laid – had gone airborne.

I was so pissed off I couldn't even look at them, but I did manage to raise a glance to send a personal mayday message, "Fuck off RAF, just fuck off." 20 minutes later they finally got the message and noisily and smellily, they fucked off to NOT rescue some other poor civilians.

Things improved after that.

I ran out of guts to chuck.

The wind dropped to a mere force four.

The waters near Lundy were calmer.

The island was lovely. The sheep and lambs and deer and horses were friendly. The scenery was breathtaking. And we convinced ourselves that the black and white specks, we were no closer to than on the mainland, were puffins too.

As we boarded for the return journey I was ready for a repeat performance. A really nice woman offered me a sea sickness tablet, saying she couldn't help but notice I'd been ill on the journey out. I turned it down more in shyness and shame than good judgement. But it was calmer and warmer and no one was ill. Not even me.

I stood up and walked to the front of the ship for part of the journey home. I fooled myself I was Ben Ainslie after all and a puffin or two flew by as if to reward us, or flick V signs and call us wankers, one of the two.

So, although this story might have come to an end with chips in Ilfracombe harbour and hysterical laughs, as Trish declared she had a pair of gloves in her bag and I declared, "I could have puked in them," it ends about 10 days later. It ends when the postcard my wife didn't know I'd sent from the Island arrived home.

She was delighted it had its own Lundy stamp and was delivered to the mainland by helicopter.

It read, *'Dear Trish, when I say we've had our ups and downs, I mean the boat trip to Lundy. Mark xx'*

~

Mark Rutterford's Biography

Mark Rutterford has been writing seriously since 2008, learning his craft (the hard way) via a couple of unpublished novels. Juggling work and volunteering commitments at a wildlife charity, Mark kept his writing going through short stories. He learned a lot from listening to some fabulous writer-performers, before eventually writing something short enough – and with story enough – to perform.

Since his first appearance in January 2014, Mark has established himself as a regular performer at storytelling events in Bath and Bristol, UK. His stories are honest, funny, romantic, with a bit of heart-ache and twists you didn't see coming. A collaboration of inspiration from Tony Parsons, Cecelia Ahern, Roald Dahl and 1,000 songs.

JUDGES' STORIES

AWAY DAY

Judge's story, by Mike Scott Thomson

It's a day that will go down into legend – and with exactly 32 people in the department, it must have been destined.

Yet if Becky the Babe hadn't joined the previous week, the whole crazy concept wouldn't have worked. Had we done a pub quiz or personality profiling or those god-awful "trust falls" – you know the ones, where you're supposed to fall backwards into the arms of your waiting colleagues – well, who knows? Maybe things would have turned out different.

My name is Peter Piper, by the way. Yes, I know all the jokes. I too used to work for Benedict Prospect, but I'm long gone now. I suppose I was only ever passing through, my fifth job in as many years, constantly on the lookout for office totty. But I'm putting in the hours now. It falls to me to write an account of that fateful day, which I shall save for posterity on the shared 'J' drive.

Since you're reading this, you'll know all about the exhilarating, white-knuckle rollercoaster ride that is insurance sales. I doubt much has changed since my time. All I know is that Charley-Ann is no longer there, and that must count for something.

Oh, many a day did I mull over the qualities, or lack thereof, of our esteemed general manager. What an endless source of procrastination that was. Chin in hand, I would stare intently at the Word document in front of me, the screen as blank as my face, looking for all the world like I was working my smelly socks off. What I was actually doing was asking myself over and over: what was it about Charley-bloody-Ann that made her so bloody annoying? Was it her insistence that we spend an hour a day filling in our timesheets, with the timesheets themselves containing a special category for filling in timesheets? Could it have been the infuriating way her voice fluttered into a falsetto, indicating, without fail, that she was right, everything she said was right, and everybody else, by virtue of being everybody else, was wrong? Maybe it was her habit of spending our entire drinks budget on fresh bunches of gladioli for the breakout area?

Yet the answer to all these questions was No. What really got me were those damn letters, added to the nameplate on her office door: "MBA". *I'm more important than you*, they taunted. *I've earned my right to be here. You haven't. That's why you work for me.*

Master of Bugger All, the rest of us reckoned.

Everyone, that is, except Kiss-Arse Kev.

But then came the day of human chess.

We were well curious when the email came round. A rare missive from Sir John Benedict himself, the subject line simply said 'Away Day'. According to the message, we were to learn 'the importance of team working', and by extension, 'personal development'. Bright and early the next Friday morning the entire sales department were to be whisked off to a hotel in deepest suburbia.

Five minutes after the email, Charley-Ann came strutting through the open-plan office, Kiss-Arse Kev hot on her heels and carrying her clipboard. "Well, I'm glad," she cooed. "I thought it was about time. I've been asking for ages for something like this."

Sure you have, we all thought in unison. Everyone, perhaps, except Becky the Babe, but she was learning fast.

Becky, as I've said, had only just joined. This in itself was nothing unusual; on average we would lose, and have to re-hire, one member of staff a fortnight. Vigilant like a vixen but with puppy-dog eyes, Becky was brunette, petite and, excuse me if words fail me for a moment, *well* fit. As she walked into our department that first Monday morning, every male pair of eyes lingered a beat too long on her hourglass figure. Even Kiss-Arse Kev tore his attention away from Charley-Ann long enough to register his own confused approval. Becky, savvy as she was, knew she'd got us in the palm of her hand. But for me, she presented – whoa – a challenge. I'd have to move fast on this one.

Who else do you need to know about, before we address the burning issue? Of course, Round Bob. With his 60-inch waist and 20 years of service, you could say he was literally part of the furniture. Every lunch break he would think nothing of sinking five pints of Spitfire and carrying on as sober as he was before. Yet he got the job done, much to Charley-Ann's annoyance, who never managed to find an excuse to fire him (a deed that would have considerably lowered the average weight of the department).

So, that's me (Peter Piper), Becky the Babe, Charley-Ann, Kiss-Arse Kev and Round Bob. Are they all the major players in this little game? Yes? Then let battle commence.

*

Only copious amounts of alcohol would make this trip bearable, and nobody could rely on Charley-Ann to stump up for a round. I checked my bank account at an ATM that Friday morning; a grand total of £11.52 flashed up on the screen. Could this not have been on payday? Grumbling to myself, I withdrew my last tenner and boarded the coach. One hour later, we were there.

We started with crate-stacking, which immediately put Kiss-Arse Kev in a sulk because he couldn't get more than six high. We were divided into four teams of eight, each of us given plastic boxes and told to pile them as high as we could, one person being harnessed up as they ascended the growing tower. Charley-Ann was handing Kev the crates, with Round Bob and a few other guys supporting the bottom, when Round Bob did one of his world-famous sneezes, a cacophonous blast of wind and phlegm, and set the entire structure tumbling. Kev was a picture as he dangled by his harness, his face turning purple. I've never heard such awful language. Boy, is that dude competitive.

Anyhow, all that business was just the prelude. Next

came the main task. In a courtyard out back was an enormous chessboard, each square at least two-feet wide. At the start of the day we'd been given dinky button badges to wear – some white, others black – and now it was starting to make sense.

"Chess," announced the leader of the training centre, a skinny kid in a baseball cap, "the ultimate in tactical nous, forward planning and strategy. Indeed, not unlike the world of business. But here's the difference. This time, you are the pieces, as well as the players."

With this guff rattling in my brain, I stole a glance at Becky. Though we had hardly exchanged a word over the past week, she returned my look. Something mysterious was going on behind those deep brown eyes.

"Two teams," announced Baseball Cap. "16 pieces per side. Arrange yourselves on the grid, and away you go."

I was black, alongside Charley-Ann, Kev, Becky and a bored Round Bob. We clustered at one end of the board as Charley-Ann took control.

"I'll be queen," she declared. "All the Band three employees are pawns. Kev, you be a knight."

"Right you are," Kev sniffed, clearly disappointed at not being made king.

A voice piped up. "I'm county chess champion," said Becky.

Charley-Ann droned on. "The rest of you, decide which pieces you're going to be and get on the board. I'll announce the moves. I used to play when I was at Oxford University."

"I'm county chess champion," said Becky again. Although she didn't seem too flustered, I couldn't let it pass. Now was my chance to get in her good books.

"Charley," I said, forgetting the 'Ann' which I knew would get her attention, "I think you should listen to our new recruit."

The 16 of us parted to reveal the trim figure of Becky, standing at the back. "I'm county chess champion," she said for the third time. "If we want to win, let me call the moves."

Charley-Ann glanced with barely concealed disdain at the newbie. Finally, she shrugged. "Fine," she said. "You make the moves. But I'm still queen."

"Deal," said Becky.

We got into place, the whites having arranged themselves ages ago. I was a castle, just behind Becky who took a pawn position on the outer edge. Round Bob was the biggest pawn the board had probably ever seen. "Sacrifice me first," he whispered to Becky as we settled into our squares. "I want a bloody drink."

"Can do," said Becky with a wink. She turned to her square and faced forward; impassive, determined.

This was going to be better than I thought.

Becky the Babe was true to her word; Gary Gilligan's white knight took Round Bob's black pawn only three moves into the game. "Thank fook for that," said Round Bob as he wandered back to the bar. Kev, surprisingly, was next off. Becky moved him to square E5, where he was rudely taken by Martin McCabe's white pawn. The fleeting look of hurt which came over his face would have been, if it were anyone else, a heart-breaking sight; as it was, I had little sympathy. Charley-Ann, having not yet moved, merely raised a quizzical eyebrow. Kev looked at his shoes and trundled away towards the crates. Becky's eyes followed him as he went. I still couldn't tell what was going on inside that mind of hers.

Then things got interesting.

"Queen to H4," called Brian Bale, the tactician for the whites. Their queen duly came trotting over our end, stopping on the right-hand side. They were on the offensive. Becky paused for a moment, her usually milky-smooth brow furrowing with thought.

Eventually, she called, "Queen to F3." Charley-Ann made her first move, shuffling diagonally along.

The next few moves, I realise now, were the calm before the storm. Martin McCabe took another of our pawns; Becky finally moved me up the board, to the far end. It was clear to none of us but Becky, least of all to Charley-Ann, that our queen was in danger.

"Pawn to F3, queen capture," announced Brian from the other end. An astonished murmur arose from the players as Martin edged into Charley-Ann's space, nudging her aside. Charley-Ann, for once, was rendered speechless – her mouth fell open – and as she marched off, she shot Becky such a vicious glare that if looks could kill, the souls of every living organism within a 15 mile radius would have permanently taken leave of their bodies. Becky, in response, just smirked.

So when 10 minutes later Becky advanced herself to the other end of the board, thereby promoting herself from pawn to queen, Charley-Ann saw a chance for revenge.

"Good," she chimed from the side-lines, the falsetto back in her voice as she flounced onto the board. She sidled up to Becky's advanced position and stood there, hands on hips. "Well, go on then."

"Go on where?" replied Becky.

"I'm the queen," said Charley-Ann. "So go on, scoot."

Becky the Babe, it was my pleasure to see, stood her

ground. "I'm queen now," she responded. "So you scoot."

The chess pieces held their collective breaths.

Charley-Ann straightened her back. "I see," she said. "We have an insubordinate in our midst. I'm sure Sir John Benedict will be absolutely disgusted."

Becky's response was immediate. "Don't tell me what my father thinks."

Silence descended. Confusion etched itself over the face of our boss.

Becky continued. "And I think our little exercise is complete. I've found out all I needed to know this past week, and will be able to give my father a full account of the reasons for the high staff turnover in the sales team." She turned to face the rest of us. "Game over, everyone."

Charley-Ann, though, was not listening. Something had caught her eye, something in the distance, by the crates in the far corner…

We all turned. Kev, clearly riled by his earlier failure and his premature exit from chess, was perched atop a stack of crates, a record-beating 11 high, wobbling five metres off the ground. Round Bob, having been roped in to helping, was at the base of the stack, loading more boxes on to the pulley.

That he'd built a new tower wasn't the problem. The fact his new construction was leaning Pisa-like towards the car park, most certainly was. Having deemed a safety harness an unnecessary luxury for use only by sissies, Kev, the stupid prat, was headed for a hospital visit – or worse, an early grave.

Chess forgotten, we watched in horror, frozen to the spot.

It was Charley-Ann who reacted first. "Jesus Christ,

Kev." And off she went, her chubby legs sprinting her away.

She got there just as the tower buckled. Kev, who until that point was swinging his arms wildly in an attempt to keep balance, succumbed to gravity, flipping himself theatrically to the side. Now to my mind, it was always ironic we called him Kiss-Arse Kev, since when he landed, bottom first on Charley-Ann's head, it was very much a case of her kissing his. With both of them splayed on the floor, a shaking Kev struggling to his feet next to an unconscious Charley-Ann and a confused Round Bob chest-deep in several dozen plastic boxes, that image tattooed itself upon my mind and shall remain there for as long as I live.

I said it then and I'll say it again: now that's what I call a trust fall.

*

So, the ambulance came and took a concussed Charley-Ann away, Becky lingered on the phone (presumably to her powerful father), while a disconsolate Kev, Round Bob and I hovered by the coach.

"You're gonna be a hero, mate," I told Kev. "You knocked out our boss."

I didn't expect his response. "Why do you hate her?" he said. "What has she ever done to you?"

"Well," I said after a pause, "she has that stupid obsession with timesheets, and..." I stopped. Despite my endless hours of procrastination about Charley-Ann, I couldn't think of anything else. I stood there, puzzled, looking at Kev, wondering vis-à-vis this strange new feeling brewing inside me.

And then, like a parting of the clouds, it became

clear.

"Just ask her out," I said. "You're clearly in there."

Kev's face mottled with anguish and embarrassment. "How?"

I glanced over at Becky the Babe, the undercover pawn. Power and beauty, an irresistible combination. It was now or never – and I could show Kev a thing or two at the same time.

"Watch this," I told Kev. I strode over to Becky, her phone conversation finished, and wore my most winning smile.

"How," I asked her, "would you like this Peter Piper to peck your pickled pepper?"

Her response was to violently connect the palm of her right hand with my left ear. I blinked stupidly as she glared back. That line had always worked before. Clearly I wasn't the man I once was. I returned to Kev and Bob, hell's bells ringing in my ear, my face flushing worse than Kev's.

"Nah," said Round Bob, smacking his lips. "What you need to do, Kev my son, is get one of them bunches of flowers she likes, then write her a note saying, 'You'll always be my queen.'"

Kev and I stared at him. "Bob, you old honey-dripper," I said. 40-stone Round Bob just shrugged.

"I don't have any cash," said Kev, a hint of desperation in his voice.

I took pity on him. Never thought I'd say that about Kiss-Arse Kev. "Here," I said, producing my last 10 pound note from my wallet. "Use this. Go."

Kev took the note and dashed away.

*

And apparently, Crazy-in-Love Kev did exactly that. With my tenner he acquired a large bunch of gladioli, wrote the note with words by Romeo Bob (as I now think of him), and paid an immediate visit to Charley-Ann in the head trauma unit. Clearly she's a more forgiving sort than we'd given her credit for, since the two of them, at the time of writing, are still together. And you know what? As you read this, weeks, months or even years later, I hope they still are. I really am not the man I once was.

As for Benedict Prospect, it underwent, shall we say, some changes. Bob, true to form, is still there, but he's the only one. Charley-Ann, Kev, Becky, they're all gone, and I will be too, once I hit 'save' on this report for the last time. I guess I need some personal development of my own.

But before I do, I should put this on record: that legendary away day was a success. Beforehand, we were no more than random strangers, thrown together within grey office walls, our true selves obscured behind the labels we attached to each other. And afterwards? Well, put it like this. Never mind pawns, castles and queens. We all should have been black knights that day. Dark horses, every one of us.

~

Mike Scott Thomson's Biography

Mike Scott Thomson has been a writer of various forms for as long as he can remember – which, depending on his state of mind, is either a very long time, or not nearly long enough. After many years dabbling in blogging, travel writing, and music journalism (his first published works were talking audiobooks of some disparate pop groups, very much of their day), he started writing fiction in 2011.

So far his short stories have been published by a number of journals and anthologies, including The Fiction Desk, Litro, Prole, *Stories for Homes* (in aid of the housing charity Shelter), and the National Flash Fiction Day anthology, *Landmarks*. Aside from being the proud winner of the inaugural To Hull & Back short story competition, other awards include runner up prizes in contests from both InkTears and Writers' Village. (His only other first prize was to win Riptide Journal's ice-themed six-word-story competition in 2014, with an entry which went: *When the loch thawed, it awoke.* He tells you this not merely to squeeze in an extra story alongside 'Away Day'. Banish the thought.)

Based in south London, he works in broadcasting.

Mike's website: www.mikescottthomson.com

~

Mike's Competition Judging Comments

There's an "inspirational" quote for everything, these days.

"When we are judging everything, we are learning nothing" reads one.

"Every moment spent judging somebody else is precious time wasted" goes another.

"Baloney," says I.

Of course, I'm being a bit disingenuous, but my point stands. Not only has it been a pleasure and incredibly rewarding to read these shortlisted entries, but also a valuable learning experience – both for me as a reader, and a writer.

I admit in the past to having an over-active imagination when my own stories failed to make competition shortlists. Vividly I pictured miniature basketball nets in the corners of judges' otherwise austere studies, into which (via well-practised throwing arms), they unceremoniously tossed crumpled double-spaced manuscripts, simultaneously bellowing (in the booming voice of the giant from *Jack and the Beanstalk*), "What fresh doggerel is THIS?"

Thanks to my involvement as a judge in To Hull & Back II, I finally realise: double-baloney. I thoroughly enjoyed, and respected, all the stories I read – it really was hard to put them in any kind of order.

Never again shall I judge the judges. (So, those inspirational quotes were right after all. Darn.)

BAG PACKERS

Judge's story, by Christie Cluett

Don finished stacking empty boxes in the far corner of the supermarket car-park and checked his stop-watch: four seconds off his personal best. He sighed, his breath clouding in the cold air, and let his hand slap back into his thigh. How was he ever going to get a job as a bag-packer if he didn't get better? He glanced over at the harassed woman trying to fit a toaster into the clothing bin and for a moment let himself dream of thank-yous; for a loaf of bread not squashed, for tins double-bagged. All that, and the warmth. The warmth of being inside and the warmth of Polly's smile of pride at having the best bag-packer at her till. Instead he watched as his stacked boxes slowly collapsed and wondered if he'd ever be allowed inside.

Don pulled his hat on and snaked his long line of connected trolleys through the car-park, stopping at the main trolley park just outside the supermarket doors. He stepped to the side as a crowd of early morning shoppers rushed past him, almost through him, eager to get out of the cold. Don rubbed his hands together, the fingers numb despite the thick gloves he wore, and looked into the warm glow of the hustle and bustle inside.

"Morning, Don."

Don turned with a smile that ebbed and surged with an eagerness that was out of control.

"Hello, Polly," he said as she came towards him. She walked with a rolling gait, on shoes that were meant to help her lose weight. Don couldn't imagine how that worked, unless the shoes were incredibly light.

"Cold, isn't it?" Polly said, as she stumbled past him, trying to keep her balance. Don watched her in slow motion. Her thick brown hair swung like a curtain of hot Bovril and her blue eyes shone with tears from the cold, her cheeks pink and her nose red. Don sighed and thought he could look at her forever. She pulled her thick coat, tugging it until it was almost closed.

"It's a bit nipply... nippy. I meant nippy. No nipples," Don said, wondering why his mouth was trying to sabotage him. He decided to dig himself out of the hole. "You're alright though, aren't you, with your thick layer."

Polly's face dropped, sagging further into her neck.

"I didn't mean..." Don pointed at her and wanted to say that he didn't mean she was fat, that he thought she was the most beautiful woman he'd ever seen. Instead, he just kept talking. "I'll see you inside soon, though, Polly. There's a bag packer's job with my name on it."

Polly's smile was strained as she nodded politely.

"Maybe I could pack the bags on your till," he said.

"Maybe," Polly said quietly before turning and walking away.

*

A week later and Don was back in the corner of the car-park, by the recycling bins, stacking bags of empty cans and half ripped up boxes. He stood back to contemplate the wall of perfectly stacked recycling he'd made and smiled. He knew a bag packing job wasn't just going to fall into his lap but Don was a man in control of his own destiny, and so he'd been practising; time trials, awkward spaces, everywhere and anywhere. Now his fridge, his sock drawer and his DVD collection were a precisely packed homage to space saving, and Don was ready.

After a morning that dripped by like Chinese water torture, it finally reached 12.30: lunch-time. He hurried towards the main building, tugging his gloves off as he went. Today was the day he was going to speak to his manager, the day he was going to get inside and begin the rest of his life. He sighed as an old man suddenly careered wildly into his path.

Errol had worked for the supermarket for 45 years and had recently been demoted to trolleys. Don was always worried that one day he was going to find Errol frozen to death, being wheeled about by a distracted mother who'd inserted her two year old into Errol's elasticated waistband. A tragic yet befitting death for a dedicated employee.

"Alright, Errol?" Don asked, trying to take his elbow and steer him off the collision course he was on with a Vauxhall Corsa.

"Get off me. Get off me," Errol shouted, swiping at Don's hand.

"Right you are, Errol. Just try not to walk into that..." Don didn't bother finishing his sentence, as Errol sagged over the bonnet of the car. Once Errol had managed to straighten up, the two men carried on their passive fight in the general direction of the automatic doors.

*

Inside the warmth rushed towards Don and hugged him from his fingers to his toes. Aisles of colourful products expanded towards the back of the store and a happy jingle was playing over the speakers. He listened to the chatter and the rhythmic beeps while his eyes automatically searched for Polly. She was sitting at her till, swiping at a stain on her uniform. The light of the fluorescents overhead sparkled on her shiny forehead and Don was mesmerised as she tucked a strand of hair behind her ear and let out a giggle that lifted his heart. He stood there for a moment, as she turned her head and smiled, a proper smile that he could almost imagine was for him. Then a customer moved out of the way and Don saw who she was smiling at. Jason. Don's chest constricted so tightly and so quickly that he felt his hair stand on end.

"Move. Move." Errol gave him a shove in the back

with a bony finger and Don blinked. He nodded to no one in particular and, catching sight of the Floor Manager up ahead, strode towards her.

"Janet," Don called as she pivoted on her heel and began to walk in the opposite direction. He hurried to catch up, then leaned back slightly as she turned. Janet had drawn her eyebrows on slightly too high, covered her eyes in white and rimmed them with black, making her look like Ming the Merciless.

"Janet." Don tried not to breathe on her for fear of making her face melt. "Janet, what's Jason doing on bags? He's only been here a day. I was supposed to be on bags next."

"Oh hi, Don. Sorry? What?"

Janet was a rubbish actress, he thought.

"Bags, Janet," he said, wondering why she was being so difficult. "I thought I was going to be on bags."

Janet tried to raise her eyebrows but there was nowhere for them to go. "Oh, bags, right. Well, I can't very well put Jason outside on his first day, can I? Don? Can I?" She looked over to where Jason was standing, with a smile that suggested she wouldn't kick Jason out of anywhere. Don thought he'd like to kick him in the balls. Jason's hair stood up in a confident, youthful wave that made Don feel like a bag of potatoes that had gone soft and were sprouting tubers. Jason was wearing the regulation trousers low, the belt tied around his thighs like a slipped tourniquet.

He turned back to Janet, who was watching Jason too. "He's doing it wrong. Look. Bread should go in last, not under the tins." Don pointed with a shaking finger that he immediately put down.

"I'm sorry, Don. Maybe tomorrow. OK?"

He knew Janet didn't mean it but Don was

determined not to spend much longer outside.

*

The next morning Don was outside, ignoring the couple of boys doing *Titanic*, as he timed himself packing used cans into a ripped plastic bag. They spun past him, one standing in the front of the trolley with his arms spread wide as his friend pushed him towards the big white iceberg of a recycling bin.

"I'm flying, Jack," the boy cried as the trolley smashed into the bin. Don looked at his watch and hurried towards the supermarket. It was time.

*

Don marched past the basket stacks, along the front of the line of tills. He'd stayed up late last night, preparing, cramming, and he was ready. His purposeful step only paused for a second when his steely gaze fell upon Jason. He was dumping eggs, pastries and tins into a bag while he leant his skinny hips against Polly's till. Don swallowed hard and walked faster.

"Jason," he said loudly when he reached them; *this was something everyone should hear*, he thought. "I challenge you."

Jason flicked his long fringe out of his eyes before it settled back in exactly the same place, like he'd got a peek at a world he didn't have time for.

"What?" he said.

Don cleared his throat and gave Polly a wink that made her eyebrows rise. "I challenge you to a bag-packing duel. At the end of the day the person with the most satisfied customers, as determined by the short survey on these cards I've made, gets the job. The other goes outside... collecting trolleys." Don put the cards down on the end of the till with a little nod of triumph.

"No," Jason said.

"What?"

"I said no. I'm already a bag packer, and you're not, so why would I give it up? That's stupid."

"But I challenged you... You have to." Don couldn't look up, couldn't look at Polly. There was a loud crackle and then a sing-song voice spoke loudly over the Tannoy.

"Colleague announcement. Would the Trolley Collector please report outside for trolley collecting duties. Thank you. Happy Shopping."

Don didn't know what to do. Jason was looking at him, well his haircut was turned in his direction, but Polly was staring at the artichoke in her hands. The Tannoy sounded again. Janet's mouth was now closer to the microphone, the sound distorted.

"Colleague announcement. I repeat, this is a colleague announcement. Would Don please report outside and collect the trolleys before another trolley collector is found that will collect trolleys. Thank you. Happy Shopping."

Don reached slowly into his pocket and pulled out his heavy gloves. He buttoned up his pink high-vis jacket and walked slowly outside.

*

It was getting dark and the wind had picked up. Don pulled the collar of his jacket up around his cold ears as he waited for a woman who'd inexplicably stopped in front of his line of trolleys. A hand clapped onto his shoulder, a pinch grip.

"Don't worry, son," Errol said. "Not all women want a bag packer."

"Maybe not, but they definitely don't want a trolley collector."

"What's wrong with being a trolley collector? You're a free man, out in the open air, in the wild, answering to no man, just the call of the trolleys." Errol's voice trailed off as he stumbled back towards the edge of the car park from whence he came. Don watched him go and wondered what the point was.

"Don?" The voice was like an angel singing, one who had a slight cough.

He turned around and the light of dusk got a little brighter for a moment. Polly stood looking at her feet. Don looked too for a second and thought, *what marvellously large feet*.

"I'd like to see your packing, Don," she said.

Don shrugged and looked off into the distance. "Well, I'm sure Jason's is much better. Anyway I can't now."

Electricity jumped up his arm as she touched his sleeve. "You can show me out here. I like it outside. It's nicer."

Don smiled and she smiled back.

"But don't you want to be inside with Jason?"

"Nah. He seems like a prick." She put on her mittens and together they walked to the recycling bins so Don could show her how fast he could stack empty boxes.

~

Christie Cluett's Biography

Christie is one of the founding members of Stokes Croft Writers, is on the organising committee for the Bristol Festival of Literature and performs at story-telling & comedy events around Bristol. She was shortlisted for the Magic Oxygen prize, by *Writer's Forum* and published by Mash Stories.

She writes humorous fiction about odd people in normal situations, which are mainly based on the lovely loons that she calls friends (whether they like it or not) or oddballs that pop into her head and march about like they own the place.

She has just finished her first novel, writing short stories in between. At all other times, she can be found chasing balloons, clapping to work out which way is left or lying on the sofa exhausted from it all.

Christie's website: www.christiecluett.co.uk

~

Christie's Competition Judging Comments

Judging was particularly difficult this year as the standard of writing was so high, but I powered through. You're welcome. Competition was stiff so well done to everyone that made the shortlist. There was a great variety of genre and topic, with some really interesting and original ideas that I really enjoyed reading. This competition is great because it celebrates humorous stories in all their glory and I'm really proud to be a part of it. Looking forward to next year already.

CENTRAL LINE BETTY

Judge's story, by Steph Minns

The rails sang the signature tune of the approaching train and the expectant passengers began to shuffle towards the edge of the platform. As the tube train burst from the tunnel, the bag lady's greying hair whipped around her face with the draught. She sat alone, shunned, on the platform bench, shrouded in her tatty layers of coats and jumpers. Her bright green eyes followed the commuter bustle with keen interest as she rested, surrounded by her court of bags. Plastic bags, canvas bags, a smart handbag found among a pile of chuck-outs left outside a charity shop on Regent Street. Her bags carried her world up and down the Central Line each day.

"All stations to West Ruislip," the synthetic voice announced over the Tannoy. "Stand clear of the closing doors."

The next train, she knew, would be less crowded as this was the tail-end of the morning rush hour, so she waited for this one. The train's warm breath as the doors hissed open was a welcome relief from the draughty platform, and Betty climbed aboard to go through her usual routine, shuffling down the carriage, her plastic cup held out hopefully to the commuters.

"Spare any change please?"

The eyes that she tried to meet, coax a little humanity from, mostly shifted quickly away or didn't even raise their gaze from their newspapers and smartphones. She could sense the prickling unease, the irritation and embarrassment that her presence provoked among the commuters. Occasionally someone would return a cold glare or mutter a comment about dirty winos or stinking tramps. But Betty was no drinker. Nor did she smell. She had dignity, and anyone who did bother to engage her in conversation would note her clear, soft voice, the intelligent perception in her watchful green eyes. They would realise they were talking to a woman with some clarity of thought and a compassionate heart.

"Just some coppers would be welcome, sir."

She offered her cup to the city gent who was fumbling in his trouser pocket, but he pulled out a handkerchief, not a wallet, and began to snort into it, ignoring her. She recoiled, embarrassed, but a young auburn-haired woman, sitting in the seat opposite him, leaned forward to drop a couple of pound coins into the cup.

"Bless you, love." Betty smiled. "Bless you for your kindness. May good fortune smile on you and yours."

During that brief connection, Betty saw sadness and a deep exhaustion in this woman's soul. She glimpsed an image as the woman's fingers touched her cup, of a sick child in a wheelchair and she understood the daily pain this woman battled. Good fortune would indeed smile upon this lady, Betty decided, as she moved on up the train, her mouth set in a determined line.

Two jeering lads tried to trip her up as she passed them.

"Gis' a look in yer bags, love. Any dirty knickers in there we can sniff?"

No one intervened and she glared at her tormentors, seeing only stagnant shadows in their hearts. They felt flat, as if made of cardboard, to Betty's keen senses. Best move on, she thought, mentally shuddering, and carried on her ramble up the train, her cup held out hopefully.

The train hummed into Oxford Circus and Betty turned to the doors to get off. The top of the escalators here always offered good pickings, especially from the German and Japanese tourists.

"Oxford Circus. Please change here for Bakerloo and Victoria lines," the announcement chimed.

As the doors slid open, she was nearly knocked over by the sudden onrush of eager tourists. Dropping one of her bags, Betty wailed in panic as it was kicked thoughtlessly away by the trampling feet of the on comers. It was her favourite bag and it held her special things. The tourists had not even considered her, taken her into account as they'd shoved past, but a tall young man with face piercings spotted her plight. Bending down, he scooped up her bag as the people seated themselves, calling across to another man with wild dreadlocks, standing by the doors.

"Hey mate, can y' hold the doors a sec. This lady was trying to get off. Cheers."

The other man obliged by jamming his foot over the sill, forcing the doors to automatically re-open, stopping the train from moving off. The trampling feet, having found their seats, now filled the carriage with a rainbow of chatter as the two men gently helped Betty onto the platform. Her fingers brushed against the pierced man's spiked leather glove as he handed her bag over to her, and she saw a gem in this one, a shining seed buried deep beneath his skin. She knew many people misunderstood him because they failed to see past the book's cover. Betty, however, could see beneath the cover of the people she encountered on her travels up and down the tube. She could read something of their past, their hopes and dreams, their fears. Betty could read their very soul, and beneath the tattoos and piercings of this rock-god dressed in black leather was a kind man who loved his family and friends with a fierce loyalty.

The older, dreadlocked man carefully guided her across the gap between train and platform with a hand under her elbow to steady her.

"There you go, love. Mind how you go now."

He grinned a gold-toothed grin at her and, as she turned to thank him, she saw in her mind's eye boisterous youths gathered around him, and understood that he was some kind of outreach worker for kids who'd lost their way. She felt the waves of compassion he radiated, his non-judgemental desire to help others, but also a certain sadness about him. She knew that he'd love to take his elderly father for one last holiday to see family in Jamaica, but he just couldn't afford it right now. His wage wasn't a big one, but he wouldn't change the job he loved. *So much generous giving*, Betty thought, *always thinking of others and how he can help.*

"Good deeds will always be rewarded," Betty muttered, as she watched the train vanish down the tunnel. "Rewarded tenfold."

Carefully balancing her cluster of bags, she headed resolutely for the escalators, hoping no more thoughtless tourists would send her flying before the day was done. There was nearly enough money in her cup now for a hot coffee and the staff that served at the little station kiosk usually let her have a sandwich left over from yesterday before it went into the bin.

*

In an abandoned side tunnel that evening, Betty struck a match to light a candle. She knew this warren of tunnels like the veins on her scrawny arms. No trains travelled this tunnel now, only mice and rats. Off in the distance, she could hear the last Central Line train thunder past the junction. In a while the night maintenance crews would be tramping past there too. Pulling her special things from her bag, she laid them out in a circle in the grime before her. To the uneducated they just appeared to be some smooth, round stones, a stick, a shard of worn glass with a symbol scratched onto it. She called to mind the faces of those worthy souls she'd encountered that day and sent them each something magical, a gift from the universe.

Sad, auburn lady would find a winning lottery ticket in her bag tomorrow, one she wouldn't remember buying. But imagine her delight when she went to check it? She wouldn't win a fortune, but it would be enough for her to take her sick boy to Disneyland, spend some precious, joyful time together.

Pierced leather lad would find he'd won a holiday in a magazine quiz he'd also forgotten entering, so he could send Gran and Mum off on a week of hotel luxury in Devon. He wished he could do more for them, but the spa break would be a treat they'd never be able to afford.

The dreadlocked youth worker would also find a winning ticket on his kitchen table when he got home. He'd assume his fiancé had bought it, although she'd deny that later, saying she had no idea where it had come from. It would pay for that trip to Jamaica for them all.

Betty's green eyes glowed with a strange inner light in the darkness of the tunnel as she scooped her precious things back into her bag and snuffed out the candle. She smiled quietly to herself, her work here done for now. If anyone had been watching, they would have seen the ragged bag lady transform into a younger, radiant woman, an ethereal mirror of the form she took during the day in the earthly world. Then they would have seen a glimmering portal to another realm open just where the special things had been, and the magical Betty step through it, back to the dimension she called home.

But Betty would be back again soon, resuming her bag lady guise. Our drab world always needs some magic, after all.

~

Steph Minns' Biography

I've been a keen reader, writer and artist since childhood. Originally from the suburbs of London but now living in Bristol, UK, I work part time as an administrator and spend my spare time writing. My previous incarnations have included gardener, magazine editor and web designer. My dark fiction stories range from tales set in future dystopian realities to classic ghost and horror.

My professional publishing history to date runs to several short stories and a novella, in both e-book and print, accepted by notable independent publishers Dark Alley Press, Grinning Skull Press and Almond Press. My competition wins have included winner of the Dark Tales March 2014 international competition, and an honourable mention in the Darker Times November 2013 competition. I've also been featured on Writing Short Ficton's website as a debut author.

Steph's website: www.stephminns.weebly.com
Facebook: www.facebook.com/stephminnsfiction

~

Steph's Competition Judging Comments

It's been a real pleasure to read all these stories and a real struggle to mark them, as the content has been so varied. I try to remember when reading that someone has put their heart and soul into their writing, as I do, but there were some outstanding stories. All the shortlisted stories were great so, even if you didn't win this one, keep writing and entering competitions.

DEVIL'S CRUSH

Judge's story, by Christopher Fielden

1

The problem with inhabiting a body with legs for 35 years is that I became accustomed to having legs. When those limbs were taken from me, I thought my subconscious would catch up quickly, and I'd instinctively regard myself as legless. I was wrong.

It's been almost two years since my date with the

grenade. Yet still I wake up oblivious to the fact that I'm missing limbs. Moments ago I swung myself out of bed, thinking to walk to the kitchen for a drink. With the dexterity of an out-of-date tin of Spam, I embraced the morning (and the floor) with a thud. I swore, I cursed, I laughed. What else could I do? If I were unable to laugh at the ridiculous broken mess I've become, I think I'd deteriorate like Steve. At war he lost an arm, a foot and half his face. Back home he lost his mind. Watching him deteriorate into a lifeless husk was hard. Could I watch my own body wither along with my personality? No. The same will not happen to me.

I struggle into my wheelchair, making a mental note to invest in some sumptuous 25 millimetre tufted-twist-pile carpet to make my morning routine less painful, and trundle into the kitchen.

The first thing that strikes me is the stink of fire. I can see no smoke, no blackened furniture, no indication of a blaze. Aside from the smell, the kitchen is exactly as I left it, apart from one small detail. A bottle now rests in the middle of the kitchen table.

I edge my chair forward to look more closely. It's small and filled with red liquid that dances like fire within the glass. On the front is a label that says, 'Devil's Crush'.

Intrigued, I pick the bottle up and almost drop it – I wasn't expecting it to be hot. But it's not searing, my fingers can bear the heat. I sniff the bottle, trying to determine if it's the source of the burning smell. It isn't. I turn the bottle over. On the back is another label. Underneath some text which is too small to read, it says, 'Made in Hull'. Somehow, this seems apt.

As I study the strange liquid, wondering if the 'u' in Hull might be a misprint, I hear someone clear their throat behind me. Instantly, I drop the bottle into my lap and swing my chair around. The 9mm Browning L9A1 I keep tucked beneath my chair's cushion is in my hand without me having to think.

As I take in my surroundings I realise the bottle had captivated my attention so fully that I'd forgotten my training. Questions fill my mind. Why didn't I clear the room? Why had the bottle intrigued me so? And how could I have failed to notice the demon in the corner?

There are black hoof-prints scorched into the kitchen's tiled floor. He's sitting on a chair which appears to be made of iron. It glows beneath his bulk. His presence makes me realise I'm dreaming. At least, I hope I'm dreaming. Either that or I'm French kissing insanity.

I know the demon is a he because he's naked. He's a he with the right to be proud of just how much of a 'he' he is. His skin is the colour of burnt rust, his body slender yet muscular and he wears a goatee on his chin more like the animal it is named after than a man. His two horns are long and curved like warped blades of molten rock, his hairline a mass of flickering flames and in his eye sockets are two glowing coals which ping and hiss like the embers of a dying fire in the breeze. He is the source of the acrid stench which fills the room.

"I'm sorry to interrupt at such an ungodly hour," he says, his voice as deep as hell's gong. "Put the gun away. It is useless to you."

I do as he commands, not because I want to, but because I am unable to disobey. There's a mesmerising quality to his voice which I realise I will have to fight if I want to act of my own free will.

"You are Sergeant Joshua Purvis?" he asks.

I'm aware that I'm gawping. I try and say, "Yes," but

all that emanates from my mouth is a kind of slurping mumble. I decide to forget talking for a moment and just nod.

"Do you know who I am?"

"Satan?" I guess, pleased that I manage not to drool as I force the word from my mouth.

He snorts laughter, smoke spiralling from the holes in his face which I assume must be nostrils. "No," he says. "My name is Colin."

I hear myself snigger.

"I've taken a human name to seem less threatening," Colin continues, in a tone that suggests he is only imparting this information so he won't find it necessary to tear my head off. "Names aside, you must concur, my master has excelled with the physical manifestation conjured for my eternal servitude?"

I find myself unable to disagree. Colin rises slowly from his chair and takes a step towards me. His horns score black marks into the ceiling.

"I'm dreaming," I state, rather than asking a question to which I may not like the answer.

"No," says Colin. I can feel my scepticism manifesting itself as a squint about my eyes. Seeing this, Colin moves forward and pinches my arm. I scream in pain, not just from the pinch of the serrated talons which are Colin's fingertips, but at the impossible heat which emanates from his body.

He takes a step backwards, politely waiting for me to stop swearing, then says, "Point taken?"

I nod. At least the pain has helped me to focus. I can think and speak again. "Why are you here?"

"To deliver the Devil's Crush."

"To me?"

"Yes. It's a gift."

"From?"

"My master."

"Why is your master sending me gifts?"

"You possess a skill we wish to employ."

"So this isn't a gift?"

Colin smiles, as if pleased with me, revealing a myriad of teeth like needles. "It depends on which way you look at it."

I pick the bottle back up and watch the fiery liquid writhe within. "Am I supposed to drink it?" I ask.

"I believe so."

"What happens if I don't?"

"Nothing."

"What happens if I do?"

"Your legs will grow back."

Now he has my interest. "And what must I give in return?"

Colin subjects me, quite literally, to a burning stare. "Oh, you know," he says, "the usual stuff about the sale of your soul. It's all in the small print on the back of the bottle."

Immediately my instincts tell me to say no. I've never heard a story where the selling of one's soul ends well. But I can feel hope prepping to run a marathon inside my mind and I don't want to stop it. I've been to Afghanistan. I came back broken. Living in this body is a lonely misery beyond imagining. I have no doubt there is trickery behind Colin's offer, but could it be worse than the life I currently endure? I could have my legs back. To me, that sounds more appealing than a sauna full of voluptuous nymphomaniacs. At least with legs I could enter said sauna without fear of humiliation. At the moment I can barely summon the courage to leave my home. Day by day, although I fight it, I increasingly understand the mental spiral that eventually led Steve to take his own life.

"I must press you for an answer," says Colin.

"Deal," I say. Before Colin can say anything else I uncork the bottle and swallow the liquid. It burns, sweet mercy, it burns so badly. I fall from my chair, coughing, gagging. I clutch at my throat and try to scream before my consciousness goes AWOL.

2

I'm on the floor. My head throbs and my mouth is dry, my tongue swollen. I'm in the kitchen, my chair tipped over on its side. I rub my eyes and look around. The stink of fire is absent from the air. There is no bottle, no scorched footprints on the floor, no Colin.

A mirthless chuckle escapes my lips. These new anti-depressants have some weird hallucinogenic side-effects. I struggle to my feet and walk to the bathroom. It isn't until I'm dropping my trousers that I realise I have legs. Not just any legs, they're my legs, right down to the scar on my right shin and the two freckles on my left kneecap.

I look at myself in the mirror and fight not to giggle like a madman. The feeling of elation rising in me is frightening. It's not that I'm scared of the joy this moment holds, I just feel weird because I realise how long it's been since I've felt any happiness.

Pulling up my pants, I run out into the kitchen and smell the stench of burning.

"Hello, Joshua," says Colin. He is as he was before – tall, hot and demonic.

"Shit," I say.

He shrugs, "Should have read the small print."

Then Colin rips my head off.

3

I have legs and my head is back where it should be. I'm on top of a colossal tower. It's the tallest edifice in the endless cityscape before me by some order of magnitude. The city is a sprawling mass of twisted buildings, all incredible and hewn from rock the colour of the moon. They look like they've been designed by an architect with a dependency on narcotics.

"Where are we?" I ask.

"Helven," Colin replies. He's standing next to me, smouldering.

"Oh, I get it, a cross between heaven and hell."

Colin shakes his head, as though I've said something stupid, "There are no such places. There is only Helven, the city of angels and demons."

The mention of angels brings back unwanted memories, for I've witnessed them dying. It's how I lost my legs. One second my division were shooting at people who were shooting at us. The next second, a mother and child ran into the line of fire and we were shooting at them. Somehow they made it into the middle of the street without being hit and huddled, confused and scared, dressed in rags. Then I caught site of a grenade in the downward arc of a lob. I ran forward. I still have no idea what I hoped to achieve, they were too far away. I saw the smeared tears on the child's cheeks. Bang. They were consumed by the explosion and I parted company with my legs.

"How else do you think we maintain balance?" Colin continues, "Nature doesn't just rule on Earth. She rules here too. If there were places where only good or evil existed, well, it just wouldn't work, would it?" He talks so bluntly, I find myself believing him, although his voice still carries that hypnotic edge.

Hypnosis aside, I've never been a big believer in heaven and hell. If I'm honest, I didn't know what to believe. All I can say with certainty is that whatever I expected, this wasn't it. Helven is magnificent, but Colin seems to belong here, which gives the place an alien quality I find unsettling.

"So, what happens now?" I ask, wanting to think about anything other than the sense of panic building in me.

"There's a debate in progress at which your presence is required. The voice of Fire is arguing about cacodemons' rights with the leader of the opposition. They are very badly treated here, particularly by an extreme right-wing group of sprites."

"Cacodemons?"

"Yes." I nod like I understand, which prompts Colin to motor on, "Then there is some argument to be had about volcanic eruptions on Earth – the Fire party feel there are too many humans now and a catastrophe would help restore balance, whereas the Light party believe humanity should have another chance to address the problem themselves. Then there's the manifesto of the murdered, decreeing the laws of vengeance—"

Before my brain cells can join forces with my sanity and organise an escape plan to tunnel out of my skull, I interrupt, "So what do I have to do?"

Colin moves over to an opening in the vast roof space. "Follow me."

Moving towards him, I see fairy-tale stairs spiralling downward. As we descend the stairway widens.

Eventually we come out into a gargantuan chamber resonating with the sound of voices in disagreement. To my right is tiered seating carved from sunlight, filled with spirits of purity and beauty. To my left is an abyss of darkness brimming with fire, talons and misshapen abominations.

Astride a monstrous dais in the centre of the chamber two huge beings sit in facing thrones. They exchange arguments, their voices as loud as storms, speaking a language I cannot understand. One is wreathed in light, his eye sockets a mass of lightning, the other is cloaked in night, her face a mask of flame.

Feeling smaller and more insignificant than I ever have before, I look up at Colin.

"This is the Chamber of Vindication," says Colin, his voice just audible above the thundering voices.

"What am I supposed to do?" I ask.

"Do as you will."

There is a new distance in Colin's voice. I feel I am on my own, as though something is expected of me, although I know not what. Then I see a flaming ball arcing through the air like a whispering Spitfire. Its trajectory gives no definite idea if the parties of Light or Fire are responsible for throwing it. I feel a sense of déjà vu as I run forward. There is no thought involved, no consideration. I'm simply doing what I must. Unlike the grenade in Kandahar, I see it with time to make a difference. I run towards the dais. Angry voices boom around me. I see the flaming blob fly towards me. It isn't as big as I first thought, more the size of a melon than a fighter-plane. I throw myself on top of its molten mass. Bang.

I'm on my back, my body aflame with pain. Light and Fire look down upon me. Both are frightening yet magnificent to behold. Colin approaches, drawing their attention.

"Are you responsible for deploying the Devil's Crush?" spits the leader of Fire, no longer using the strange language of their arguments. Colin nods. "You do not have the authority."

"I did so at the bequest of my master," says Colin.

"Who do you serve that has the right to–"

Colin clears his throat. Twin tongues of fire flicker from his nostrils. "Nature."

The demeanours of both Light and Fire change instantly and they bow.

"My apologies," says Fire.

"Accepted," says Colin.

"His actions show hope," says the leader of the Light, looking back down at me after a moment of contemplation, "as I have argued."

"They do," the leader of Fire concedes. "So it is decided."

The two beings move back to the dais and retake their seats. As my consciousness fades, an announcement is made from the fiery abyss to the left, in that alien language. Both leaders listen to the point and then the thunderous arguments begin once more.

4

I wake in my bed, glad the nightmare is over. I roll out from under the sheets, remembering I don't have legs a second too late. Wallop. "Tufted-twist-pile, tufted-twist-pile," I mutter, hoping it might help me remember.

"Morning, Joshua," Colin's voice rumbles from the kitchen. So it wasn't a dream.

I pull myself into my wheelchair and trundle into the kitchen. He's watching the news, sitting on his iron chair. It's a story about how a change in seismic activity means Yellowstone's super-volcano is no longer expected to imminently erupt.

"I'm alive," I say.

He nods, "Enjoy."

"I have no legs."

"How would you explain them if you did?"

I'd never thought of that, but, "I'd find a way." Colin just shakes his head. "What about my soul?" I ask.

"What about it?"

"I was hoping—"

"Should have read the small print," says Colin.

I'm beginning to wish I had. We watch the news report for a while. Scientists seem confused, people seem pleased. "Did I act as Nature intended?" I ask.

"You did as you did. There was no right or wrong outcome." Standing, Colin says, "However, your actions have merely postponed disaster. I hope your race is wise enough to do as you did, and make the necessary sacrifices."

"What can I do?" I ask.

I receive Colin's smouldering stare one last time, "What can anyone do?"

Then he, his chair and the stench of flame are gone.

I feel different. It takes me a while to realise it's nothing physical. My thoughts are positive. What can I do with my life? How can I make a difference? As I put the kettle on, for the first time, I find myself considering how I can best lead a life without legs.

~

Christopher Fielden's Biography

I was born in the 70s, which is too long ago for my liking.

I grew until I was old enough to attend school. I generally disliked learning. Somehow I passed a few exams.

I played drums in a rock band for 15 years and was fortunate enough to tour all over the world. I'm sure this was more educational than university or a 'proper job' could have been.

After the band stopped being a profession and became a hobby, I started writing fiction. I self-published my first book, *Wicked Game*, in 2010. To avoid a mental breakdown, I then started writing short stories as they're a lot easier to finish.

InkTears will be publishing five of my short stories ('Devil's Crush' is one of them) in their *Showcase* collection alongside some other wonderful authors in the near future, which makes me very happy.

Due to my success with short story writing, I recently wrote and released a book called *How To Write A Short Story, Get Published & Make Money*. It uses my published stories as case studies, so writers can see how all the different tips and advice in the book were used in practice to achieve publishing success. You can learn more about the book here:

www.christopherfielden.com/books/how-to-write-a-short-story.php

By day my job is in digital marketing, where I spend most of my time trying to avoid wearing a suit. By night I play drums in a multitude of rock bands. In between, I ride motorcycles, write and run my website.

Chris's website: www.christopherfielden.com

Chris's Competition Judging Comments

There were 216 entries into the 2015 To Hull & Back competition, compared to 94 in 2014. Because of this unexpectedly large increase in entries, I have changed the closing date for next year's competition to the 31st of July. This is to give me more time to read the last minute entries and compile the shortlist. I received 74 entries in the final week, 27 of which were on the closing date of the competition, so I had to take a week off work to get through everything. Writers and their deadlines... Meh. I'm guilty of the same.

Overall the competition made a small profit this year. Prizes are 1st: £200, 2nd: £100 and 3rd: £50. By the time you take out PayPal charges, video production costs, costs associated with publishing the anthology, the costs of putting on a book launch and, of course, the loooong ride to Hull and back, there ain't much left. Still, a small profit is an improvement on last year's small loss.

Due to the growth in entries, I've decided to invest this profit into next year's competition and increase the prizes for 2016 to:

- 1st: £1,000
- 2nd: £150
- 3rd: £75

I've also upped the entry fee to £7 in the hope that I can make the competition break-even overall.

The long-term aim is to provide a five figure top prize to help the competition become more well-known and give humorous short stories a respected platform to holler from. Due to the amazing amount of support all the entrants have provided so far, I'm hoping that will be achievable over the next few years. I'm also considering asking Harley Davidson if they'd like to sponsor To Hull & Back, seeing as I'm currently giving them free advertising for their glorious two-wheeled motorised-monster-machines. Maybe in 2017...

The judges have all given very positive feedback about the stories they've read. It really was very difficult to choose a shortlist. If you entered the competition and didn't make the shortlist or get a special mention, please don't be disheartened. I could have easily included 100 writers in the special mention list. Just remember, judges are human beings and have different tastes. Keep entering those stories elsewhere. Many have an excellent chance of being published.

That's it I guess. I chuckled a lot while reading all the entries. This is something I like to do, so all the writers who entered have made me very happy. Thank you.

NIGHT RECEPTION

Judge's story, by Andy Melhuish

Norman was the night receptionist at Oldhill Hospital, an ancient mansion hidden behind rows of giant evergreens on a vast estate near the city. Many men and women had thought they knew what the night receptionist role entailed, and they'd all run away, because the hospital had once been Oldhill Lunatic Asylum – and some part of it still remembered. Despite the good work done during the day, it remained a mad house at heart, possessed by old ideas of insanity and a relaxed attitude to the finality of death.

"Woooah," came the ghostly scream through the darkness.

"12:30?" said Norman to himself. "Jean's running a bit late tonight."

He stood up and left his game of solitaire half-finished on the computer screen. IT were threatening to upgrade the system soon, and he'd heard chilling stories that solitaire would not be included in the new package. He shook his head and left the reception desk, making his way along the main corridor with its high, curved ceilings. The games rooms and lounges along here were locked and dark as they should be.

"Jean?" he said softly. "Where've you got to now?"

"Woooah," came another scream from upstairs.

"Urgh, OK," said Norman, and he took the broad marble staircase up to the dormitory levels, unlocking and locking behind him the wire mesh security doors. The long-term patients were sleeping soundly, as always, their prescriptions and sports programmes having worked like magic.

"Jean?" said Norman, approaching the end of a corridor where a pale figure may or may not have been standing at an arched window in the moonlight.

"Woah," came a disinterested moan.

"How's the view tonight, Jean, eh?" said Norman, using the voice he reserved for visiting his grandma.

"They... hurt me..." hissed the figure of Jean, whose decayed face poked out from a white shawl.

"Ooh, skin's flared up again, eh? Have you been using the cream?"

"Didn't have the... proper biscuits..." hissed Jean, her skin disintegrating before Norman's eyes. It had been disturbing the first time, he would admit, but only because there were no cleaners on at night and he didn't want to go around with a mop. But the bits of Jean just vaporised as they fell, so no mess. She now stared at him imploringly, he guessed, but her permanent skeleton grin and lidless eyes made expressions difficult to interpret.

"What's that Jean? Speak up, dearie."

"...didn't... the biscuits..." whispered Jean.

Oh, thought Norman. *It's the biscuits again.* "I thought we'd got past this, eh?"

As far as he could piece together, Jean had wound up here because a tea shop once served her the wrong biscuits. Based on the varieties she occasionally mentioned, he figured this was somewhere around the mid-Victorian period. It seemed to Norman that back then the authorities would throw the word Lunatic at anyone prone to making a fuss – especially the old, the poor and the homeless. From Jean's initial altercation, it had been a number of cantankerous scenes, misunderstandings, and finally telling a doctor that his collar was dirty, that landed her in Oldhill. A number of refreshing ice baths later, and she soon learned to keep her gob shut, but by then it was too late, of course.

"Come on, poor thing," said Norman, "Before you wake someone up."

Jean raised a hand which was little more than bone patched with frozen blue and rotted green flesh.

"Need a wee?" asked Norman.

"Wooah," sighed Jean.

"Come on then, dearie." Norman pretended to take her non-existent hand and they walked slowly in the direction of the old shower block. But by the time they arrived he found himself walking alone in the dark, his hand slightly raised for no one.

*

Norman went down for a cup of tea and laid a few more cards in solitaire. What was he going to do without it – play actual solitaire, with actual cards? That sounded like a lot of effort and they wouldn't do that little dance at the end when he won. Crosswords, maybe. He thought perhaps he was reaching crossword age.

"So who's next?" he asked the ceiling. It might be any of them.

The heavy thump that came from above could have been ignored. Could be nothing. But the short dragging sounds that followed could only have been Reg in the store room again. When Norman finally arrived at the door, he took a deep breath to steel himself from the horrors that awaited. Reg was a talker.

"Ah, Norman, pull up a pew, old chap." Reg wore the striped pyjamas adorned with medals, and the uniform cap, that apparently all incarcerated soldiers had been required to wear. Norman couldn't help rolling his eyes at that, even as he tried to avoid breathing the stench of rotten cabbage and booze.

"Haven't seen you for a while, Reg, been busy?" Norman sat down on a mega-multipack of toilet rolls across from Reg, who'd brought his own foldout chair.

"Oh, no more than usual," said Reg. "A lot of letters to write, you know. A lot of letters." Under the single 40 watt bulb Reg looked even deader than usual, though Norman had yet to figure out exactly what caused his death in the first place. Terminal romance, perhaps. "Care for a drop?"

The 80-year-old whisky was slightly tempting, but Norman wasn't much of a drinker. Also it wasn't there.

"Go on then," he sighed. He found a tube of plastic

cups on a shelf and plucked one out. Reg's black-veined hand poured three shaky measures for Norman and about two on the floor. Norman pretended to wince as he took a sip from the factually empty cup.

And so began Reg's story. Again. The war; the specific dates; the intricate descriptions of items that no one makes or owns anymore; the dames when he was on shore leave; then the bomb that almost ended it all. All of this he told with the vacant stare of a lonely drunk and melting corpse. By the end Reg had usually come close to finishing the bottle and gave Norman a final top-up. And by this point, Norman was usually starting to wish the whisky was real.

"Shell shock," shouted Reg, forcing Norman's sleepy eyes to open. "That's what they called it. Unpredictable behaviour? Well, what did they expect? Every time I close my eyes I see that... oh, but she was a sweetheart. Clerical nurses, you know, always brightened the day."

Norman had been waiting for this bit, which had been genuinely touching the first time but now signalled that it was time for him to leave. "What was her name, Reg?"

"Was it... Bobby? Christine?"

"I thought it was Beryl?"

"Oh, Beryl," said Reg, wiping a tear of blood from his yellow eye.

"Plenty more fish in the sea, as they say." Norman hated that, but the important thing he'd learned about palliative care was the stuff you're supposed to say when you don't give a shit, as much as what to say when you do. He stood up to leave, but Reg was having none of it.

"Nooo..." he moaned, drunkenly. He shifted a few boxes around and hit some dishcloths off a shelf.

Then came a loud smashing noise from down the corridor. *Urgh*, thought Norman. *Susan. Is it that late already?*

"Reg, old boy, I've got to be on my way."

"But... noooo... I've got... unfinished business." Reg really dragged those words out.

"You had a brief flirtation in 1944. That's not unfinished business. Truth be told, I quite fancy the day receptionist. But that's never going to happen, because she's 20 years younger than me. And she works in the day."

The old man was already gone, to sulk and sleep it off wherever it is they go. *Seriously*, thought Norman as he turned off the light, *the hours I've spent proofreading his war poetry.*

*

There was another smash, but *exactly* the same as the previous one – the same length and shatter pattern. Norman quickened his pace up the stairs and along another endless corridor to Female Toilet Room 3B – incidentally the room most distant from his desk.

"You all right in there, Susan?" he asked, trying to sound more caring than annoyed. "Susan?" He gave it the usual 10 seconds then quietly unlocked the door with his key. "I'm going to break the door down," he said, with no urgency whatsoever. He faintly shoulder-barged it for effect, then casually opened it.

Susan's ghost lay in a patchy mess of blood and smashed mirror. She'd broken two of them above the long line of sinks. "Two?" said Norman. "I was on my way, you didn't have to die twice in the same night." He could swear he saw her smile. Attention seeker.

She'd originally slit her wrists sometime in the 1980s, or so they said. Norman had worked out that they were roughly the same age when it happened. Now here they were.

"Oh, dear me, look at this mess," he said, hoping the skinny form would have received enough fuss by now and so begin to fade. He didn't feel comfortable picking up bits of broken glass around her revealingly short nightdress. "Bloody teenagers, I don't know."

He collected up the bigger shards then stopped to look at himself in one of the identically broken mirrors. "What a tired old man I've become. And here's you, Susan, dying every night and never getting any older."

Norman's genuine remorse for his own mortality seemed to be enough for Susan, whose corpse and spilled blood soon disappeared. Norman got the yellow danger cone from a cupboard, and put it outside the door, then he locked Female Toilet Room 3B.

It would soon be light outside, and the hallways looked their saddest at this hour, but Norman thought that might just be end-of-shift blues. Back downstairs, he took a quick look at the screen and moved a few cards around. He could probably win the game right now and watch the timeless cascade of numbered faces before clocking out, but he liked this feeling and wanted to live with it for a while longer.

~

Andy Melhuish's Biography

I've most recently focussed on my travel writing and improving my live storytelling, which to me is more important and enjoyable than publication. Amongst other things I've had some short plays produced, worked with multimedia artists, and won the occasional small competition whenever I could bother entering. To facilitate the next patch in my chequered life, I've recently stepped down as Editor at a financial publishing firm and moved to Oxford to do a second degree.

Samples of my creative and copy writing can be found on my website.

Andy's website: www.eloquentbear.com

~

Andy's Competition Judging Comments

It's been very eye-opening to see what comes out of so many different brains with just a single guiding purpose. The variety of styles and approach to humour is heart-warming, as I imagine all these individuals typing away in their own, equally idiosyncratic, lives.

WONDER WOMAN'S BIRTHDAY PARTY

Judge's story, by Mel Ciavucco

I pick up my bass and glance over at Jeff, our drummer, who's on his fourth pint already. He's gulping it back so fast it's dribbling from the sides of the glass and onto his Clash T-shirt. Dave, guitarist and vocalist, is fiddling around with his amp again. Dave likes to think we need hours for sound-checking, as if it's Wembley or something, but it's not. It's a working men's club and we're about to play at a 40th birthday party to a bunch of pissed-up 40-something losers.

"Rob, make yourself fucking useful," Dave calls to me, motioning to my amp.

"What? I'm ready," I snap back. "I've been ready for the last hour,"

Jeff glances at me, unimpressed.

This is my Saturday night, nearly *every* Saturday night. It's fair to say I'm familiar with most of the town halls, tennis clubs and working men's clubs in the Midlands area. Boy, does that look great on my CV. Then there's all the hotels. The weddings. I fucking hate weddings. People are either so pissed they fall over on the dancefloor, or so pissed they fall asleep in a corner, or both.

Tonight, it's a 70's theme birthday party for someone called Tracy who's dressed as Wonder Woman. Her husband, dressed as Batman, keeps groping her arse; I can see his hand moving under her cape. His costume has extra padding around the arms and chest, sewn in to look like he's got a six pack. He's red-faced and grinning under his mask, probably ecstatic that he finally gets to grope Wonder Woman.

There are a couple of other Wonder Womans at the party. Tracy had given them evils before hugging them and thanking them for coming. Some people have gone all out on their costumes. Maybe it's one of the few nights a year they get to leave their kids at home with a babysitter. Some of the less enthusiastic guests sit in the corner, picking at their sausage rolls, glancing at their watches to work out if they've stayed long enough to be polite. There's a group of guys, some dressed as T-

Birds and one dressed as Elvis. They're swigging back cheap lager like they're 18 again. I've seen this type before, the air-punchers. Soon they'll be attempting to mosh to the music they probably used to call too 'mosher' to like back in the day. Knobheads.

I realise Dave is shouting at me. "Blur first," he says.

"I know," I shoot back.

Of course I know; we always start with Blur's 'Country House'. Then we follow it with Oasis, the two being ying and yang. Or rather, just equally shit.

Considering it's a 70's themed birthday party, we weren't actually told to play any 70's songs. Tracy sent us her own list full of the usual rubbish. I could've guessed most of the bands on it before I read it, they're the 'cool' tunes we have to play every week. Well, let me tell you - Oasis, Kaiser Chiefs and Blur are not 'cool vintage classics'; they're for people in their thirties and forties pretending they're teenagers again. It does make me wonder though, in the future, if the golden oldie equivalent to Neil Diamond will be Liam Gallagher with his whiney little bitch voice? I'm not sure which is worse.

We start playing and people congregate on the dance floor. They're all pretty pissed already, despite it being early, so they get straight to dancing. I should be enjoying this, shouldn't I? Entertaining people? This is what I wanted ever since I first learnt 'Come as You Are' by Nirvana on the bass. I was going to be in a cool band, and write songs, and tour...

But now a sweaty man in half a Chewbacca costume is dancing in front of me, grinning.

Now this right here, this is my 'why am I here' moment. I have one of these nearly every weekend. They're all smiling and dancing to music I'm playing, but

It's not the music I've written, is it? I'm the first to admit that our versions of these songs have managed to make them even shitter than they originally were. We're a joke. Why the hell am I doing this?

My lack of enthusiasm must be showing as Dave keeps glancing over with a disapproving expression. I give him my perfected 'fuck off and die' look. Jeff sees and laughs. Don't think we're being mean, it's not that we don't like Dave, we've been mates for years. It's just that working with someone puts a special kind of strain on a friendship, especially when it involves this shit every weekend. Oh. Now Princess Leia is gyrating against David Bowie. I can't believe I'm here.

We're storming through the set list but I'm not even sure which song we're on. My fingers just automatically do the work for me now; I'm like a pre-programmed musical clown. I glance over at Jeff who looks just as bored as me but more pissed. His eyes are drooping. I wonder what would happen if he just fell asleep. In fact, what if I just fell to the floor, shut my eyes and drifted off into a world where fancy dress doesn't exist?

We're onto The Fratelli's 'Chelsea Dagger' now. I can tell as they're all air-punching and chanting, "Dur-da-du, dur-da-du," and, oh God, Elvis is playing air guitar. He and the T-Birds form a circle which is almost a rugby scrum, arms locked around each other. They start to jump. This is going to end badly. I remember a brief time when The Fratelli's were good before 'Chelsea Dagger' got claimed as a kind of chanted mating call, expressed mostly outside Weatherspoon's.

I'm still playing, though in my head I'm curled up in a dark room. I don't feel like my fingers are moving, but I glance down and see they still are. I wonder if my head is still attached to the rest of my body, if not then who's controlling my fingers. Am I actually going insane?

We start 'I Predict a Riot' by Kaiser Chiefs. Elvis and the T-Birds laugh and glance over at Tracy's sister who's dressed as a giant Can of Spam. They're puffing out their cheeks and bellies, looking at her, chanting, "I predict a diet." The fuckers. Again, my fingers feel numb, but I presume they're still moving, until I look down. Then I notice Dave and Jeff are staring at me. I've actually stopped playing this time. I'm standing with my hands dangling by my sides and the bass hanging around my neck. People on the dance floor are staring at me. A fuzziness takes over, and I attempt to flex my fingers.

Dave and Jeff stop playing, Dave looking bewildered. The birthday girl looks confused, and then some of the T-birds start to boo. That's it. It's over. In one swift motion, I hoist my bass up over my head and bring it crashing down onto the middle of the dance floor. The sound is deafening. The entire rooms stops dead and stares at me.

"What the fuck?" I scream, at nobody in particular, more the whole room.

"You." I point to the group of guys, but realise my finger is shaking. The rest of my words come out as a stutter. "Stop it... alright. Just fucking... stop it."

I'm suddenly aware that my knees are shaking and sweat is dribbling down my back and into my arse crack. It's not unpleasant if I'm honest.

"Chanting and punching the air doesn't make you cool," I shout, "especially when you're wearing a fake quiff." I look at their T-bird jackets. "Grease is set in the 50's anyway, knobheads."

One of them murmurs, "It was *made* in the 70's..."

I ignore him and move on to the birthday girl, aka

Wonder Woman. "Who the fuck has a 70's party with no 70's music? This stuff you say is *not cheesy* is the shit we play at every fucking party, every fucking wedding, all the fucking time. Your party isn't original, it's just shit."

She looks like she might explode, and so does her husband, Batman. Before he can, she launches onto the stage and I duck out of the way of her fist. I fall back into the drum kit with a crash of symbols, managing to dodge her. Jeff jumps over to me to help but Dave just stands there in shock. Wonder Woman advances on him.

"I'm sorry," Dave cries. "I don't know what's wrong with him, he's acting like a dick... probably just drunk..."

"Your band is shit," she says, "and you've ruined my fucking party." She pushes him over into the middle of the dance floor and a kerfuffle starts. Jeff helps me to my feet, but I notice the T-Birds are laughing at me.

Another sudden burst of rage takes over and I run straight into them, managing to nearly slap Elvis in the face before the others pull me off. A T-Bird punches me in the stomach repeatedly; it's the school playground all over again but with more hair gel. Suddenly the Can of Spam and her friend wearing a Psychedelic Playsuit jump on the guys, trying to pull them off us. The Can of Spam punches Elvis in the face. The Psychedelic Playsuit wrestles one of the T-birds, and I manage to punch another in the arm. Even through the leather jacket it still hurts my hand. I notice Wonder Woman has Dave in a headlock, but Princess Leia is trying to pull her off. Jeff is wrestling Batman, but to be honest looks as if he's rather enjoying it.

Elvis grabs me and the Can of Spam and Psychedelic Playsuit keep trying to fight off the T-Birds. We struggle for a while until I manage to get him on the floor and pull off his quiff wig. I push it into his face, into his mouth, hoping he'll choke on the thick polyester hair... until he actually does. He starts gasping for air and I stumble back in shock, dropping the wig. What the hell have I become? I just tried to suffocate a man to death with a novelty quiff. The Kaiser Chiefs may be shit but it's not worth all this.

"Stop," I yell. "Please stop, I never meant this to happen."

Everyone ignores me and continues fighting. It's a mess; tables and chairs tipping over, blood splattered on the dancefloor, torn shirts, but for a moment I revel in the fact that I started all this. Then, I go and save Jeff from Batman. I pull his cape and wrap it around my arm, and he stumbles back choking. Capes are such inappropriate fighting attire. Jeff escapes and we head towards Dave who is actually now straddling Wonder Woman, trying to wrestle her arms to the floor. Oh God, what the fuck is he doing? Batman is about to swing for me but then notices the straddling. He pushes Dave off Wonder Woman and helps her up.

"Come on Dave, let's get some fresh air," I say, steering him towards the door.

"Are you kidding me?" he says, pushing me off. "This is all your fault."

He pushes me, I push him back, and then we both wrestle on the floor in a six-year-old play fight sort of way. Jeff pulls Dave off me, but Wonder Woman isn't done yet. As her fist swings towards my face, I can tell she's determined not to miss this time. It collides with my nose and I fall back, feeling as if my head just exploded. I guess I deserved it.

Wonder Woman cradles her hand, and I take a bit of

pleasure knowing that must have hurt her quite a bit too.

"Get the fuck out of my party," she says. "And don't think you're getting paid for this."

"Fair enough," I mutter.

Jeff helps me up.

The fighting dies down and the guests watch us as we walk out the front doors. The bar staff hiding in the car park, smoking, are now staring at us. I hear police sirens. Oh bollocks.

I turn to Jeff and Dave. "Can't we just go back to playing Nirvana in my garage like old times, eh?"

~

Mel Ciavucco's Biography

Mel Ciavucco is a Bristol based author, screenwriter and blogger. She's had short stories published both online and in print, and she recently performed on a comedy BBC Radio show called *Speechbubble*. She has written a novel and a screenplay, plus short stories and short film scripts, and she writes a column for *Zusterschap* – an online lifestyle magazine.

Mel is a co-founder of Stokes Croft Writers. They run a bi-monthly storytelling event in Bristol called Talking Tales.

Mel is the founder of Freesized – a website promoting body positivity and gender equality.

Mel's website: www.melciavucco.weebly.com

~

Mel's Competition Judging Comments

I'm honoured to have been a judge for a second year. It's been an absolute delight to read such brilliant stories – they're all written to such a high standard. Congratulations to all the writers, and thank you for making me smile. I look forward to the release of the anthology so I can read them all again.